Seasonal
HABITS OF HUSBANDS & HONEYBEES

EMMALINE WARDEN

EMMALINE WARDEN LLC

Digital Edition ISBN: 979-8-9874003-4-0
Print Edition ISBN: 979-8-9874003-5-7

Cover design by Lily Bear Design Co.

FIRST EDITION
Print Edition

To the baddest bitch out there for doing the damn thing.

(It's me, I'm the baddest bitch)

To the Let's Get Critical Group, I can get through anything with you all by my side.

To Jackson Wang, who will never read this, nor know it exists.

You'll never know how grateful I am to you.

#TeamWang

CHAPTER ONE

February, 1822
London

"PHOEBE, YOU SIMPLY cannot ask a gentleman if they are aware of the mating habits of bees. We're at a ball for heaven's sake!" said a sharp voice, the shrill reprimand determining it to be a lady of questionable years.

The cigar that Lord Harrison Metcalf had raised to his lips paused in midair at what had to be the most absurd sentence he had ever had the misfortune to overhear. So much for enjoying his cigar in the cool evening air, in blessed solitude, away from the crush of the ballroom.

"I was merely stating that bees use dancing to give direction to food sources while we have relegated the action as a form of a mating ritual. It is only logical that the next point of discussion would be to point out that when it comes to mating, a queen is the one who populates her hive with the secretions of many male bees as opposed to a single individual and that there is very little courting in their process of procreation," a seductive voice answered.

Second. It was the second most absurd sentence he had ever heard, the first place now going to that mesmerizing paragraph, spoken by a smokey voice that should make him think of dark rooms and intoxicating touches. Not bee secretions.

"You'll never marry if you continue on in this manner," the sharp voice responded.

"I'm not sure I understand why that is a problem," the seductive voice said.

Harrison leaned against the wall; his cigar forgotten as his ears pricked up at the unusual conversation. He had surely never heard of a societal miss uninterested in procuring an affluent marriage. That is, if he did not count Margaret Reedy—now Ludlow, the newly appointed Marchioness of Greenwood. And he did not count her, for she was a kind of holy grail that no one would ever be able to touch, including him.

The sharp voice sighed. "How is it that you are my daughter, and yet I still don't understand you? Compose yourself into a respectable young lady and then join me in the ballroom, Phoebe. And please, no more nonsense about bees."

"Yes, Mama," replied the seductive voice.

The balcony grew quiet and Harrison returned the cigar to his lips and took a deep puff, the tip turning a burnt orange. Silence embraced him, and he was glad to be alone once more.

"I'm told it's rude to eavesdrop," the sultry voice said.

Harrison sputtered, the cigar falling from his mouth. Stubbing the thing with the toe of his slipper, Harrison stepped out from the darkened alcove to stand before his accuser. The outspoken miss looked nothing like her absurd comments, her blonde hair pinned in a loose chignon while a demure pink gown, absent of lace and fripperies, hugged a body that would make Botticelli weep. The darkness masked her face, the light of a single torch merely cupping her soft jaw the way the hand of a lover should.

"Normally I'd agree, but in this circumstance, I believe it is you who is in the wrong. I was on this terrace before you arrived. Perhaps, before having such a…" Harrison paused, his gaze scanning the sky as he searched the darkened night for the proper word.

"Preposterous?" she supplied.

"I was thinking private, but preposterous might fit a bit better." Harrison waved his hand. "Before having a preposterous conversation as the one I just overheard, you might check that you are alone."

The woman said nothing, the silence filling the space in an uncomfortable haze. Adjusting his cravat, Harrison took a step closer. The shift in position gifted him a faint glimpse of the woman's eyes, their wide gray gaze stopping him in his tracks. How someone just talking of mating rituals could appear so innocent would forever plague him, the oddity of it rather perplexing.

The woman frowned at him. "Isn't it the responsibility of a gentleman to ensure that women are at ease by announcing their presence? Especially once it becomes obvious that the conversation being had is one of a private matter?"

Harrison raised a brow at her words. "So I am supposed to announce that I am there?"

"Yes, I believe so."

He shook his head. "That is utterly absurd. All of this could have been avoided if you had simply ensured you were alone before beginning such a ridiculous conversation."

"No. All of this could have been avoided if you had removed yourself before the conversation veered toward ridiculous. Why do men tend to place the blame upon the woman when they are in the wrong?"

"I beg your pardon, Miss—"

"Lady," she corrected, the word flat. "Lady Phoebe Kent." She said the sentence without harsh tone or barb, as if talking of the weather, and Harrison was taken aback. Young ladies, no matter their age, happily corrected anyone who assumed them lesser, but not Lady Phoebe. If anything, it was as if she were resigned of the fact.

"Lady Phoebe, perhaps we've gotten off on the wrong foot. I merely meant—" His words were interrupted once more at the onslaught of giggles that joined them on the balcony, their volume getting louder as the pair came closer. Grabbing Lady Phoebe, Harrison steered her to the dark alcove he had hid in only moments before.

"Stay quiet," he whispered in her ear, the scent of honeysuckle tickling his nose.

Thankfully, the miss kept silent as the young women's voices came toward the spot they had occupied, their chittering setting Harrison's nerves on edge.

"I hope Mr. Greene recovers from his dance with Lady Violet. The insipid girl plodded his feet endlessly during the reel," one voice said.

"Tabitha," the second voice said with a giggle. "What if someone hears you?"

"Oh hush, Minnie. Who is going to hear us over here? Everyone must be inside watching the Marquis of Greenwood dote upon his new wife. Strange that Lord Everly hasn't joined them."

"I'm certain I saw him earlier this evening," Minnie whispered. "I hoped he would dance a waltz with me. He is unbearably handsome."

Harrison rolled his eyes at her words, choosing to ignore the precious comment about him. He would greet Meg and Oliver when he damned well felt like it, and at present, he had little interest in doing so.

"Did you hear what Lady Phoebe said about bees? Her mother's face practically turned the shade of a strawberry," Minnie said with a high-pitched squeal. "The girl is an absolute nightmare with her unadorned dresses and tufts of cotton sticking out of her ears."

"Her family should be ashamed, parading her about this season with the rest of us. She has no decency, spewing every iota of nonsense that pops into her head. Did you see her fanning herself? One would think she were perishing of heat in the desert instead of in a ballroom in London. Her father should have committed her to a nunnery. She'll never marry, of that, I'm sure. I'd place money on it," Tabitha said, sounding every bit the future matron she no doubt planned to be.

"We should start a pool," Minnie said, her laughter ear splitting.

"No one would win. Poor dear might as well join the shelf now," Tabitha said with a snort.

Lady Phoebe stood tense beside him, her breath shallow as she listened to the two women insult her. Her every movement sent tingles of awareness coursing through him, even in the darkness. Especially in the darkness. Her body pressed against his, her warmth spreading through him through the layers of cloth, and when she took a sudden deep inhale of dismay, his jaw clenched. Harrison was sorely tempted to intervene as the two girls gossiped, but his presence would only add kindling to the fire no doubt already swirling around Lady Phoebe, and in truth, he was not a knight who slayed dragons for young ladies.

"We should go back in, Tabby. I'm sure my mother is already looking for me."

Tabitha sighed. "Let's hope we marry this year so we can truly enjoy all the offerings of Lord Brinsley's ball."

Minnie giggled, the sound softening as the pair retreated back inside.

Harrison turned to Lady Phoebe, uncertain whether the miss would faint at what she had heard, or become a raging storm. Much to his surprise, she was neither.

"I wish there was a better way to go about this whole matrimony bit," she mumbled, stepping away from him and back into the spotlight the moon created.

"What do you mean?" he asked, following her.

"All of this, the balls and the courtship." She waved her hand to the inside. "It's all an act devised to cover the true purpose of it all."

Harrison felt the corner of his mouth quirk up in a smile. "The true purpose?"

"Yes. Marriage is a business deal. A contractual entity and nothing more. Sure, there are the occasional love matches, but most of those people in there searching for a spouse aren't looking for love, they're looking for a merger. Why must there be all this fuss with rules and manners and uncomfortable garments when we can simply come to an agreement as one would do with a company? It would certainly be a more comfortable affair for everyone involved."

"I thought ladies liked balls and courtship? Flowers, chocolates, strolls through Hyde Park. Sweet treats at Gunter's?"

Lady Phoebe blew a raspberry at his statement, thusly proving all the more that this was not the setting for her. "I can do those things for myself."

"Yes, but isn't it nicer when they come from another?"

She shook her head, her face alight with exasperation. "Not when the meaning behind them is empty."

Her words echoed, bouncing around in his head, striking the bits that wanted nothing to do with emotion anymore. With a frown, he looked at her. "All right, Lady Phoebe, then what is the perfect solution?"

"A contract," she said, matter of factly as she began to pace back and forth on the stone balcony.

"Isn't that already done?"

"Between the men, absolutely, but I mean a contract between the two parties tied together in marriage. One with rules and regulations, a map so both know what they are agreeing to without all the nonsense that is required in a season."

"Isn't that rather cold?"

She looked at him then, her piercing gray eyes ablaze with indignation. "And this is not?" Lady Phoebe made a deep curtsey, her light pink skirts fanning against Lord Brinsley's stone balcony. "I should return to my mother."

She did not wait for his agreement, but took her leave, the hem swishing at an almost sullen pace as if it too did not want to return to the ballroom. Harrison watched the woman until she disappeared into the crowd, then resumed his spot on the balcony, his gaze searching the night sky.

He had come out here for a moment of respite, a second's reprieve from watching Margaret Ludlow, the woman he had loved, be fawned over by the man she married, but instead of quiet, he had found her. Where others might have found her forward thinking harsh and unnerving, Harrison had enjoyed it. She did not dance around a subject but instead voiced her thoughts openly, uncaring that the world around her would think her bold. It was a refreshing change from the simpering debutants inside the ballroom.

Which made it all the more a pity in his eyes. Lady Phoebe would most likely never marry and end up a spinster, just as the two girls suspected. London society had very little liking for bold and brash. No doubt, the young woman certainly had a perilous journey before her, and while he felt for the girl, there was very little he could do. He was no knight in shining armor. More than likely, he was the sad fop who would go about the rest of his life pining over what could have been. The maudlin jester. And no one would ever want to be rescued by him.

CHAPTER TWO

March, 1822

THE ALCOVE INSIDE Lord and Lady Halliwell's library was quite uncomfortable, the cushions severely under-stuffed and the pillows uneven in all the worst places. No amount of plumping changed the shape of the saddened lumps, and given the earl's depressing offerings with regards to literature, it was little wonder that the room was so gloomy. But it was a room that did not include a multitude of debutants who smelled like an appalling number of florals mixed with body odor, and it did not include men who laughed openly when her mother paraded her before them, intent on making her converse about trivial matters. No, no matter how uncomfortable or sorely lacking the earl's library was, it was still a better place to be than their ballroom.

It was the third event of the week, fourth if she counted her mother dragging her to the modiste to try on another bloody ballgown. Phee chewed on her bottom lip as she looked out the window onto the garden below, the book in her lap forgotten. There truly was no kind way to put it to her mother and father that perhaps it was time they gave up on their daughter marrying. True, they were only a month into the season, but given the exceptionally lacking welcome she had already received from the ton, it did little to bolster her confidence that a match would be made. Even she could see they were wasting their money on a fruitless endeavor. The endeavor, of course, being her.

With a sigh, Phee removed the small timepiece she had tucked into her reticule, disappointment flooding her when she noted she had only been gone fifteen minutes. It would take more than that to convince her mother that she suffered from a sour stomach and finally be able to take her leave.

As a child, being the only daughter to the Earl of Youngly had been heavenly, her eldest brother Jonathon, Viscount Hunt, gaining the lion's share of attention as the heir, allowing her the freedom to explore. And explore she had. There was not a book in her father's library, in both the London and Sussex home, that she had not read. Not a meter of ground that had not seen the soles of her boots. Not an animal nor insect she had not encountered. It had been a heavenly childhood that had quickly been snatched away as she neared sixteen. Then, her days had become irritating lessons, dancing and etiquette, training on household management and wifely nonsense. Her boots for exploring had disappeared as quickly as her freedom, all due to their senseless hope that she make an advantageous marriage, but she knew without a doubt that those dreams were fruitless. Were she able to find love, which seemed as possible as finding the end of a rainbow, perhaps her future would be more certain. But given the ton's regard for marriage, she knew her value would be far lesser than the new gaggle of debutants that flooded the market this year.

Yes, for the betterment of all, it was best her parents gave up the dreams of marriage for their daughter. Perhaps, if she pled her case, they would banish her to Sussex, the unfortunate daughter who never made a match. Then they all would be content.

The click of the door opening had Phee pulling the navy drapes surrounding the alcove closed, hiding her from the interloper's view. Hopefully, it was a footman taking a reprieve from his duties, but given the clinking of glass from the liquor cart, she doubted it.

Placing a hand over her mouth, Phee leaned against the wall and closed her eyes, pleading to every god and deity that she not be caught. It would only be one more strike against her to be found here, the earl's odd daughter sequestered away in Lord and Lady Halliwell's library, hiding from the eyes of London.

A crash sounded, followed by a muffled *fuck*. The voice was familiar, its smooth sound enticing, but no matter how intrigued she was to see the man in question, Phee kept still. It would do very little good for either of them to be found alone together. She would be labeled a villain, accused of trapping any man possible into marriage.

The room fell silent and while Phee was certain she had not heard a door open and close, the eerie stillness certainly must mean she was alone once more. Right? With a sigh, she let her head fall against the wall of the alcove. Just as her eyes fell to the book in her lap, the curtain swished open, the tinkling of its metal rings shaking the room from its slumber.

"I thought I smelled honeysuckle," a man said, standing in front of her, a glass of amber liquid clenched in his hand. "We meet again, Lady Phoebe."

Phee squinted at the man, searching for any familiar feature, but the only item that niggled at her brain was his voice and the touch of citrus and cigar smoke that permeated the air. "You again." The balcony bounder stood proudly before her, his sandy blond hair rakishly pushed from his face, his jacket and cravat the epitome of class. A smile lit his face but never reached his eyes, an odd juxtaposition given the humor he had displayed at the Brinsley ball.

"Another accusation from the lips of Lady Phoebe," the man said, clutching at his lapel, his body swaying from the drink. "One more harsh charge from you and I shall turn into a pile of dust at your feet."

Phee stood and stepped closer to the rogue, the heavy scent of alcohol on his breath making her nose twitch. While he reeked of a distillery, the man appeared rather well put together, his hair styled rakishly with small pieces falling before his brown eyes in an alluring manner. His tall, lean build, clad in a black jacket and breeches, hinted at strength, but with the way he was swaying, Phee had to wonder if that was simply an illusion.

"How is it that we've managed to sequester ourselves with one another yet again?" she asked, stepping away from the intoxicated scoundrel.

"Tis fate," he said, waving the hand that contained the cut crystal glass in the air. "The gods must know when I am in distress and send me to you so that you may further my torment." Collapsing into a chair before the fireplace, he sipped at his drink, or what was left of it.

"You are a dramatic man," Phee said.

"Can you blame me?" he asked. "It's not my fault you happen to be in my vicinity every time I'm miserable."

Eyeing the man, Phee weighed her choices. She could escape the library and return once more to the hell that was the Halliwell ball, or remain here with an albeit drunk, but seemingly harmless man, and while away a bit more time before finding her mother.

Moving toward him, Phee took the tufted chair next to his and watched him. His brown eyes were soft, his movements almost sleepy as he eyed the empty fireplace of the library. "Why are you miserable?" she asked, intrigued by the forlorn man before her.

His gaze never left the empty cavern. "Love," he said. "Loss." With a shrug, he finished his drink and set the glass down on the pilled red rug. "Isn't is always those two?"

Tucking her feet beneath her bottom, Phee rested her head in her hand. "Sometimes."

His head fell back against the white fabric, his eyes rolling to the side to look at her. "How goes the search for a business partner?"

A smile tugged at her lips. "Isn't it obvious? Why else would I be hiding in here?"

"Hard to strike such a heavy deal alone in a secluded room, Lady Phoebe. Why not get out there and pander your idea to every available man in society?"

Phee laughed. "I tried. Lord Bright laughed, but when he realized I was serious, he excused himself quickly. My mother nearly had an apoplexy."

"Dead mothers can be a bit of a problem. For what it's

worth, I find what you're looking for a rather brilliant notion."

Phee's head shot up at his words. "You do?"

The man nodded. "You sort out all the nasty business beforehand. Gets rid of the surprising bits and everyone is on equal footing from the start. No one is expecting love or monogamy, especially once the line is secured." He clapped his hands together. "Just a simple agreement between two individuals with a likeminded goal. Rather efficient."

"Mm," Phee said. "If only the rest of society agreed with you."

He sat up and looked at her then, his brown gaze drilling through her. "It's not as if you're asking for unattainable items, right?"

Phee laughed. "Wouldn't you agree that love is the unattainable item?"

"Perhaps. It might be easier to ask for the moon. Or perhaps the king's jewels."

With a small smile, Phee shook her head. "All I'd like is an amicable partnership."

He sat there silent, his eyes penetrating. "A friendship of sorts? Well, come on then. Give me your list."

Phee raised a brow. "What?"

"Your list. What would a marriage contract with Lady Phoebe Kent look like?"

"You're making fun of me."

He laughed. "Not at all. Come on, I'll write it down for you." He stood and scoured the room for paper before returning to his seat and removing a graphite pencil from a small case tucked inside his jacket pocket. Using his leg as a table, he began to write. "Marriage contract to Lady Phoebe Kent. Article one." He paused to look at her, his expression expectant.

"No children."

His mouth curled into a smile. "Starting the negotiations strong I see. Most men within the aristocracy would balk at the demand for no offspring. You know how much value we place on our heir and spare."

"That's a non-negotiable, I'm afraid."

"You don't like children?" he asked as he wrote on the paper.

"I adore children, but I don't think I'm the right fit to be a mother." Phee tilted her head and scrunched her face as she searched for the right words. "I have no interest in being a mother. I'd rather be a doting aunt, surprising my nieces and nephews with gifts and games, being the silly one they play with."

The man wrinkled his brow in thought. "Hmm."

"Do you want children?"

"This isn't my list, it's yours," he said, looking at her. "What's next?"

"I shall only attend one ball a month during the season, and it shall be one of my choosing. My spouse is more than welcome to attend any events they feel inclined to partake in, and can give my excuses if necessary."

He nodded his head in agreement as he wrote the next article on the paper. "Do you dislike social settings that much?"

Phee smiled. "I detest them."

"Why?" he asked, his focus still on the paper.

"I don't do well in large settings like balls, and in

truth, I dislike the social necessities required to partake in one. I don't understand their purpose." Phee shook her head. "My mother thinks I intentionally say odd things to get out of being invited to such occasions, but in truth, I merely say what is on my mind at the time. It isn't my fault my words happen to be wrong."

"Doesn't everyone detest large crowds and noise at one time or another?"

Phee pinched her lips.

"It isn't just the large crowds and noise. People say things that have an altogether different meaning, and they smile as they mutter something cruel. And I don't detest the noise, it makes me feel sick. My skin crawls and my palms sweat. It's somehow so very loud and yet I can hear the rustle of every scrap of fabric, every conversation around me, and the clink of dishware at the same volume as the person speaking right beside me. I come home feeling exhausted, as if I've been torn to pieces in the time I was gone."

He set down his pencil and looked at her. "Have you told your mother this?"

With a smile, Phee shook her head again. "Yes. She told me everyone feels this way at these events but surely that can't be true. Not everyone is walking around with stuffing in their ears." Waving her hand, she motioned to the paper on his lap. "Next item?"

With a raised brow, he looked at her, his gaze accessing. With a sigh, he picked up his pencil. "Article three?"

"Bees."

He looked up. "I beg your pardon?"

She shook her head. "No, that's too specific. I must be

allowed to pursue any hobby I would like."

With a quirked brow, he set down the pencil and picked up his glass, frowning as he found it empty. Refilling it at the bar cart, he looked over his shoulder at her. "You said bees?"

Phee nodded, a smile on her lips. "Perhaps I must also be allowed to dictate the design of the gardens at the properties as well, just to ensure proper habitat."

Sitting back down, he nodded. "Right. Right. Should that be one item or two?"

With a laugh, Phee leaned forward to look at the paper. "Two."

He wrote down the rest of her list, then set the pencil to the side and looked at her. "Is that it?" When she nodded yes, he cocked his head to the side, examining her. "What about intimacy? Does that not get addressed in this contract? Is that a separate contract?"

Phee looked at her hands. "Intimacy will not be part of the contract at all. Whoever I married, I'd expect them to get that from someone else."

"Rather cold."

She shook her head. "Why is that? I'm not sure physical intimacy is required in this sort of marriage. Marital congregation is only necessary in the making of children, and seeing as how I don't wish to have any, I'm not sure it is an essential piece."

Lord Everly smirked at her as he leaned forward and said in a low voice, "You do know that physical intimacy isn't just about procreating. It's a hedonistic activity that can be very pleasurable for all involved."

Phee's cheeks heated as she met his gaze, his brown

eyes soft and sleepy in the firelight as they danced over her face, and she swallowed at the tingle of want that overtook her.

Clearing his throat, he sat back in his chair with a sigh and looked at the paper before him. "It's a rather simple list, Lady Phoebe."

A corner of her mouth lifted in what she hoped could be perceived as a smile. "I want a rather simple life." Glancing at the clock on the mantel, she cursed under her breath. It had been nearly an hour since she had excused herself to the ladies' retiring room. Her mother, no doubt, was likely looking for her. "I must return to the ball, I'm afraid. It was a pleasure to divert my time with you once again…" She paused, her brow furrowing. "I don't believe I've caught your name, sir."

"Lord Everly," he said.

Phee paused, her eyes assessing him once again, now with the knowledge of who he was. In the three seasons that Phee had been out in society, she had overheard her share of stories about the charming Lord Everly. When the Marchioness of Greenwood had made her strategic reentrance into society, Lord Everly had been by her side, a staunch supporter, as Lady Greenwood had chaperoned her younger sister through her season. On more than one occasion, gossip had been spread that the pair were secretly together, a rather heart wrenching love story given their inability to ever marry, but when Lady Greenwood married the marquis, the ton's interest in him faded to nothing more than speculation of who would be next to grab the dashing earl's attention.

"Right. Well, good evening, my lord." Giving a curtsey, Phee left the library in search of her mother. If she had looked back, she would have seen Lord Everly watch her leave, his once smiling face now a reflective frown as he folded up the piece of paper that held her contract and tucked it inside his jacket.

CHAPTER THREE

MOUTH DRY AND head pounding, Harrison sat in his bed the next morning, certain that if he repeated his nightly endeavors of drinking to excess, it would eventually kill him. Each evening he started out certain that he was fine, determined to carry on as if his heart did not ache with loneliness, and each morning he wandered back into his Mayfair townhome with drunken regret for what was about to come. The headache and nausea were nothing a strong cup of tea and hardy breakfast could not handle, but the notion of his behavior was the thing that tormented him, and last night was not any different.

Except for one thing.

Folded on his nightstand was Lady Phoebe Kent's list of demands.

She had once again found him wallowing in his desolation, and once again, her intriguing conversation and smokey voice had given him a small relief from the agony he put himself through. The woman was an enigma, her unapologetically bold way of talking odd but captivating, her ways of thinking even more so. She had made him laugh and smile, an unfamiliar notion these days, and in truth, he found it very easy to be in her presence. With her departure from the Halliwell library, she had not seemed to realize that she had left her list of demands with him, and even now, the sheet of paper called his name, begging him to look at it again.

Her notions of marriage, while entertaining, seemed absolutely ridiculous. Yes, marriage was a contract, but for things like money and family lineage, not beekeeping and child rearing. And yet, were those not the things that made up every marriage? Harrison frowned at his cup of tea.

In the end, the decision to lead a contented marital life resided between the individuals who exchanged vows, so did it not make sense that both parties were in agreement as to what that would look like? And in turn, would not marrying someone with a mutual understanding be a much simpler endeavor than the courtship dance she so obviously hated?

Harrison shook his head, his pounding mind racing with thoughts and questions, and in their center was a woman with gray eyes and a husky laugh. It was her fault he was thinking so heavily in the morning, her fault he was contemplating how a marriage like the one she proposed would work. And her fault that he could not shake the idea that perhaps Lady Phoebe Kent was onto something.

Throwing back the covers, Harrison stood, pausing to let his stomach settle at the sudden jolt. Snatching up the paper from his nightstand, he opened it and scanned its contents. No children, one ball, and the ability to do whatever hobby she wished. Nothing demanding love, nothing demanding gifts of adoration, not even a note requiring fidelity. It was nothing at all like he had hoped marriage would be. It was simple. Could it be that simple?

Pursing his lips, Harrison folded and unfolded the paper. A marriage such as this would bind him to a stranger for eternity, removing any chance he may have at love. But as of late, he had begun to wonder if a love such as the ones he had read about were even possible for him. With Lady Phoebe's proposition, at least it would guarantee that he would never be alone, even if his wife was someone he barely knew. And given her lack of interest in emotional and physical requirements, there were parameters in place that would keep him safe. Stop him from forming any sort of connection other than their business arrangement.

Ringing for his valet, Harrison waited for the man to arrive, pacing his room with even steps as he read the contract over and over again, his mind calculating the possibility that a marriage like this could even be successful, while his heart screamed at him, certain of his folly, unwilling to give up the idea of a love match. When Roger, his valet, arrived, Harrison had talked himself into and out of his plan so many times he was not certain what to do.

"My lord?" Roger said.

Raising his gaze from the paper, Harrison looked at Roger. With a breath and a final glance at the contract, he nodded. "Right. Help me to dress."

Roger raised a brow, but set to work setting out a pair of buckskin breeches, a freshly starched cravat, along with a shirt, waistcoat, and jacket. After two hours of meddling, followed by a hearty breakfast, Harrison stood before the mirror of his bedroom put back together, his sandy locks styled artfully and his face clean of stubble.

While his head still pounded and his stomach rolled, those ailments had little to do with the decision he had come to.

Calling for his carriage, Harrison set his driver toward James Street where Thomas Kent, the Earl of Youngly resided. While the footman delivered his calling card, Harrison sat inside his carriage, his leg bouncing with nervous energy, and when the footman returned stating that Lady Phoebe and her mother would see him, his breath caught. What the devil was he doing? But the contract burned his chest where it resided in his coat pocket.

Answers. He was simply looking for answers.

Inside Lord Youngly's drawing room, Lady Youngly and her daughter both stood to greet him, Lady Phoebe's mouth forming a small circle before she glanced at her mother, her eyebrows raised.

"Lord Everly, it is such an honor to have you grace us this beautiful morning," Lady Youngly said, her voice soft.

Lady Phoebe stood with her hands clasped before her, her mouth flat as she inspected him, as if ascertaining what his presence meant. Her blonde hair was pinned in a simple coiffeur, nothing at all like the tightly rolled styles that had become popular as of late, and she wore a modest yellow day dress that appeared to have been made of linen with not a ruffle or flounce in sight as it curved and caressed the lines of her body. She was even more beautiful in the sunlight, a smattering of freckles skipping along her cheeks and nose and her gray eyes lined with dark lashes.

"Lady Youngly," he said with a bow. "Lady Phoebe. You both look stunning."

Lady Youngly motioned to the yellow sofa where Lady Phoebe stood. "Please, sit. I've rung for some tea and cakes."

"Tea would be lovely, thank you," he said, taking the seat beside Lady Phoebe.

Harrison's leg resumed its bouncing. "Did you attend the Halliwell ball last night, my lord?" Lady Youngly asked.

"I did. It was a lovely evening with very diverting conversation," he said, with a quick glance at Lady Phoebe, who sat uncharacteristically silent, her gaze unmoving from the hands in her lap. Christ, how did one make small talk when they had such important questions to answer?

"It was a lovely evening," she said, glancing at Lady Phoebe. "It is a shame we had to leave early."

"I hope everything was all right?" he asked, avoiding glancing at Lady Phoebe again, certain the motion would give him away.

Lady Youngly smiled, her gaze taking in her daughter. "Oh yes, everything was fine. I simply became tired and unfortunately my daughter was forced to come home with me."

"Ah, yes," Harrison said, peaking at Lady Phoebe who looked at her hands as she linked and unlinked her fingers together.

A knock sounded before a maid entered the room pushing a tea cart. Once the dishes were set out and the tea poured, the maid hurried away, the click of the door closing piercing like a gavel.

Lady Youngly poured everyone tea before picking up her own cup and taking a sip. "What lovely weather we're having," she said.

Harrison's teacup rattled in its saucer as he set it down on the table before him. "I beg your pardon, my lady, but would it be possible that I speak to Lady Phoebe alone?"

Lady Youngly paused, her teacup halfway to her opened mouth, frozen as if he had stunned her into silence.

"May we have fifteen minutes and then you can return?" Lady Phoebe asked, her voice quiet.

Lady Youngly nodded, a bright smile taking over as she set her teacup down on the table. "Of course. Why not make it twenty? No use in hurrying through this wonderful visit." She glanced at Harrison. "My lord?"

Harrison nodded, hoping the smile on his lips was reassuring. When she left and only they remained in the room, Harrison turned to Lady Phoebe, removing her contract from his coat pocket.

Taking in the piece of paper before her, she asked, "What is that?"

"The contract. Your contract," he said, the words pushed from his lips on a breath of air.

Lady Phoebe shook her head and stood. "Are you returning it to me or do you have something more nefarious in mind? You wouldn't be attempting to blackmail me, my lord?"

"What?" Harrison said. "No. God, no. I wanted to ask you something."

Lady Phoebe stared at him, her fingers opening and closing around each other. "Go on."

"Is this truly all you want in a marriage?"

Lady Phoebe rolled her eyes. "I told you as much the night before. I'm not certain what the point of this is—"

"I'll do it," he said, standing from his seat. Lady Phoebe froze like prey before a lion as his words reverberated around the room. "I'll do it. I'll marry you."

"Why on earth would do you do that?" she asked, her gaze focused on him.

"Because it's just as you said. I'm looking for a wife and you're looking for a husband. Your terms seem reasonable, I don't dislike being in your company, and it would give us both what we're looking for."

Her wide eyes scanned the room, her hands fluttering in a panic. "I don't want children, my lord."

Harrison stepped forward. "That's fine. I'm not too interested in having them myself."

Her head swiveled to look at him. "You're the earl. You're supposed to carry on the line. You're supposed to have children."

He shook his head. "I have a cousin with three young boys of his own who I'm sure would be more than happy to take over the title," he said, taking another step closer. "You were right, Lady Phoebe. This is our life and we should have a choice in the way it goes." Taking one of her hands, he squeezed it gently, noting the faint tremor in her delicate fingers. The soft warmth of her pale skin was soothing beneath his touch and she emitted a soft gasp as his thumb swept over her knuckles. "If you've changed your mind, I understand."

Lady Phoebe shook her head. "No." She looked at their clasped hands, her brow furrowed in confusion. "No, I haven't changed my mind," she said, gently removing her hand from his.

"Then marry me?" he asked, the words more a plea

than a question.

She bit her lip as she stared at the white carpet that covered the floor of the drawing room. "What are your conditions?"

Harrison smiled. "I'm glad you asked." Removing a pencil from his coat pocket, he retook his seat at the yellow sofa and bent over the table, his pencil raised over her list. Looking at Lady Phoebe, who had not moved from her spot, Harrison motioned to the sofa on the other side of the table, and waited for her to take a seat. "I'm amendable to all of this. I would, however, like to add a few things for myself."

"Go on," she said.

"At the balls you do attend, you must dance both waltzes with me." Lady Phoebe wrung her hands, her gaze focused on the contract. "Will that be a problem?" he asked.

"No," she said, her focus never wavering. "Anything else?"

"Yes." Harrison paused, uncertain of how to put the item into words. "Each night." He cleared his throat. "That is, each night, you are to play a card game with me before we go to bed." It was the one requirement he knew would make her pause. The one addendum that could change her whole mind on the contract, but he could not fathom another night alone with only his thoughts to entertain him.

Lady Phoebe looked at him then, her mouth open in protest. "Each night? And what of the nights that you're out? Am I supposed to wait up for your return like a dutiful wife?"

One corner of his lips tugged into a smile and he looked at the paper to hide it. "I shall be home every night at a reasonable hour for our card game."

"Do you plan for us to remain in London indefinitely?"

Harrison thought on her question. "If that is amendable to you? I feel more at ease in the city, but if you'd like, we can follow the ton and only remain during the season?"

"No, London is fine." She took a deep breath, then looked at her hands once more. "And what about intimate matters?" she asked, her fingers opening and closing about each other.

"Oh. Well…"

"I ask because it seemed to be a pertinent part in our discussion last night."

Harrison paused, allowing himself to focus on the notion of an intimate relationship with any woman who was not Meg. His throat tightened, and a pang coursed its way through the area where his heart supposedly resided. Given that he required a connection to have any interest in physical intimacy, it would appear that his future was one of celibacy, the same as Lady Phoebe. "Intimate matters will not be required."

"Very well. And how are we to announce our marriage? Not a single soul has seen us interact, and in truth, I'm not sure I can do with a whole courtship façade."

Harrison frowned, mulling over the problem. "If I were to ask for your hand right this moment, do you think your father would be amiable?"

A corner of Lady Phoebe's mouth rose in a smile. "Yes.

I've had offers from the usual fortune hunters and social climbers, but I've always dissuaded him from accepting. If he knows that this marriage has my approval, I'm certain he'll get down on his hands and knees and thank you profusely."

With a nod, Harrison added his articles to the list, then signed his name at the bottom of the contract before standing and handing the pencil over to Lady Phoebe. Her penmanship was concise, tight and neat as she scrawled her name beside his and it did something odd to Harrison's stomach. The rolling emptiness that resided there settled, as if given a soothing tonic. Yes, this was most certainly a good decision for both of them. A marriage of convenience that would give them each the life they wanted without the nonsensical requirements of society. It was brilliant, really, and Lady Phoebe, his future wife, had been the mechanism for the whole thing.

Once her signature was finished, Lady Phoebe set the pencil down beside the paper that had started it all, wiped her hand against her skirt, then stuck it out to him. "We have an agreement, Lord Everly," she said.

Taking her hand in his, Harrison shook her hand, a sense of calm overtaking him. "Indeed, we do, Lady Phoebe. Indeed, we do."

CHAPTER FOUR

April, 1822

THE WEDDING OF Lord Harrison Metcalf, the Earl of Everly, and Lady Phoebe Kent was unimaginably boring and decidedly simple, exactly as Phee had wanted. While her mother had toiled over every nonsensical detail required for a wedding, Phee instead chose to plan the layout of honeybee hives for her new home. And when her mother mentioned a wedding trousseau and gown, Phee simply shrugged and said not only did she have no need for a trousseau, but that her peach day gown would work just fine for the ceremony. Her mother had stood stunned, the two lines between her eyebrows deepening at her daughter's absolute lack of regard for her own nuptials, but Phee could not find it in her heart nor head to care.

It was a business transaction, after all, and the only rules she was required to follow were clearly outlined on a simple sheet of paper that now resided in her copy of *Treatise on the Nature, Economy and Practical Management of Bees*. As far as she was concerned, the wedding was nothing more than a Tuesday. Which is why, as the well-wishers, if one could call them that, flooded her parent's front parlor, each vying for a glimpse of the odd newlyweds, Phee stood still beside her new husband, her clammy, gloved hand resting lightly on his arm, the corded muscles beneath his wool coat giving her fingers something to trace. With a smile on her lips, she remained motionless as she was inspected with curiosity as to what she could have possessed to ensnare the Earl of Everly. It, of course, made little sense to the ton that the eyesore of the season would make such an advantageous marriage, especially when they had never been seen in each other's presence.

Phee's body buzzed, the blood rushing through her veins creating a pounding sound in her ears as each minute she was required to be on show passed. There were too many people, too many bodies stuffed into the small space, their pungent smell filling her nose, and no amount of fanning her scent of honeysuckle could push away the aroma. Phee's mind raced and she focused on the lists of necessary preparations for when they finally were able to make their way back to Lord Everly's Grosvenor square home, praying the familiar would ease the ongoing discomfort. And given the time reading on the small pocket watch she had stowed away, they were in for another hour of this torture before they could even move on to the wedding breakfast.

"Are you all right?" Lord Everly whispered in her ear.

Phee forced a smile to her lips and looked up into his brown eyes, which were currently scanning her face. With a nod, he smiled softly at her. "I think we're done here, my lady. Are you ready to head home?"

Not waiting for her response, Lord Everly removed her gloved hand from his forearm and headed over to where her mother and father stood with a group of guests. With a bowed head, he said something to the pair before bowing and returning to Phee's side. "I've made our excuses and the butler is bringing around your things. Is there anything else you require before we depart?"

"No," Phee said, the word released in a single breath.

After procuring her spencer and hat, Lord Everly took her hand and guided her outside to where his carriage waited, handing her into the conveyance with haste. Inside the conveyance, Phee pulled in a breath, Lord Everly's citrus and cigar scent permeating the air, filling her lungs like a hug of relief. While the slight throbbing at her temple did not ease, her shoulders relaxed and her stomach stopped churning as soon as the door closed behind her new husband.

"How did you know—" she began to ask, but Lord Everly interrupted her.

"Your mouth becomes pinched and you flinch at the sharper voices in the room. Do you truly not know you have tells when you're overstimulated?"

Phee blinked. "No, I didn't." She rubbed at her temple, willing away the pulsing that resided there. "Is it obvious?"

"Only to those paying attention," Lord Everly said, removing the white gloves from his hands and moving beside her on the bench seat. "Is your head bothering you?"

Phee nodded. "I usually get a headache after these interactions."

"May I try something?" Lord Everly asked as he reached out his hands.

Phee pulled back. "What are you doing?"

"You look as if you are in pain and I only hoped to

ease it," he said, his hands still outstretched. "Is it all right if I do?"

Phee nodded even as she felt her forehead wrinkle into a frown. Lord Everly's warm fingers slid along both of her temples, the slight pressure he applied creating a soothing rhythm to the aching areas. Sunlight filtered in through the carriage window, casting a spotlight on her new husband. His sandy hair turned platinum where the sun kissed it, reminding her of the straw Rumpelstiltskin spun in an old fairy tale her nanny used to read to her. Flecks of gold danced in his brown eyes which were framed by pale lashes, his gaze focused on where his hands resided. He was an unbearably attractive man, this husband of hers, almost exactly what she pictured the prince would look like in the storybooks.

"Does this feel all right?" he asked, his voice quiet.

Phee forced herself to focus on his ministrations instead of the work of art that sat before her. His fingertips were soft, nary a sign of callus or scar, and as they worked in a circular motion, easing the incessant pain, Phee closed her eyes and allowed the rhythm to entrance her. "It's helping," she said, the truthful words slipping easily between her lips.

Lord Everly chuckled, the sound heavy and deep like the beating of a drum. "I'm glad." He remained quiet for a time, the silence filling the carriage comforting in an odd sort of way, so when he spoke again, Phee startled at the noise. "You said you get these headaches after every society affair?"

"Mm," she said, hoping the sound was affirming and that he did not stop the soothing motions upon her skull.

Lord Everly released a sigh, the slight hint of peppermint mingling with the citrus and cigar that already danced in the air. "I cannot imagine the pain you must go through every time. It's little wonder you ran away at every possible convenience." He paused and Phee released a sound of frustration that prompted his motions to start once again. "Little wonder you deemed limited interaction in your contract as such a necessity."

His words lifted the foggy haze that clouded her brain, and Phee pulled back. Even if this man was her husband, it was a business transaction, and surely it did not include skull rubbing. At least, she was certain it was not anywhere in their contract. "Thank you, my lord. My head feels much better."

Lord Everly's hands were still raised in the air where her head had resided and with the quirk of a brow, he lowered them into his lap. "I'll have the housekeeper fetch a tonic for you once we arrive at my home." He chuckled once more. "Or perhaps, I should say, our home, my lady."

Phee felt the muscles between her eyebrows contract at his statement, and the pounding in her head resumed at the action. Blast and drat, she would need to get that motion under control if she wanted to get rid of these horrid pains.

As the carriage began to slow, Phee removed her pocket watch once more and glanced at the time. A small smile tugged at her lips as she watched the big and little hand nearly straddle one another as they pointed at the twelve. Surely her delivery had arrived, and hopefully fully intact. Biting at her lip, she pushed down the urge to jostle her leg in impatience and waited, as a fine English lady would, for a footman to open the door and her husband to hand her down.

The entire staff of Lord Everly's Mayfair townhome stood on the steps, a stern looking woman in a brown dress standing to the side presiding over them. Laugh lines bracketed her mouth, contending with her severe appearance, and her eyes brightened as Phee moved toward her.

"Lady Everly, this is my housekeeper, Mrs. Beatley," Lord Everly said, motioning to the figure before them. "She's been with the family since I was a young lad." The woman dipped a curtsey, a smile taking over her face as she raised her gaze to Phee.

"My lady, it is a pleasure to meet you," Mrs. Beatley said.

Lord Everly smiled. "And this is my most dutiful butler, Sterns," he said, nodding to an older man with a wrinkled forehead and kindly smile.

The butler bowed to her, his soft expression comforting, and she smiled at him in return. "A pleasure to meet you both," she said, the expression slipping easily from her lips as if it had been hammered into her skull for years, which it had.

Sterns, gentle smile still in place, looked at her. "My lady, a delivery arrived for you. I had the footmen set them up in the garden as per the instructions I was given," he said. The housekeeper winked at his pronouncement.

"Thank you," Phee said.

"Delivery?" Lord Everly asked. He looked at Sterns. "You made no mention of a delivery before I departed this morning."

Sterns smiled at Lord Everly. "The delivery arrived while you were at the ceremony, my lord. A most exciting delivery, indeed. I've never seen hives before."

"Hives," Lord Everly said, the word full of amusement. "Any reason why I was not privy to this addition?"

The question was directed to Sterns and Beatley, but Phee answered for the pair, uncertain where the confusion lay. "I'm afraid that's my fault, my lord. Seeing as how it was in our contract, I made the assumption that I would not need your permission." Lord Everly looked at her with a frown marring his beautiful pink lips. "I am allowed to pursue any hobby I like as well as have full control over the design of the garden."

Lord Everly shook his head, a smile overtaking his face, before turning and striding into his elegant Mayfair townhome. Phee trailed at rapid speed behind Lord Everly, barely looking at the home's design, her peach skirts swishing with the force of a broom against the marble floors. Lord Everly threw open the doors to the balcony and gardens below, and Phee's breath caught at the onslaught of colors and perfumes that assaulted her senses. Flowers of every shape and size danced at the slight breeze, trees bearing luscious flowers stood strong against the onslaught, the impressive branches reaching toward the sky. It was a paradise full of potential, and Phee nearly giggled in delight.

Two *Huber* hives sat on wooden tables in a section of the lawn, the individual frames of each hive open like a book, empty, as if awaiting their words. The hives were spaced nearly two meters apart, the setup appeared more like the face of a dice than the imagined enterprise of beekeeping Phee had dreamt up, but it was merely step one in a complex series, and would have to do for now.

Lord Everly stopped at the sight, his face a journey of emotions as he absorbed the contents of his gardens and while Phee desperately longed to examine the hives and make adjustments to the layout, she instead paused beside her husband and waited for him to speak. Lord Everly took his time, and Phee clasped her hands before her, her fingers pulling at the tips of her white gloves in impatience.

Clearing of his throat, Lord Everly turned to her, his eyes crinkled at the corners. "Lady Phoebe, what is this?" he asked.

With a smile, Phee turned and looked at the setup of her hives. "Isn't it obvious? This is my hobby."

"Bees," he whispered with amazement. "That's what you meant by bees."

CHAPTER FIVE

EVEN THOUGH THE hives were obviously empty, Harrison swore he could hear a buzzing that sounded like a swarm of bees had taken up residence in the space between his ears. Shaking his head, he laughed at the image before him. This was fine. No doubt his newly acquired wife would become bored of her hobby like all aristocratic wives. After all, she did not specify what her hobbies were. No… No, he was certain the contract said hobbies, as in many. Certainly, it had.

With a smile on his lips, he turned toward the stranger that was now bound to him for eternity. "How delightful to learn another interesting facet of you, my lady."

Lady Phoebe seemed unaware of his words, her eyes focused on the hives, a smile forming near the corners of her mouth. She was removed from their conversation entirely; her whole being drawn to the hives like a bee to a luscious flower. She moved toward one table, her gloved finger tracing over a frame that lay open exposed to the sun.

"They're empty," he said, moving to stand beside her.

"Yes. I'm still looking for colonies to fill them." She smiled as she looked at the pair. "Wouldn't it be wonderful if a colony made one of these their home all on their own?"

"Is that likely to happen?"

"It might," she said, looking at him, "if I do it right."

"That sounds rather mystifying."

She frowned at him and Harrison puzzled at the display. Had he said something wrong?

"Well, I'm excited to see what comes of this," he said to her. "May I escort you inside so you can relax after today's festivities? Perhaps join me in some refreshments since we did not partake in breakfast?" He extended his elbow toward her, waiting for her to take it, but she shook her head instead.

"No, I think I will remain here, thank you."

Harrison blinked, his arm still extended as his brain attempted to understand what he had heard. "You wish to stay out here?"

Lady Phoebe nodded, removing her gloves as her eyes examined the hives. "Yes. The placement of the hives isn't quite as I'd like them to be, and I would like to speak with the gardener regarding the types of flowers I'd like for him to use around the area."

"I'm not sure I understand," he said, lowering his arm to his side. "You're planning to take this section of the lawn and surround it with flowers?"

She released a small sound, a giggle that was terribly childlike in its resonance. "Of course. How else are the bees expected to nourish themselves as they settle into their homes?" she asked with a smile. She was laughing at him, but it seemed he missed the joke.

"I'm not sure why my confusion amuses you," he said, the words filled with perplexion.

The smile on her face disappeared as swiftly as a

breeze, her eyes losing any glimmer of joy they might have held. "I'm sorry, my lord," she said softly before executing a curtsey. "Please excuse me."

Her skirts swished with gentle dismay, as if they too were summarily dismissed, and Harrison frowned. The interaction made no logical sense. One moment she was laughing and the next, the light in her eyes disappeared as if he had admonished her, like a nursemaid does an unruly child. It was perplexing and irritating, and if he were honest, a bit saddening. What had this poor woman been up against that she mistook a simple comment of confusion for something else?

Harrison stood frozen in his spot, uncertain whether to follow and remedy whatever miscommunication they were having, or give her space to compose herself. "Better out than in," he said, the words whispered as he took a step in the direction she had gone.

"My lord," said Mrs. Beatley.

Smoothing the wrinkles that graced his brow, Harrison turned toward his housekeeper with his practiced smile in place. "Yes?"

The older woman glanced toward the direction of his wife, then back at him. "I had Cook start hot water for baths for you both." She glanced once more toward where Lady Phoebe had gone and smiled gently. "But I can see her ladyship is currently preoccupied. Perhaps something to eat while she examines the gardens?"

The housekeeper's concern was understandable. With a final glance toward his new wife, Harrison returned his gaze to the housekeeper, his tone bright as he addressed her. "My wife is rather excited over the arrival of her hives, but I'm certain once she has arranged the garden to her likings, she would enjoy a bath and some refreshments."

She nodded her head. "Very well, my lord. I had the countess's rooms aired and cleaned and her maid is currently settling the lady's items to rights, so all shall be ready when she does wish to bathe."

The sentence was simple, its tone erring on the side of bored, yet the moment his ears heard it, his heart picked up speed and his breath became labored. What surely must have been a hand gripped his throat making swallowing, let alone uttering a single word, possible. Forcing himself to nod and smile, Harrison croaked out the word *good*, then swiftly removed himself from the terrace.

Inside the study, he threw the lock before pouring himself two fingers of scotch and taking a seat on a plush brown leather arm chair. Sipping at the fire-like liquid, he called himself every name in the book as he forced bit by bit past his lips, willing the concoction to loosen the grip around his throat.

It was merely a bedroom. A bedroom, he reminded himself, that had been subjected to occupancy by many countesses before his time, and yet... And yet, his imprudent heart kept chiding him, reminding him that the bedroom beside his, the one meant for the Countess of Everly, had once been Meg's when she had been his uncle's countess. The blue papered walls covered with daisy's, the light pink linens that graced the bed and windows had been meticulously picked out by a woman that not only no longer resided there, but had moved on. Had married another and by all appearances was happier than she ever had been. Yet the room still smelled like her, a spicy vanilla scent that hung about like a specter, and his brain would not stop replaying the image of her standing in that space, no matter how much time had passed.

He was a ridiculous man no doubt bound for Bedlam, for he could not stop thinking about a future and a wife that would never be, could not stop thinking about the moments when he should have taken a chance and not been so scared. If he had not been so afraid, had confessed that since the age of twenty he had been in love with Margaret Reedy, the Countess of Everly, his uncle's wife, perhaps the path he had ended up on would have been different.

It took very little time for Harrison to understand that he was a sap, a lovesick dolt chasing after a woman who not only felt nothing but friendship toward him, but had fallen in love and married another man. A future duke. Scoffing, Harrison threw back the last of the drink. Oliver Ludlow's title had very little to do with the reason Meg adored him, but Harrison was certain it helped.

And the worst part, the bitter piece he could not stomach to chew, was that if he had merely not been such a coward and spoken his true feelings for her sooner, his future quite possibly could have been different. If he had confessed to Meg that he loved her from the very beginning. If he had followed her to Woodingdean instead of staying behind as she had asked, if he had helped her repair the dilapidated manor his uncle had left her instead of merely offering funds. If he had been there before bloody Oliver Ludlow swooped in and snatched her attention...

If only. If only... It had become a bloody song in his head, a nightly ritual that chanted at him, calling him tens kinds of a dunce as he replayed every opportunity he missed. And it had been his biggest reason for agreeing to Lady Phoebe's contractual marriage.

But now? Now Lady Phoebe was going to take residence in the final piece of Meg he had. Her scent would take over the room, sweeping the familiar vanilla spice away and replacing it with the sweet aroma of honeysuckle. She would no doubt choose new paper for the walls, new linens for the bed, and within little time, Meg's presence in the home would be removed entirely, especially given that his uncle had made sure Meg had little say in the home's décor. And for that, Harrison hated the man even more.

Perhaps he had not thought this marriage thing through enough, not given it the proper focus required for such a life altering decision. And now, he had a wife who surrounded his garden with bee hives and within a matter of hours would erase the final piece he had of the woman he loved. A harsh laugh broke through his lips as he heard himself, the role of Shakespearean protagonist looking less and less appealing on him each day, but no matter what he did, he was reminded of his mindlessness. Of his cowardice.

No. Perhaps this was for the best. Let Lady Phoebe cast out the final specter of Meg that resided in this house. Let her presence fill the home and banish away every remanence of the former countess. There was little sense in delaying the inevitable, and it was only right for his wife to occupy the countess's rooms. And, like it or not, Meg would never be his countess. He would rather her be in love and happy than trapped once more in her gilded prison.

Setting the cut glass down on the sideboard, Harrison straightened his jacket, adjusted his cravat, and sighed before forcing his practiced smile back on his lips. This was fine, everything would be fine. He was moving on.

Healing, one might say.

Leaving the study, he kept the smile plastered to his face, calmly navigating through the rest of the day with his typical jovial demeanor as he attended to estate matters and periodically checked in on his new wife.

Dinner that night was an utterly awkward affair, Lady Phoebe choosing to place her focus on the meal before her rather than converse, and the silence was nearly deafening as she sat on the opposite end of the table, the distance palpable. The need for distraction from the rampant thoughts in his head was making his signature smile twitch at the corners, and even the delicious roast chicken before him did very little to help.

"How was your meeting with the gardener?" he asked, cutting the meat on his plate into several bite sized pieces.

"Beneficial," she said, before placing a piece of carrot into her mouth with her dinner fork. In the upper corner of her place setting sat a pile of discarded silverware that Lady Phoebe had inspected before settling on the dinner fork, dinner spoon, and the knife.

Harrison's eyebrow twitched at her one-worded answer. "What did he think of your idea for the flowers?"

"He was amenable." In went a potato.

Placing his knife and fork to the side, Harrison forced

a smile and looked at his new wife. "I'm terribly sorry, Lady Phoebe, but are you all right?" She looked at him then. "It's only that you seem a bit out of sorts." She frowned at him. "Is there anything I might do to help you feel more at ease?"

Lady Phoebe set down her fork, her lips pinched, eyes scanning her plate as if searching for the proper words. "I'm not used to conversing at meal times."

"Why?" he asked.

"My attempts at conversation would make the lines between my mother's eyebrows deepen, so I thought it best to say nothing at all."

"Like bee mating?"

A corner of her mouth lifted. "Like bee mating."

For Lady Phoebe, it would seem that the silence was a necessary evil, one she had acclimated to given her penchant for odd conversation topics, but for Harrison, the silence was hell. He had spent every moment in this home in utter silence with only his thoughts for company. Whether his uncle were alive or not, it mattered very little, for he was always lonely. One thing he could not do was live another moment in that home in silence.

"This is your home now, and in truth, I'd prefer conversation, even on bee mating, rather than silence. Just because this marriage of ours is contractual doesn't mean we cannot treat one another as friends. Think of ourselves as accomplices."

She raised a brow at him as she picked back up her fork. "Accomplices?"

Harrison took up his fork as well. "Yes. Accomplices in marriage." He waved the fork in the air. "Coconspirators. Companions."

She laughed then, the sound smokey. "Now you're just saying the same thing in different fonts." She put a piece of chicken in her mouth and eyed him. When the bite was finished, she took a sip from the wine glass before her. "Friends?" she asked, the word tentative.

Harrison nodded. "Certainly. Friends."

The remainder of the meal carried on in comfortable conversation, Lady Phoebe's mind working like an intricate web that on the surface, made little sense, but when one followed the string, it became crystal clear how the thoughts were connected.

"Might I ask why you've discarded some of your cutlery?" he asked.

Lady Phoebe frowned and she shook her head. "Those didn't feel quite right," she said.

"What do you mean?"

"The salad fork is too small to wield and the smaller spoon doesn't give you the right sized bite." The words were stated simply, as if it were general knowledge.

Harrison looked down at his table setting, his eyes falling to the dinner fork in his hand. It did feel different than the salad fork, its weight more reassuring in his hand and the tines long enough to support a sufficient bite. "I see what you mean," he said. "What else have you noticed?"

With a smile, Harrison watched his new wife talk, a beautiful smile on her face, and for the first time in a while, he felt hopeful. After all, he could be friends with his wife, and there was certainly nothing wrong with having friends.

CHAPTER SIX

AFTER A DELICIOUS chocolate pudding for dessert, Phee followed Lord Everly into the library. Four cozy chairs faced one another in a circle before the fireplace, which was burning low and slow, filling the room with heat but very little light. A few candles along the mantel were lit, drawing the room out of the gloomy atmosphere it no doubt could have become, and Phee's shoulders relaxed at the ambiance. Rather than intimidating, the room appeared friendly. Comfortable. Like a place one could while away the hours on a rainy-day reading.

Lord Everly grabbed a low table and placed it between the two chairs closest to the fireplace, then went over to one of the glass enclosed cabinets and removed a deck of cards. Phee's stomach knotted as she wondered what game he intended to play. While she was versed in a multitude of games as customary for young ladies, she rather detested them. They were time consuming, requiring the player to while away hours at a time to something frivolous, and while the rules of the game did not confuse her, the tittering and underhanded barbs struck at one another during the play did. Her mother assured her it was all in good fun, but Phee was not so sure.

When Lord Everly stood before a chair and smiled at her, Phee scrunched up her courage and took the chair opposite of him. The blue striped fabric and pillowy cushions surrounded her as she settled in her seat and a yawn threatened to overwhelm her at the comfort of it. This chair, no doubt, would make a wonderful place to read a book or take a nap.

Lord Everly sat across from her and began shuffling the deck of cards, a carefree smile on his lips. Phee took the moment to watch him, analyze the man she had just agreed to spend the remainder of her life with. The smile seemed immovable, as if glued to his face, and instead of chalking it up to a happy demeanor, she wondered at the purpose of it. Was he always happy? Jovial? The two times before their engagement that she had spent with him, the smile had been absent, a mask of discontent marring his gorgeous features. And gorgeous he was, for she could not lie about that. His sandy blond hair and chocolate brown eyes gave him the appearance of a friendly pup always excited to merely be in your presence. His complexion was clean, lightly tanned but unmarred by freckles or scars, as if he had been sculpted mere moments before. It was unnerving, really, just how handsome her husband was. And given his friendly disposition, she truly could find very little fault in him, except for that smile.

"Now then," Lord Everly said as he began to deal the cards equally between the two of them, "the game we are going to play is Snap."

Phee's brow rose. "Snap? A children's game? I used to play it as a young girl to learn the alphabet."

He nodded, smile unmoving, as he finished dealing the cards. "Mine were pictures of animals." With a shrug, he said, "Just because it is a game for children doesn't mean adults can't play it."

"But it is such an easy game," she said, perturbed. Did he think her incapable of playing something more complex? "I assure you, sir, I can play other games that require more of a challenge."

Lord Everly looked at her, his smile transforming, the corners of his lips raising in devious pleasure and a small dimple appeared in one cheek. "Shall we make it more challenging?"

Phee rolled her eyes. "I assume you mean wagering?"

He nodded. "Something like that. Loser of a hand shares a secret about themselves."

She stared at him, uncertain whether to laugh or wonder at her husband's lucidity. "Why?"

He shrugged. "We are married, which means we've got a lot of time to be together. Don't you think one of the requirements of friendship is knowledge about one another? How else would you propose we were to learn about each other's likes and dislikes?"

Phee squinted at him. "I see," she said, the words tentative as she picked up her stack of cards. "Who draws first?"

"Higher card?" he asked, motioning to her deck. "Count of three. One, two, three."

They both flipped their cards over and Phee swallowed a squeal as she saw the king she had turned over, summarily beating his nine.

"Well done, my lady," he said, with a mock bow and Phee chuckled, then paused at the sound.

She stopped, her thoughts turning inward as she assessed the situation. She was comfortable, nearly the same as at her parents' home. Her heart was not racing, its beat strong, and her palms were dry and hands steady. She shook her head, confused by the notion. She was comfortable.

"Lady Phoebe," Lord Everly said, her name on his lips a whisper that still had her head shooting up to meet his gaze. "Are you all right?"

Phee shook her head and smiled at him. "Yes, sorry. Yes."

With a nod, Phee turned her card over, a five. Looking to Lord Everly, she watched as he flipped the first card in his deck revealing a seven. Their motions took on a rhythm as card after card was flipped, but when a pair of aces graced the top of each pile, Phee seized her moment. "Snap!"

Lord Everly's head shot up and a bark of laughter filled the room. "Nicely done."

Phee's skin tingled at his words, and she rolled her eyes as she swiped up the cards she had won. "It's a children's game," she said, leaning back in the chair. "Come on then, pay your dues, my lord."

Lord Everly glanced at the ceiling, his mouth forming a thin line as he contemplated, then a smile took over his lips, the dimple appearing once more. "I detest peas."

Her mouth dropped at the pronouncement. "That's your secret? You dislike a form of legume?"

He smirked. "Did you think I was planning to confess to murder, wife?"

She frowned, whether from the endearment or his secret she was not certain. "No, I simply thought it'd be more scintillating than that."

He nodded sagely. "I'll do better next time. Ready to go again?"

Phee looked at the clock that sat upon the mantel, its hands ticking slowly toward half past eight. She yawned before sitting up and taking her cards in hand once more. "Ready."

"Perhaps this should be our final hand of the night. You look nearly ready to curl up in that chair and sleep."

She met his gaze and smiled. "It's been an extremely long day."

"That it has," he said, returning her smile. "You begin."

The next round went much shorter, Lord Everly calling *snap* as a pair of queens covered the table and he danced in his seat as he collected the piles. Phee sat back and puzzled, searching for a secret but uncertain which to share. One corner of her mouth pulled up as she had a devious thought and she leaned forward, ready to share.

"I hate blueberries."

Lord Everly's mouth fell agape, silence the only thing exiting his cherry-stained lips. Phee leaned back against the chair, its cushion enveloping her, and she crossed her arms, awaiting his reply. His mouth opened and closed like a fish; his brow furrowed as he stared at her.

"I've married a monster," he said with a whisper.

"A monster?" she replied, outraged. "You hate peas, I was merely matching the topic!"

"Peas taste horrendous no matter the seasoning. Even smothered in butter they are inedible. But blueberries." He stood and paced. "Blueberries are delightful. A handful off a blueberry bush on a hot day is a summer necessity.

Blueberry muffins dripping with butter and blueberry pie with a dollop of cream are nearly heaven. How can you hate blueberries?"

Phee searched for the words only able to say, "Baked or stewed, even as a jam, you're correct. But, raw? Off a bush?" She shook her head. "No, thank you. They're too unique."

Lord Everly stopped moving and stared.

"You can never be certain what you'll get with a blueberry. Some are sweet while others are sour. Some are mushy, some are mealy, while others burst in your mouth unexpectedly. A mere handful of blueberries is such an uncertain snack. An apple is itself throughout. The same can be said for an orange, but blueberries." She shook her head. "They're unreliable."

Lord Everly fell into his chair with a soft plop, his eyes searching her face. "Extraordinary," he said.

"What?"

"You're absolutely right, how you just described them. And yet, something I find delightful about the berry is something that leads to your hatred. It's interesting, is all. You're interesting."

"You make it sound as if I'm an artifact to be studied," Phee said, crossing her arms in front of her as she looked down at the table before them, her eyes flitting to every mark and ding along its top to avoid his studying gaze.

"No. You're simply a human who is fascinating and unique. You see the world with a lens I don't possess and it's mesmerizing when I get a chance to peer through it with you." The words were said softly, but the sincerity within them was powerful. Terrifyingly so.

"I should head to bed," she said, looking at the mass of cards in her hand, then toward the table. "Where do I—"

Lord Everly grabbed her deck and returned to the cabinet, placing her stack on the right side of the shelf and setting his own deck on the left side. "So we know where we left off tomorrow," he said with a wink.

"Right." Standing, Phee looked at him. "Well, goodnight then."

"I—" he said, his hand reaching out to her before pulling back. "I'll go with you. I was rather unaware how tired I am myself until just now." Giving her his arm, he led her from the library and up the marble staircase to the floor that housed their rooms.

Phee kept her eyes on the steps before her, uncertain why she felt such an odd niggle of unease that he was walking her to bed. He stopped outside the entrance to his room, turned and smiled at her, although the effect was forced, the dimple that appeared in his right cheek failing to make an appearance. Removing her arm from his, Phee stepped back, her hands gripping one another behind her back as she looked at him.

With a nod, Lord Everly executed a small bow. "Goodnight, Lady Everly. Sleep well," he said, opening the door to his room and disappearing behind it. The wooden portal closed with a soft *snick*, his exit so unremarkable Phee was certain she imagined him being there at all.

Inside her own room, Phee allowed her mind to drift as her maid, Flora, helped her to undress before sitting her in front of a white ornate vanity to brush out her hair. Phee frowned as she ruminated on the evening with her new husband. Confusion at his somber mood change only further burrowed into her brain, replaying over and over as she analyzed what might have caused it. Surely nothing she had said could have provoked the true smile leaving his face, its faux counterpart sliding in to cover the modification.

When Flora left, the quiet of the room wrapped around her like a blanket, its surety a hug unlike any other. The comfortable ease of the evening with Lord Everly did little to dissolve the man's uncertain moods, and Phee shook her head, dismayed that she had likely entered into a situation where she would have to stay on guard and never fully relax into herself. Even his soft words of reassurance were quickly erased by his wavering emotions, which did not bode well for the future. Not at all.

Taking soft steps to avoid detection, Phee approached the door that joined their rooms. Setting her hands gently against the wood, she leaned against it, pressing her ear to the portal as she silently waited for a sound, but it was only silence that greeted her. No deep voice echoing through the door, nor the sounds of one readying themselves for bed, and Phee leaned back, frowning at the thing. He claimed she was a lens through which he could see her viewpoint, but for her, he was a door, blocking off every discovery and only leaving a muffled sound if any.

"Goodnight, Lord Everly," she said with a whisper. "Sleep well."

CHAPTER SEVEN

HARRISON HAD BEEN married nearly a week, and yet, if someone were to visit his home, they would wonder if his wife even existed. Lady Phoebe chose not to break her fast with him, but instead, took her tea and porridge in the garden, surrounded by the litany of flowers she had instructed the gardener to plant. She then spent the remainder of the day tending to one of the hives, which had become occupied by a swarm of bees that simply appeared one morning. She wore an atrocious mask and coat, and long gloves about her arms, protecting her skin from their potential sting as she monitored their daily habits in a small yellow journal that she took nearly everywhere with her. At lunch time, she removed herself to her bedroom to eat and bathe, then spent the remainder of her day in her room until dinner.

She still sat across from him and talked openly about her day and the things she was learning from the swarm as they dined, and their games of Snap arrived like the chiming of the clock, a few hands played and secrets divulged, and then off to bed, only to repeat the same events the following day. It was maddening.

The only change within the home that was slightly obvious was the incessant buzzing from the hive that one encountered as soon as they exited the balcony and made their way to the gardens. The bees were not hostile, their intentions to make food to feed the queen and hive, not start a war, but their constant *bizz* and *buzz* were less like music to the ear and more like the wailings of a small child, bothersome and grating. And grating it was, for not only was he just as alone as he had been before marrying, but now it was accompanied by the backdrop of what could only be described as a nightmare. And what was worse, Lady Phoebe seemed utterly content with the conditions.

It was unfathomable, in truth, her comfortability in nearly little to no human interaction. The woman no doubt spoke less than a thousand words each day, and most of them to him; meanwhile, he was on the verge of hysteria at the loneliness of it all. Yes, there was not a single item in the contract that required companionship, nor had he ever asked for her company, but he did hope that there would be some sort of interaction with the person he had taken vows with outside of their nightly dinner and cards. Had hoped that the presence of another person would ease the quiet that had incessantly sur-rounded him in the home.

The rooms remained untouched, for as she had stated one evening at dinner, she had 'very little interest in decorating', and Mrs. Beatley simply continued on with the care and attention to the home since his wife believed 'she was not very good at such matters'. She did nothing but bees. If she was not tending to them, she was reading about them, or adding more flowers, or studying the dance they did to make the others aware of a food source. He did not resent her hobbies, no, merely he had assumed that their marriage would mean he would be a little less alone, and as it was turning out, that was not true.

After four days of watching her focus solely on her hobby, Harrison had begun to take himself to White's, desperate for company, even just a change of sound. The men there would greet him in a jovial manner, but rarely with friendly intent unless they wanted something. It would seem his uncle's rather negative reputation in Parliament had merely spilled down upon him, and the ton seemed uncertain of his intentions. No, unless they were looking for deep pockets to place a bet or a vote from him, the majority preferred him as an acquaintance rather than a friend. Well, all but Averndale.

Jamison Crenshaw, the Viscount of Averndale, had stayed by his side from the very beginning of Eton, though Harrison could never really say why. The man, although angelic in appearance, lived voraciously, his title bestowed to him at the ripe age of two, and their paths had never truly crossed until his first year at school. An invitation to a card game had placed him directly in the viscount's sight, and whether it had been Harrison's lack of polish, or the whiskey one of the lads had smuggled in, Averndale had taken Harrison under his wing, determined to make the awkward boy into a charming rogue. Thankfully, Averndale had seen how impossible that task would be, and instead decided to continue the connection in the true name of friendship, and Harrison could not have been more grateful, for true friendship was a rare gift indeed.

Book in his lap, pages unturned since he opened it hours before, Harrison watched the comings and goings of White's, thankful for the change in setting and sound, and yet lonely just the same as he awaited Averndale. One would think that after nearly three decades on earth, consistently alone, one would become used to it, and yet the yearning never left him. The want for human interaction still nagged at him just at much at thirty as it had at thirteen, willing to do nearly anything for his mother to finally love him, but that too had been an ill-fated notion. His mother chose instead to sacrifice her son to the alter of the title, gaining the prestige of bearing the future earl without ever having anything to do with him.

In truth, Harrison could not blame his mother for her escape. His uncle, who had never once been called kind, had treated Harrison's mother as lesser, an animal only fit for providing offspring, and when it became clear that he would not produce any heirs of his own, the man saw fit to try and mold her son to his liking. It mattered very little that Harrison hated the man, intent upon never becoming the vicious monster he was, nor did it matter if he were the perfectly curated son, worthy of his mother's love, she still had left him to his fate in order to save herself.

On his own since childhood, it had been a sigh of relief when Averndale had arrived, taking interest in Harrison, not only as a human, but as a friend, so when the man in question walked through the door, Harrison closed the book with a snap and waved him over. The viscount, appearing more like a depiction of an angel than human, made his way toward him, his silvery blond hair glimmering in the candlelight, nearly turning white as he moved.

"Averndale," Harrison said, a true smile taking over his lips.

"Everly," Averndale said, his voice low and mocking.

"What are we drinking?"

Rolling his eyes, Harrison summoned a footman. "It's eleven in the morning. I'm drinking tea."

"Rather boring of you," Averndale said, ordering himself a scotch and sending the footman on his way. "This is the third time I've run into you at White's. Don't tell me you're already bored of your marriage?"

Harrison took a sip of his tea, now cold from sitting idle for nearly an hour. "I'm rather certain it is she who is bored with me."

Averndale leaned forward. "Truthfully? You cannot be serious. Ladies want for nothing more than a doting husband and a house to call their own; how on earth could she have become bored of you so quickly?"

Setting his tea cup down, Harrison pursed his lips and summoned the footman once more, ordering a finger of scotch for himself. "She's enthralled with this hobby of hers." Averndale frowned at him. "She's consumed by it. Every waking hour she has she's in the garden with the bees, worrying about the bees, reading about the bees. The only time she shows me a moment of interest is at dinner, and even then, our conversations are stilted. It's as if I hardly exist within my own home."

"Well, you certainly didn't marry for a love match, so is it any wonder she has little interest? You didn't even court the girl."

"It was what she wanted," Harrison said, the words whispered sharply.

Averndale shrugged. "Perhaps, but you've basically requested her to move into a house with a perfect stranger and then be required to entertain him. She is not a jester there to amuse you, Everly. The hobby is surely a place of comfort in an otherwise unknown setting."

"Maybe," he said, the words muttered.

"And maybe," Averndale said, taking the drink the footman delivered and taking a hearty sip, "it is time for you to find a hobby yourself?"

"Beg pardon?"

"A hobby. Needlework. Boxing. I hear woodcarving is very time consuming." Another sip, this one accompanied by a wicked smile.

"I have hobbies." It was a protest, and an awfully weak one at that.

Leaning back against his chair, Averndale crossed one leg over the other, his drink cupped in his hand. "Do tell. I wasn't aware you filled your time with anything but people watching, politics, and tending to your estate, but I'm delighted to learn I'm wrong."

"Come off it," Harrison said, sipping at his scotch.

"No, tell me. What fantastical thing is taking up your time and allowing your wife a moment of peace to get her bearings in her new environment?"

Harrison scowled at the saint that sat across from him. "Fine, you've made your point."

"Excellent. Now, finish your drink and then escort me to Tattersalls. There is a pair of Arabians I've been eyeing and I think I might let the man convince me to buy them today."

"How does that—"

Averndale raised a hand. "After, we'll head to the Western Exchange on Bond Street and ponder over what you might be able to do to fill your free time."

Harrison sighed. "The bazaar?"

"Yes. Nothing a bit of mindless wandering and shopping cannot do to wiggle free the ideas in our mind. Consider it research. Maybe you'll acquire a trinket for your wife that might increase your value in her eyes."

Rolling his eyes in exasperation at his friend's antics, Harrison knocked back the last of his drink. "Right then."

After the pair of Arabians were procured, the duo headed to the Western Exchange and walked the three storied establishment, their eyes dancing over small knick-knacks, porcelain, and paintings. The roof light poured sunshine over the stalls, setting the sparkling delicacies to a shimmer, while shoppers walked the aisles, pausing to peruse the goodies. Columns and archways separated the shops, not allowing the browser's eye to wander any further than necessary, no doubt increasing the chances of a sale for the shopkeepers.

In a back corner, a small shop, softly lit, stood nearly empty but for the shelves lined with ceramic pottery, each in varying stages. Large linen wrapped bricks stood side by side along the bottom, while small pieces of dried clay sat before them, each a different earthy tone. On the second shelf bowls, vases, and mugs, each delicately made, stood on display, some coated in a shiny glaze while others held a rough finish, as if awaiting the final trek of its journey.

Averndale, inspecting some jeweled cufflinks, seemed too immersed to care, and Harrison wandered toward the stall, pulled in by the oddity of it. The shop did not fit into the trend of the exchange, its ambiance a bit too harsh, too humble for the upward set, and perhaps that was why it drew his attention.

An older gentleman sat on a wooden stool, his fingers molding and pulling a slate-colored piece of clay and as Harrison approached him, he rose and smiled. "Good afternoon, my lord."

"Good afternoon," Harrison said, his eyes flitting from object to object while his mind wondered at the old man's motions. "Your shop is rather unique."

The man blushed at his compliment, his fingers working the clay. "Yes, my lord. I make ceramics, but in a more personalized way than transferware."

Harrison smiled. "You design them by hand?"

"Yes, my lord. Each item is designed from the very beginning entirely by the client, from the color of clay used to the glaze and image painted. It allows for a more exclusive piece."

With a nod, Harrison looked at the shelves. "A rather interesting approach for sales. I commend you. It's a hard business to be up against the likes of Wedgewood and such." The man nodded, his fingers still fiddling. "Is it difficult to do?"

"Beg pardon, my lord."

Harrison nodded to the clay in his hands. "Sculpting the piece. Is it hard?"

"Ah," he said, looking at the clay in his hands. "It can be, but I've been doing it for nearly forty years."

Harrison's eyes widened. "That is quite a long time to hone your craft."

The man chuckled. "It's a hard craft to hone. Even the best ceramists make mistakes that can ruin an entire piece." He pointed to a tall, soft pink vase that sat on the top shelf of his display. "It took me four tries to form that piece."

"Truly?"

"Aye. Bugger kept collapsing on the wheel and then cracked in the kiln. Clay is a wily mistress."

Harrison nodded, his eyes glued to the piece the man indicated. The tall vase, the color of the inside of a seashell, stood proud, its fluted opening rounding like soft petals on a flower. The glaze shone against the candlelight, the color along the ribbing in the center changing as the lights flickered. "What does it take to make something like that?" he asked, before looking back at the man.

"Lots of time and practice, I'd say. And an immense amount of patience." He smiled at Harrison, as if his question had been a joke. "Would the lordship have any interest in learning?"

Harrison returned his smile, certain he was on the right track. "He would, actually." Leaning on the counter, Harrison pointed to a pad and pencil by the man. "If you don't mind, may I write down all the things required to take up pottery? And if your schedule allows it, I'd gladly pay you any sum to teach me how to start."

Pad and pencil in hand, Harrison jotted down a list of items the man relayed: a potting wheel, clay, and kiln, along with a litany of tools each given a unique name and design. So enthralled in his list making and the potential before him, Harrison failed to notice the older gentleman's wary gaze, nor that Averndale had sidled up to the stall, a catlike smile taking over his lips.

CHAPTER EIGHT

May, 1822

SHINY, LARGE, BLACK droppings littered the table around one of the hives, the bees buzzing angrily as Phee swiped the specs into the grass, away from the frames. Rats, both literally and figuratively.

This was the third time she had found droppings surrounding one of the hives, their appearance ominous, but no more so than the dead rat that lay a few yards away from the hives, perished from too many stings after its attempted honey theft. It served the scoundrel right, taking advantage of the bee's hard work. With a sigh, Phee knew what she had to do, but was not sure she could do it. Rats had been adversaries of beekeepers for centuries, their thievery well known, and it was only right that she eliminate the problem altogether. But to hire an assassin to do the job? It seemed low, even to her. After all, rats were merely doing rat things, following the pattern that had been ingrained in them since their creation. They were innocent creatures who had no ill will or intentions, and here she was, contemplating a murder for hire situation.

But, first problem first, where to procure such an individual. One did not merely pick up a cat off the street and put the poor beast to work with no credentials or proof of ownership. No, certainly not.

Leaving the deceased rodent for someone with a stronger stomach, Phee searched for the gardener, intent to learn the proper steps in solving the issue. Mr. Drake, the head gardener for Lord Everly's home, was elbows deep in a hyacinth plant, his sheers trimming away at the dead branches that sprouted from one side of the plant. When he saw her coming, he stood, slapping together his gloved hands before removing the gloves entirely and tucking them into the back pocket of his pants.

"My lady, is everything all right?" he asked, removing his gray cap to reveal his black head of hair. His age was indiscernible, somewhere between late twenties and early forties, which told her very little. His brown eyes were bracketed with lines, but from age or the sun, she did not know, and she found it slightly dismaying that without asking him, she would never know the answer to the question.

"There was more rat refuse around the hives again, and unfortunately, the bees seemed to have killed the poor creature."

He frowned at her pronouncement. "I'll have the creature taken care of. I'm sorry you were forced to see that, my lady."

She waved him off. "I believe the best solution for this problem is going to be a cat, but I'm not sure where to begin in procuring one."

He nodded. "The household several stops down has a barn cat who recently had a litter. I'll see about getting one of the kittens for you."

"May I come with you to pick it out?" she asked. "I want to be sure we choose the right one."

"Of course, my lady," he said, bowing. "I'll inform you as soon as we are able to see them." With a smile and a nod, Phee left him, pondering other methods to save the hives from the unfortunate invaders. Perhaps a strong smell would deter them in the meantime while they awaited their new garden guard.

Walking into the house through the conservatory doors, Phee paused as she heard cursing coming from one end of the room. Following the noise, Phee wandered toward the orangery as the cursing grew louder. Peering around a branch, she spotted an older gentleman sitting in a plush red chair, his elbows on his knees as he watched Lord Everly attempt to control a lump of clay that spun at an excessive speed on a plate before him. The large phallic shaped substance flopped between his cupped hands with unruly abandon, slapping every surface it came into contact with.

"You need to push the piece down with your finger-tips, my lord," the man said, his gnarled hand pointing to the spinning mushroom top.

"It's hard," Lord Everly said, sleeves rolled up to his forearms as he wrestled the brown mass.

"Wet your hands, then use your two fingers and gently press in the center as the piece spins." The man stood from the chair and demonstrated the motion, taming the piece to his control. The phallic shape transformed into a short-rounded edge, almost like a cup, its sides smoothing as the man used his fingertips to soothe the rough edges.

"Why does it look so easy when you do it?" Lord Everly asked with a grumble.

The man laughed. "Because I've been doing it forever,

my lord. It will get easier with time."

Lord Everly shook his head. "Will it? My apron is covered in debris and these trousers are going to send my valet into fits." He sighed. "Perhaps these will simply have to become my pottery outfit." He glanced down and groaned. "Boots and all."

"I told you it wasn't easy work, my lord. If you find it too much it wouldn't be unreasonable to stop. Nothing wrong with saying you gave it a try."

Her husband shook his head, his brow stern, determined. "No. I'll not be laid low by some insipid piece of clay. I will prevail." He said it like a battle cry, certain of his success, and yet the disaster that was his outfit, and the sad state of the conservatory floor, said otherwise.

The man beside him nodded and retook his seat. "Then let's start again. Once you're able to manipulate the clay, this part will seem much easier."

"If you say so," Lord Everly said with a grunt, slapping the clay with a stern hand, the sound making her stomach do an odd little flip. With a frown, Phee stepped away, uncertain why his action sent her heart rate galloping, nor why the sight of her husband's exposed forearms, covered in wiry brown hair and corded in veins, turned her breath shallow. It was an odd reaction, one she had never experienced in her twenty-one years of life with regards to the actions of another person, and it was disconcerting.

"Now, my lord," the old man said. "Center the clay on the table. Right hand in, left hand out. Kick the wheel, and slowly lift your hands up as the clay turns."

Phee peaked around once more to watch, determined

to understand the feeling occupying her stomach. Lord Everly's mouth was a narrow line, his brow furrowed as his long fingers caressed the clay, smoothing the mold upward, the veins in his hands protruding at the effort. Phee swallowed, the room becoming hotter as she watched him handle the clay with forceful ease, and she nearly groaned as his hands cupped the top, his two fingers pushing at the center, driving the rim back down.

"Dear god," she said with a whisper.

And then, the piece he had been handling smoothly broke off in his hands, separated in half, its counterpart spinning whimsically on the wheel. Phee laughed, the look of sheer shock on Lord Everly's face erasing whatever lingering tingles she might have felt, and when his eyes met hers, block of clay still in his hands, he smiled back, his laughter filling the conservatory with such a joyful noise that she could only join him.

The older gentleman, startled by her laughter, turned in his chair, then pushed to standing and bowed to her. "My lady, I hope we didn't disturb you."

Phee smiled at him. "Not at all, sir. You must be Mr. Williams. I'm Lady Everly."

"A pleasure to meet you, my lady."

"And you as well, sir." She looked at Lord Everly. "I'm glad I'm finally able to see this the new hobby you've mentioned."

Lord Everly smiled at her, slapping the clay in his hands back down on the now still table. "Rather messy and chaotic, isn't it? I'm finding joy in learning it though. What brings you through here?"

She grimaced. "I was in the gardens inspecting the

hives and found more remnants of rat droppings. I'm now on the search for a cat to rid the poor bees of their intruder."

He nodded. "Sounds like you've got a lot on your hands as well." He looked at Mr. Williams with a smile. "I think we can call it a day, Seb. If you head to the kitchen, I'm sure Cook will happily fix you a cup of tea and some cake before you head home."

"Of course, my lord." Mr. Williams picked up a worn black jacket and rough cap from the chair he had sat in, bowed to them both, and left the room.

"He seems the patient sort," Phee said, taking a tentative step toward Lord Everly.

Dipping his hands in a bowl of water, Lord Everly scrubbed at the clay stuck to his hands, his sandy brown locks shaking with his effort. "He has to be if he's to teach me. I'm lucky to not only have found him, but for him to have agreed to teach me at all."

Phee laughed, moving closer to Lord Everly and the wheel. "And I'm sure you're paying him a premium for his services, given those circumstances." Phee inspected the clay that still sat on the wheel, its color fading as it dried in the warm air of the conservatory. "What is to be done with this?"

Lord Everly sighed. "A casualty of war, I'm afraid. I've worked so much air into the bits that they'll break the instant they feel the fire of the kiln."

"Truly?" She tsked, poking the piece, disconcerted to see that the wet mixture stuck to her finger. "What a waste."

Mouth flat, he nodded his head. "Do you need any

help with the cat issue? I'm happy to look into it," he said, dipping a small towel into the bowl of water before taking her hand. With soft swipes, Lord Everly rubbed away the clay that marred her skin, his smooth motions pulling her in closer until his citrus smell enveloped her.

"No, Mr. Drake is sorting it out for me," she said, the words a whisper as she looked up to meet his brown gaze. Swallowing, she smiled and took a step back, burying the hand he had held in the folds of her dress. "But thank you for offering."

Brow furrowed, he looked at her. "Of course. I'm happy to help with whatever you require, you need only ask. I hope you know that?" He looked away and brushed at his apron. "I should finish cleaning this up."

"Oh," Phee said, his dismissal a pin prick. The words were minute in themselves, but over time, his hot and cold moods had begun to rattle her, sending strings of uncertainties spiraling in her mind at what she could have done, or should have done to prevent it. "I'll leave you to it, then."

Nodding her head, she continued her journey out of the conservatory and to her room where she took her usual bath and read over her notes of hive examinations. Yet, Lord Everly's jumbled mood swings bothered her the remainder of the afternoon. His ever friendly, helpful nature set her up like a trap, luring her in with his comforting words, his playful smiles, and jovial disposition, but it took only a small change within the setting for that demeanor to shift, like a ghost in the room. It was as if the Lord Everly she knew disappeared, rendering nothing but a scared and uncertain man, afraid of what came next.

Brow furrowed, Phee shook her head. What utter nonsense. More than likely, it was merely her anxiety plaguing her regarding his emotions.

A knock on the door sent her maid answering the call, returning with a folded piece of paper. "Mr. Drake has sent you a missive regarding your request, my lady," Flora said.

Taking the note, Phee read, a bubble of excitement rising in her. "Fetch my gloves and hat, Flora. I'm off to run an errand."

Fifteen minutes later, Phee stood in the garden of Lord Cowden's Mayfair townhome, following the man's housekeeper toward the mews. "You truly should have sent a footman to do this, my lady. It's a rather dirty place we're headed to."

"Nonsense, Mrs. Clancy. I must ensure the right mouser is picked for this job and the only way to do that is to inspect the lot myself."

Out the gate, Phee followed to where the stables were housed, her heart pumping at the experience. Inside the stable, Phee met Lord Cowden's stable master, Smick, then the pair followed him to a far back corner stall. "The lot are inside there. Mama's keeping a close eye on 'em but they can't get too far. Still rather small to make the jump out," Smick said as he opened the large wooden door.

Inside, bales of hay were set against the wall and along the floor, decorating the space in soft yellow hair. A small black cat sat atop one stack of hay, her eyes guarded as she watched Phee and Smick enter the stall. Along the ground, five kittens rolled around in play, before pausing and hiding in the masses of straw. Phee motioned for Smick to close the door behind her, then examined the straw for cleanliness before sitting.

Back pressed against the wall, legs crossed, Phee set her hands in her lap and waited, watching the kittens for any interest. One black tuxedo kitten peeked its head out of the straw, watching her with amber eyes as it creeped slowly toward her. Phee held her breath, determined to stay still for the creature's examination. The fearless feline sniffed the edge of her dress, then stepped closer and administered the same treatment to her hands. With confidence, the dear edged toward her half boots, sniffing at the soles before eyeing the string that tied the shoe together. Bending down, the kitten zeroed in on its target, its bottom wriggling, before springing into action and capturing the string as its prize. "Well done," Phee said, the words quiet.

The kitten cared very little for her congratulations as it attempted to maim its prey, front and back claws holding the string for dear life as its small, pointy teeth chewed on the fibers.

Phee's fingers itched to scratch at the small patch of white fur that adorned the dear's head like an arrow, and instead, squeezed her fingers tightly as the beast grew bored of its prize and wandered off to find a playmate.

With a smile, Phee looked at Smick and smiled. "I believe that one will do quite well," she said, pointing to the small mite with the arrow on its forehead.

"Very good, my lady," Smick said with a nod. "I'll have a footman send it over in the next few weeks once we've weened it from its mama."

Clapping her hands, Phee stood and shook out her dress. At least that was one problem solved. If only her new husband could be handled as simply.

CHAPTER NINE

June, 1822

THE SMALL BLACK bundle of fur in his wife's arms was the first surprise Harrison received that evening. The second was when the fluff ball joined them for dinner.

"You've brought a cat to dinner?" he asked, stirring his soup.

Lady Phoebe looked up at him. "She is far too small to be left in the garden yet, and I will not force her to the mews." She looked at the creature curled up on the chair beside her. "I tried to leave her in my room but she was crying horribly. I don't think the poor dear has ever been alone."

"She?" he asked, eyeing the black blob. "You're quite sure?"

Lady Phoebe nodded as she slurped her soup. "Mr. Drake inspected her nether regions when I brought her home. I've decided to call her Mildred."

Harrison's cheeks heated at how matter-of-factly Lady Phoebe uttered the words regarding the cat's genitalia.

Mildred chose that moment to stand and stretch, then hop onto the dining table to inspect Lady Phoebe's bowl.

"Lovely name," Harrison said, his eyes following the kitten who examined the salt shaker.

Lady Phoebe picked the cat up and placed it in her lap,

stroking the arrow shaped fur on her head before the thing disappeared beneath the table on her lap. "Poor thing is barely the size of the rat I just so happened to see this morning. She'll need a bit of time to grow before I allow her to roam the gardens."

"She no doubt would be rat food at the size she is now," Harrison said, smiling at Lady Phoebe. "She seems rather content with you."

She nodded, her brow furrowing. "Yes. I'm worried we took her from her mother too soon and so she has turned to me for comfort. Hardly the proper beginning for a trained rat killer."

A bark of laughter escaped his lips. "Is there a manual in the proper way to raise a rat killer?"

"No," she said, shaking her head. "But I'm sure a cold demeanor and stealth personality are required to do the job, and I'm not sure coddling the poor thing will result in a cat who enjoys hunting." She firmed her mouth and looked at him. "I plan to start her training in the morning."

Nodding as he forced his lips to pinch and hide the smile that threatened, he looked at his wife. "And how will that go?"

"I've attached a feather tied to a string onto the end of a long stick to train her to pounce and stalk, and Mr. Drake mentioned making some stuffed rats to hide around my room for her to track and practice her killing blow."

"Killing blow?" he asked, lips shaking.

"Mm," she said, using the larger spoon to scoop soup into her mouth with one hand while the other continued to stroke the cat in her lap. "I figure a month of consistent practice will make her a stealthy ratter in no time."

The smile won, pulling his lips into a full grin as he looked at his wife, so certain she would not only train the kitten to be a ratter, but do so without gaining any emotional attachment to it. "I think it sounds like a wonderful plan."

She looked at him and frowned. "You're smiling."

"I'm always smiling," he said.

"You think this is funny?" There was a touch of confusion and hurt in her voice.

"I think you are going to be wrapped around dear Mildred's fluffy paw in no time," he said, putting down his spoon. "And while I have no doubt she will make a fantastic ratter after your training, I'm also certain that you've just gained a companion who is as much in love with you as you are with her."

"What nonsense," Lady Phoebe said, stopping her stroking to glare at the cat. "I am detached."

"If you say so," he said standing. "If you're finished, we can have dessert in the library while we play our game."

Lady Phoebe nodded, picking up Mildred and placing her on the ground before taking Harrison's proffered hand and standing to meet him. The pair walked to the library, the soft click clack of kitten nails on the marble floor making his smile grow as Mildred followed them into the room.

Inside the library, Lady Phoebe took her usual blue chair, Mildred waiting for her to settle before climbing the fabric of her gown to get to her mistress. The black hairball circled three times, then settled into the folds of her dress, long paws extended as her murder mittens retracted, showing the fine points that served as her claws. Lady Phoebe hardly noticed, her hand falling to softly stroke the white arrow on her head.

Removing their respective decks from behind the glass, Harrison handed Lady Phoebe her stack of cards, then removed his jacket and settled into his chair across from her.

"I wonder what Mrs. Beatley has planned for dessert," Lady Phoebe said, settling back against the chair.

"I believe it is a chocolate cake," Harrison said, knowing fully well that was exactly what it was. His wife had a penchant for chocolate in all forms, and when he had learned that Mrs. Beatley planned a blueberry pie garnished with fresh blueberries on top, he had intercepted that potential disaster. A simple word to the housekeeper, about not only the dire blueberry decision, but of the mistress's favorite treat, was the least he could do to help Lady Phoebe settle into her new home more comfortably.

Averndale's words had struck a chord, wiggling into his brain, forcing him to realize just how awkward the situation would be from her end, and with that knowledge in hand, he had begun inspecting their usual interactions with a more careful eye. His wife found comfort in her bees, comfort in the routine she had created and followed every day. The least he could do was ensure that not only was she content, but that any obstacles she may encounter that would disrupt her comfort be avoided.

"It sounds wonderful," Lady Phoebe said, wiggling her bottom into the couch, the motion shaking Mildred from her sleep. Her discontented meow brought her mistress's attention to her, and Lady Phoebe cooed at the thing, apologizing for her movement. When Mildred had settled, Lady Phoebe looked at him. "Ready to spill your secrets?"

Harrison laughed. "If I remember correctly, my lady, you have shared the most secrets between the two of us."

She scrunched her brow. "That will end tonight."

A soft knock at the library door had them turning their heads as a maid entered with a cart, chocolate cake and tea service filling the room with sweet potency, and Lady Phoebe turned to him, one corner of her mouth lifted. "Saved just in time from sure defeat."

The maid set the cake and tea service down on a separate table. "Will there be anything else, my lord?"

"No," Harrison said, setting his cards aside to serve the cake.

"That's my job," Lady Phoebe protested from her chair.

Harrison shook his head. "I do believe you are trapped at the moment, my lady, but never fear, I am adept at tea and cake service."

She merely shook her head at his nonsense before turning back to the kitten who held her pinned to the chair. "It would be rather hard to move her."

"She would never forgive you," he tsked. "So discourteous."

Lady Phoebe actually rolled her eyes at him. "Your humor is in high form tonight, my lord."

"Something about seeing you coddle a kitten has tickled my funny bone."

"Why?" she asked, taking the plate containing her piece of cake from him.

"Because much like your bees, I assumed you only had a sharp side, always on the defense, hesitant of the world." Her jaw dropped at his words and he rapidly continued. "However, like your bees, you are also a fuzzy little creature who cares for the helpless and attempts to cause as little harm as you possibly can. It's a pleasure to see all the different sides of you."

She pursed her lips, blowing air between them. "What nonsense."

With a nod, Harrison retook his seat, setting a cup of warm tea before Lady Phoebe before picking up his cards. "If you say so. Now eat your dessert so I can trounce you once more."

Mouth full of cake, she said nothing in reply, and Harrison smiled.

When their dessert was finished, they picked up their respective piles and began as they always did, highest card flipped first. Harrison drew the higher card, and with a smirk, winked at Lady Phoebe. Her raised brow was the only response as she watched him flip the top card on the deck. The dance of cards took over the game, the rhythm consistent until two threes lay face up on the table.

"Snap," she said, the words soft as she looked at the sleeping kitten.

Harrison set his cards down, and looked at the kitten as well. "I've never had a pet before."

"That's your secret?" she asked.

"Yes, but there's more to it." He frowned. "I asked my mother for a dog when I was seven. It was lonely, being an only child and going back and forth between being the earl's heir and not, depending on his state of matrimony, so I thought a dog would ease that."

"She said no?"

He nodded. "My uncle hated animals, and we waited on baited breath for the eventual day he would send for me and I'd begin my training to become the earl. She knew if I had a dog, I wouldn't want to leave it, and that she would be forced to deal with my uncle's dismay." He smirked. "Instead, I decided to name the pair of horses that we had in our barn Theodore and Calliope and I snuck them apples whenever I could find the time to."

Lady Phoebe frowned. "So instead of easing her son's loneliness, she opted to leave you in isolation merely because of your uncle?" When he nodded to confirm her statement, she scowled. "What a ridiculous notion. I'm surprised you didn't get a dog as soon as you took the title."

He laughed, the sound harsh even to his own ears. "I didn't really think of it. In truth, I've let the house continue to run just as my uncle did when he was alive. I don't want to put the staff to all the bother of monumental changes or the addition of an animal." With a shrug, he dismissed the depth the conversation had taken. "Who knows, maybe I'll look into it eventually."

Lady Phoebe's frown turned into a gentle smile. "This is your home, you should make it how you want it."

His shoulders tightened at her words but he forced a smile to his lips and waved away her statement. "You start this round," he said, retaking his card pile.

She took up her cards but the frown returned. The synchronization picked up once more, the slapping of cards on the table filling the space until a pair of aces sat face up. "Snap," Lady Phoebe said again.

"You're evening the score," Harrison said, smiling at her. "Hmm, let's see." He racked his mind for something light to take away the heavy feeling that clouded the room from his previous secret, but struggled to find anything. Every secret hidden within his depths held the same weight, the same sadness he had just revealed, and he would give anything to see her happy as she had been before. Grasping at something light, he said, "I think you should have gotten a pair of kittens instead of just our Mildred."

"Two kittens? Why on earth would I do that?"

"So we could each have a fluff ball to snuggle with while we play our game."

She smiled at him. "I should have known it would be a self-serving reason." Lady Phoebe glanced at the clock. "I best take this fluff ball upstairs to bed."

Harrison nodded, then returned their cards to their case, before escorting Lady Phoebe and Mildred, who now lay cradled in Lady Phoebe's arms, upstairs. At his door, he gave a small bow to them both. "Goodnight, ladies."

Lady Phoebe nodded her head. "Goodnight, my lord."

And yet, it would seem it would not be a good night for Lady Phoebe. Tiny kitten cries echoed from her room for hours after they parted, her soft murmurings doing little to soothe the distressed creature, and when the clock struck midnight, Harrison knew he could not sit idly by and let her suffer alone. Knocking at their combined door, Harrison smiled at the pair of eyes that peeked around the portal. "What seems to be the poor mite's problem?" he asked.

Lady Phoebe stepped away from the door and opened it. Her blonde hair was unbound, the golden waterfall cascading down her shoulders like spun silk. Her gray eyes were soft and sleepy and, in the candlelight, he could see she was dressed in her nightgown and robe, the latter of which contained multiple wet spots while Mildred sat cradled in her arms like a babe. Shaking his head, Harrison pulled himself from the intimacy of the environment and turned his attention to the kitten.

"Dear heavens, did she relieve herself on you?" Harrison asked.

Lady Phoebe groaned. "No, she's been nursing on the hem of my nightgown on and off. And if she isn't nursing on me, she's pacing the room and crying. I don't know what to do to help her."

Harrison followed her into her bedroom, the honeysuckle smell strong and yet the bedroom unchanged from when Meg had once lived there, a conundrum to his senses. He shook his head. Not the moment, not now. Poor Mildred mewed in protest, her nose snuffling Lady Phoebe's robe like a piglet.

"I've fed her, she's used the dish of sand Mr. Drake provided as her toilet, we even played for half an hour, but as soon as we went to settle down, she became inconsolable." Lady Phoebe sat in the chair near the fire, cradling Mildred as the small black tuft nursed restlessly on the hem of her nightgown.

"I understand, little one. I felt the same on my first few nights here. This is a big house, and it's hard to be away from your loved ones. It can be scary," he said, watching the pair.

"I felt the same way," Lady Phoebe said, and a tightness filled his chest at her admission.

Her confession struck him like an arrow, the sadness in her words reminding him of the small boy he had once been, dropped in an unknown townhome in London with nothing familiar and no one he knew to be safe. For a moment, he wanted to snatch her up in his arms much like she held Mildred and soothe her. To tell her that everything would be all right and that she was not alone. It was the words he had needed to hear as a child, the comfort Mildred no doubt required now.

"I have an idea," he said, his mind reminding him how he had found solace when he first arrived.

Returning to his room, Harrison removed a heavy chenille blanket that was draped across his reading chair, the fibers of each side soft and silky under his fingertips, sandwiching sheets of wool to create a heavy wrap. Back inside Lady Phoebe's room, he made a small nest on the floor with the blanket and carefully set Mildred into it, holding his breath as the kitten rooted around in the fabric before settling in to nurse and knead the billowy tufts. Lady Phoebe tucked her hand beneath her chin and watched Mildred, her damp robe creating spots like a leopard in the firelight. After ten minutes of nursing the blanket, the dear settled, her paws prolonged in front of her, claws extended into the blanket.

Harrison looked at Lady Phoebe, a broad smile on his face, but it faded as he saw that his companion had fallen asleep, her arms curled, creating a pillow for her head, her legs tucked up underneath her. A worried frown took over her features, her forehead furrowing, as if she still solved unseen problems even in her sleep, and Harrison took his thumb and brushed at the smooth skin, soothing the worry from her features.

Mildred released a soft meow, and he turned his attention back to her, smoothing his hand along her fur to soothe her as well. Much like her owner, it seemed Mildred fought battles whether asleep or awake. Keeping his hand on her back, her black fur tickling his hand, Harrison sat on the floor and leaned against Lady Phoebe's chair. He would only stay for a few more minutes before returning to his room. Just long enough to ensure that Mildred remained asleep and allowed Lady Phoebe some rest. Yet, the fire roared, and the small kitten purred, and Harrison allowed his eyes to close. But it would only be for a minute.

*   *   *

WHILE PHOEBE SLEPT on the armchair, her body positioned uncomfortably, Harrison dozed on and off, sleep coming and going as Mildred protested her conditions. The early hours of the morning crept by as he changed out blanket after blanket, determined to give the mite some sort of comfort, but one thing remained the same the entire time. Lady Phoebe's fingertips would find his shoulder, her slim fingers resting on his robe as if to ensure his presence remained even as she slept. Her touch became a talisman throughout the night, a necessity as he comforted the kitten, Lady Phoebe's small hand curled around the collar of his robe like a child's favorite blanket.

When the sun finally peeked through the night sky, Harrison's eyes were scratchy and his body shook with exhaustion, but Mildred had finally succumbed to slumber, her soft purrs filling the room. Resting his head against the seat of the armchair, Harrison sighed. True sleep was not going to be found, but perhaps a solid nap would help him to feel more human.

Standing, Harrison stretched his arms above his head, releasing a groan and his eyes fell to where Lady Phoebe slept, her neck twisted uncomfortably and her legs tucked up beneath her. This would not do. At least one of them should be well rested when the morning fully arrived. Bending down, Harrison picked her up, her lush body easily fitting against his own. She protested the movement in her sleep, her hand sliding up his chest and grabbing hold of his robe once more, settling as she nuzzled her head against his chest. Harrison laughed, the sound surprising in the quiet room. His wife would never know how much like her kitten she was.

Setting her down on the bed, Harrison pulled up the coverlet but even then, she protested the loss of him, her fingers reaching out. Sitting beside her, Harrison watched her sleep. Her hair was fanned out against the pillow, the strands determined to find freedom and her small cupids bow of a mouth was parted as if she were in the midst of explaining one of the beautiful thoughts that went on in her head. It would take very little to place Mildred in the middle of the large bed and then take over the other end himself. Made sense even for him to remain on the chance the kitten awoke once more, but something about the comfort of the night, the familiarity of the action, and the grasp of her hand on his lapel had him standing.

Call it fear. Call him silly. But the coziness he could so easily slip into had just turned into the very thing he could not afford to do.

CHAPTER TEN

PHEE AWOKE IN her bed, Mildred and her nest tucked alongside her. With her sleeping companion still in the land of dreams, Phee sighed. What had started as a harrowing night had turned to ease thanks to Lord Everly and his blanket.

Lord Everly.

Phee pushed up and looked around her room but found it to be empty except for her and the kitten. He must have returned to his room after she had fallen asleep. Except, she had been in the chair the last she remembered. Surely, he hadn't... No. He could not have possibly moved her to her bed and tucked her in with the kitten, and yet, all signs pointed to yes.

There was no use in ruminating on the meaning behind his kindness for that way led madness, and quite possibly heartbreak. Leaving the bed, Phee performed her ablutions, then returned to check on her companion, who finally decided to join the land of the living. The beast noticed her and stood from her bed, stretching her paws in front of her before pulling her body forward to stretch the backend. Her excited meow as she walked toward Phee was a sudden change from the inconsolable creature of last night.

"You seem pleased with yourself," Phee said, stroking

the white arrow on her head. "I did not appreciate our midnight adventures, Mildred."

Mildred meowed, brushing up against Phee's hand, and she could not help but smile at the kitten's antics. "I'll forgive you, but only because it was your first night in a new home. Let's be sure to make a better go of it this evening, yes?"

Readying herself for the day, Phee snatched up the stick with a feather on its end and dragged it across the floor, forcing Mildred to give chase down to the breakfast room. Lord Everly sat at the table, a paper before him, his tea frozen before his face as they entered the room.

"Good morning," Phee said, setting the kitten down on her chair before heading to the sideboard to make herself a plate.

"You've never joined me for breakfast," Lord Everly said, the words soft.

"Hmm?" Phee asked. "Oh, the smell of kippers tends to upset my stomach, but Mildred seems rather famished after her night of nonsense so I thought it better to bring her directly to the food."

"You never joined me for breakfast because you don't like the smell?"

"Yes. I thought it best to remain elsewhere so you could enjoy your breakfast and I could avoid a stomach upset."

He shook his head, his rakishly brushed back hair falling over his forehead. "I'm happy to adjust the menu so it doesn't cause you distress if that means having breakfast with you. I enjoy your company."

"Oh," Phee said, spoon of potatoes paused over the

plate. "I didn't—That is, I wasn't sure—"

Looking to a footman, he said, "Please remove the kippers from the room and open a window to clear the smell." Lord Everly rose and met her at the sideboard. Gently taking the plate and spoon from her hand, he finished the job she had started, his citrus scent masking the odorous kippers.

"I can do that," she said, eyeing her plate in his hands.

"I know, but I like caring for you. And I like the idea of us eating breakfast together." He walked along the side board, shooting her a devastating smile, his dimple winking at her. "We know the inconsistencies of blueberries, and the smell from kippers, but what other items should we add or remove from the menu? Bacon? Toast?"

"I quite enjoy those," Phee said, looking at him, warmth filling her at having someone attend to her needs for their own pleasure rather than treating her as someone incapable of caring for herself. While he appeared his usual put together self, he seemed tired. "Did you sleep well last night?"

"I'm afraid not," he said. "Our darling Mildred was rather testy regarding my choice of blanket so I attempted several different ones until I found the right combination."

"I'm terribly sorry. I wish you had woken me so I could have relieved you of your guard duties."

"No need. You were comfortable." He chuckled. "Well, as comfortable as one can be in an arm chair. I'm certain there was a moment where it was unclear whether you or Mildred were the most perturbed by your sleeping conditions."

"Is that why—"

"Why I moved you to your bed? Yes. It started to hurt my own neck watching you sleep like that." He set her plate down on the table and pulled back the chair for her.

Phee took her seat and began to eat. When a steaming cup of tea was placed before her, she looked up to say her thanks, surprised to find Lord Everly the distributer of the beverage. "Thank you," she said in a whisper.

His mouth quirked up at one corner in a smile. "Of course," he said softly, stopping at the chair beside her to tickle Mildred's chin. "And what would this mischief maker like for breakfast?"

"I've been feeding her scraps of chicken that Cook had left over from our supper the other night and a dish of water for drinking." Lord Everly nodded to a footman who set off quickly to deliver Mildred her breakfast.

Phee sipped at her tea and nearly sighed. The brew was perfect, a touch of milk with a slight sweetness from the sugar. "You made my tea to near perfection."

Lord Everly smiled. "I'm happy to hear it, however, I shall strive for perfection in the future, my lady."

"That's- That's not what I meant." His smile paused as his eyes assessed her. "This is the second time you've given me a cup of tea exactly how I like it. You've remembered how I take my tea."

He waved away her comment. "That's nothing."

"It's not," she said, with a small shake of her head "It's not nothing. Thank you."

He frowned at her, but nodded just the same before returning to his chair.

Phee had become used to catching others' notice, of course never for the right reason, but Harrison's awareness was not like the others. There was a sense of care in the things he noticed, a type of awe as he took in the way she perceived the world around her. That he noticed her, not because of what society would deem a flaw but because of who she was, was a kindness she had only found with her family.

They ate silently, Mildred the only dining companion to not only devour her food, but have the indecency to clean herself afterward, and Phee chuckled as she watched the dear, happy to see that her night of discomfort had not ruined her experience at the home.

"Are you planning to continue your usual schedule?" Lord Everly asked her.

Phee nodded, but her gaze went to Mildred once more. "I'll have to keep her inside while I tend the hives. I wouldn't want her making mischief and upsetting the bees. Or getting lost," she said, imagining the worst.

"She'll do just fine for a few hours alone. I'm sure she'll take a much-needed nap after last night." Lord Everly smiled at her. "Don't worry. She'll be all right."

"And what of you?"

"Back to the potter's wheel, I'm afraid. Off to damage more clay in an attempt to create something."

"Is Mr. Williams planning to return for another lesson?"

"Not today. I shall be on my own this time, forced to control the unwieldy beast and make it into something useful."

Phee smiled. "What do you have in mind?"

Lord Everly's brow furrowed. "A bowl, perhaps. That shouldn't be too hard, right?"

"I have every faith you will accomplish your goal to-day," she said, wiping her mouth before pushing back from the table. Leaning down over the chair beside her, she picked up Mildred, cradling the small kitten in her arms. "I wish you immense luck in your battle, my lord," she said, giving a small bow.

"Thank you, madame. I shall return a conqueror of my latest enemy."

With a giggle, Phee left the breakfast room, taking Mildred upstairs to her bedroom. After ensuring the dear used her box, and had plenty of water in case she was thirsty, Phee changed into her work dress, an ugly brown thing her mother had fondly called "the dirt collector", laced up her ankle boots, and grabbed her bee veil, padded coat, and gloves. Bidding farewell to Mildred, who had curled up on the sofa in a sunbeam, Phee headed to the garden to examine the progress the bees had made, all the while, a smile pulled at her lips, no doubt a reminder of the joy she had found at breakfast.

The hive was active, bees coming and going from the frames, their buzzes like a lullaby as they zipped around the garden, tending to their homes and queen. Marigolds and cornflowers surrounded one side the hives, lush and teeming with flowers, while fennel and poppies grew along the other end, luring the bees in with their sweet scent and supple nectar. Planter pots full of tansies stood at each corner of the garden, completing the extensive array of options for the fuzzy pollinators. Later in the fall, dahlias and ivy would ensure the bees stayed well-fed for the winter, but there was still time before then. Phee hummed, sparks of joy dancing in her veins as she watched the hive carry on its daily work. Yes, the other hive was still empty, but it was wonderful just the same.

Being careful not to excite the bees, Phee wandered around the box, searching for signs of rat droppings or ants. In truth, it was less work caring for the bees as it was guarding them from thievery. Yet both tables showed little traces of invaders, and the bees showed no signs of alert, which boded very well for their rat problem. Perhaps the rats had found a new eatery in the neighborhood and Mildred could instead live her life inside the townhome. Phee shook her head, chuckling at the thought. Mildred was a barn cat, with the instincts of a killer. She would never be happy indoors, boredom consuming her as she did nothing but lay about all day. No, as much as Phee wanted to coddle the poor dear, nature would no doubt take its course.

A glance at her pocket watch showed nearly an hour had gone by, and while the garden was a peaceful place to be surrounded by bees and flowers, her brain niggled at her to check on Mildred. Inside, however, she found her bedroom empty, with Mildred nowhere in sight. Checking all the possible hiding places proved fruitless, each empty space filling her with a tinge more panic, and Phee bit her lip as her stomach knotted with anxiety, certain the kitten had been led to her death.

Hurrying from the room, Phee headed to the conservatory. Perhaps Lord Everly had seen her and if not, perhaps she could enlist him to search. Inside the conservatory, the scraping sound of ceramic on metal from the pottery wheel, accompanied by a sloppy wet sound, played as a map to Lord Everly, and as Phee rounded the corner, she pulled to a stop, her franticly racing heart skipping at the sight before her. Lord Everly sat at the potting wheel, a shallow bowl being carefully molded before him, and in the red chair Mr. Williams typically occupied, sat Mildred, her paw raised as she attempted to shape the bowl as well, her swats causing slight curves along the rim.

"Unbelievable," Phee said, the words sharp.

Lord Everly looked up at her, the wheel slowly rolling to a stop as he pulled his hands back from the piece. "Lady Phoebe, are you all right?"

She scoffed. "No. No, I'm not all right. I thought she was lost. I thought she was dead, and she was here with you the whole time?" She marched toward him, hands on her hips. "Why is she down here?"

Lord Everly stood, rinsing his hands in the bucket of water beside the wheel. Wiping them on the apron he wore over his trousers and shirt, he stepped out from around the wheel. "The footman outside your room alerted me that she was meowing for fifteen minutes before he came to get me. It seems that merely a moment after you left your room, she started working herself into quite a ruckus, crying at the door and trying to get out." He came to stand before her. "I thought it would be best if she came to sit with me while I worked. I'm sorry to have worried you and will make it a point to tell you my plans next time."

Phee looked to where Mildred sat, her heart racing. "Is it even safe for her to be in here? There are so many things that she could get into or hurt herself on, she could have gotten out."

Lord Everly touched her chin, turning her gaze to him

and her heart kept up its errant pace. "I kept the door closed and my eye on her the entire time. She's shown a bit of interest in the wheel but I made sure she stayed on the chair while it was spinning."

Phee shook her head. "I thought I'd lost her. I thought she had escaped the house and gotten out into the yard. My mind raced with so many scenarios where she had perished." She was shaking, fear and worry filling her veins as she squeezed her hands, her nails biting into her palms.

"Lady Phoebe," Lord Everly said, but Phee could not control the onslaught her body wrought at the potential disaster. "Phoebe," Lord Everly said once more, pulling her into his arms. His arms tightened around her as she shook, her breathing sharp against the front of his shirt as she rocked her forehead back and forth, trying to calm herself. Lord Everly whispered against her ear, soothing words as he held her, one hand stroking her hair while the other remained tight, a coil of strength that she clung to with every fiber. "It's all right, Phoebe. Everything is all right. Mildred is safe," he said. "I'm sorry. I'm sorry I didn't tell you. I'm sorry I made you worry."

She stood that way for some time, Harrison holding her close, his arms tight, a comforting embrace that surrounded her until the storm slowed to nothing but a calm sky.

"Are you all right?" he asked.

She nodded, her forehead sliding against the soft cotton of his shirt. "I'm sorry."

He sighed, pulling her in closer as his head rested on hers. "You have nothing to apologize for. I should have told you I had her. I'm sorry, Phoebe."

Phee scowled into his shirt, her name on his lips something she had never expected to hear, and hadn't realized, until that moment, how much she wanted to hear it. They were accomplices. Two individuals who had entered into a mutually satisfying agreement, and yet…

And yet they talked and laughed just as friends did. They took interest in one another's activities like friends, and they both cared for Mildred, no matter how poorly it was done. Stepping back, Phee looked at him, his hands messy from the clay that still sat on the wheel, awaiting its form, and yet, he stopped to help her. To comfort her in a way no mere friend ever had. No one outside of her family. "You called me Phoebe." There was a touch of awe to her words.

His brow raised. "Did I?"

"Mm." She took a step forward, her hand raising to brush at a smudge of clay at his jaw and she paused as she touched his warm skin, her gaze meeting his.

"Is it all right that I do?" He angled his head, a warm smile on his lips, his dimple playing peekaboo.

"Yes," she said. "What would you like me to call you?"

He paused for a moment at her question before answering, "You can call me Harrison."

"Do you think—" She took a breath. "Do you think we are truly friends?"

He chuckled. "I'm starting to think we are."

"I am as well," she said, a frown tugging at her brow.

"You seem perturbed by that notion." He looked down at himself and brushed at the bits of clay that marred his apparel. "Am I that disappointing?"

She shook her head and smiled. "No. It's only that I've never had a friend before."

"Surely that cannot be—" he said, but stopped as Sterns appeared, a silver salver in his hands.

"I beg pardon, my lord," he said before turning to Phee. "My lady, a letter from your mother has arrived."

"Oh," Phee said, taking the note and opening it. "It's an invitation. It would appear my mother is planning to host her yearly ball in three months' time and she has requested that we attend to show familial affection." Phee's stomach knotted at the thought of her mother's yearly ball, the attention that would once again be placed on her. The crush of bodies and veiled conversations. She swallowed and looked at Harrison. "I should respond to this."

"Your mouth is pinched," he said, stepping closer. "Is everything all right?"

Phee looked to Sterns, then back to Harrison. "Everything is fine. Please excuse me." Picking up a sleepy Mildred, Phee left the conservatory, kitten and letter clutched in hand. Mildred made a mew of protest at the tightness of her grip and Phee loosened it. "I'm sorry, pet."

In her room, Phee set Mildred down on the floor after closing the door, ensuring she would not disappear again. Sitting at the small writing desk, she removed a sheet of paper and taking up her quill, opened her ink canister and dipped the metal nib in the pot. Yet, the words for her reply never came as she stared at the blank sheet, ink dripping, forming black dots of death, a sure sign of how she truly felt at her mother's request.

It was time once again for her mother's yearly ball, and not only was it a ball, but a familial one. One where she and her brother, along with their spouses, would be paraded and critiqued by society. One where, given her quick nuptials, the ton would pay sharp attention to her behavior and the behavior of her husband. One where she would have to mask every impulse in a setting where her senses would be overwhelmed.

Heart racing in her ears, Phee shook her head and set down the quill, her hand shaking at the mere notion of what was to come. The exact definition of hell, that was what. No amount of practice, no amount of deep breathing could contain what was always a rather immense stimulation that could be called her mother's ball, and although the event was three months away, her every nerve jingled like it was to happen that very instant.

She sighed as her head fell into her hands, her heartbeat racing in her ears, a resounding drumming, a crescendo that did very little to help her anxiety for what was to come. This was why she only surrounded herself with bees.

CHAPTER ELEVEN

P HOEBE'S SUDDEN DEPARTURE from the conservatory left
Harrison perplexed the remainder of the day. As he
cleaned up his pottery wheel and dumped the gray water
into the yard, as he bathed, scrubbing the last bits of clay
from his body, and as he readied himself for dinner, Roger
busily starching and pressing his garments for the McKinley ball he was set to attend later that evening.

Sitting across from his wife at the table, Mildred occupying her usual seat as she too partook in supper, he
watched Phoebe for any sign that something was off, but
her smile remained serene, her laughter at Mildred's antics
consistent, and her conversation unstilted as they volleyed
back and forth about their day and their charming dinner
companion's despicable manners.

"You're going to the McKinley function after our
game?" she asked, sipping at her wine.

Harrison nodded, wiping his mouth with his napkin.
"Yes. Averndale has asked me to accompany him in his
weekly duty to his grandmother."

"Weekly duty?"

With a chuckle, Harrison set down his napkin and sat
back in his chair. "Yes. His grandmother has requested
that he show his face at a public setting with her once a
week, and while he hates the spotlight, and certainly wants

nothing to do with marriage just yet, he adores his grandmother. So he humors her."

"My mother has said that most affairs such as these help to dissuade the loneliness of the older set."

"I'm sure it is that, but I think, secretly, she hopes that these events will spark his interest in finding a wife."

"Why do you suspect that?"

"Because she mentions matrimony every chance she gets," he said with a laugh. "No doubt tonight will be no different, especially given my attendance. She'll most likely use my state of matrimonial bliss as an example to why he should do the same."

Phoebe chuckled. "If only she knew the true state of the matter."

He raised a brow at her comment. "Who's to say I'm not blissfully married?"

"The woman you married?"

He leaned forward and rested his elbows on the table. "Marriage to you is blissful. I enjoy your company, our conversations are interesting, and you make me laugh. What more could I ask for?"

Her lips turned down. "A wife who attends these events with you? Who's actually interested in societal ongoings?"

Her words struck, but not in the way she intended. No, instead, they made his heart ache at how very little she thought of herself and their marriage. "I never asked how it is that you attended so many functions when they leave you feeling as you do?"

"I have a list," she said, as if it were the simplest idea.

"A list? A list of what?"

"Everything," she said, one shoulder raising. "A list for getting myself ready. Making sure my hair isn't too tight and my dress isn't too itchy. Ensuring I've used enough perfume to fan up for myself if the smell is unbearable. I have a list of items that go into my reticule; tufts of cotton, my fan, a bracelet with charms that move that I can fiddle with."

"It sounds as if you are readying for war."

"A ball is a lot like war." She paused, her eyes searching the room as if to find the answer there. "Have you ever been to a fireworks show and been too close to where they set them off?" He shook his head. "When you're that close to a noise that loud, it takes over your senses and you cannot focus on the brilliance of the view because you're overwhelmed from the noise."

She looked at him as if to see if he understood. He nodded.

"Going to a ball is like that. The noises are amplified tenfold, the smells, the senses. My body becomes so focused on the discomfort of the sensations that I can't enjoy the good parts of the ball, so I prepare as best I can."

"The good parts?" he asked. "I wasn't aware there were any."

She looked down at her plate. "Dancing. I love dancing, but at a ball..." She shook her head. "It's just too much." She smiled brightly at him, her eyes alight, their sharpness softening. "When I was learning to dance, I used to spin around the ballroom for hours after the instructor left, humming tunes to myself as I executed the steps. I'd pretend I was at a ball and my dance card was full, and I would get lost for hours on end as I waltzed around the ballroom."

Harrison leaned forward in his chair at her words, her eyes dancing with delight at her description and he wondered for a moment what it would be like to be the cause of that joy. What it would take to be the one that brings that bit of bliss to Phoebe's face. "I didn't know you liked to dance."

She shrugged. "You've never asked." With a sad smile, she looked at him. "We probably never will."

Harrison's heart tugged at the sight, at the heartache. A ball, for all its glamourous appeal, was a sensory overload for anyone in general, but Phoebe's description sounded like the whole ordeal was placed under a magnifying glass. As if attending the opera and being forced to sit directly next to the orchestra, or a horse race, but your only place of seating was near the gun. Her love for dancing would no doubt be less enjoyable given those circumstances. Was it any wonder she denied herself?

Standing, he walked to her chair and held out his hand. "Come with me."

"Where?" she asked, taking his hand.

"Trust me," he said with a smile as he led her out the dining room and down the hallway toward the ballroom, Mildred hot on their heels. Grabbing a candelabra from one of the sideboards, Harrison headed inside, lighting several candles before setting the original on top of the piano, and returning to Phoebe. Her brow was raised, and when he took her hands and led her to the center of the room, she met his gaze and smiled. Picking up one of her small hands, Harrison placed it on his shoulder, the weight of it light against the fabric of his coat, like a butterfly. She blinked as she watched him take her free hand into his, the warmth of her palm a beacon to his cooler one. As he placed his hand on her waist, pulling her in close, she took a small inhale of breath and his chest tightened as her skirts brushed against his legs. Humming "Greensleeves", he began to move.

Phoebe said nothing as he turned her about the room. It was as if all the words inside her had simply vanished into the air, but the smile on her lips and the gleam of joy in her eyes spoke volumes. Her body relaxed against his, and he took charge, whirling them around with steps engrained in his body since he was a lad but, in their ballroom, only filled with ghosts and a kitten, he decided propriety and polite societal rules be damned. Her soft giggle had him focusing on her, his legs taking over the steps while his eyes watched her. The way her blonde hair flew at the smallest wisp of a turn, how her gray eyes turned to a smokey ash color in the candlelight, her pale skin taking on a slight hint of pink at the cheeks from exertion. She was a fairy queen and he was under her spell, the joy that spilled from her filling all the cracks and crevices of his soul until he was whole again.

She sighed and looked at him, and Harrison was not sure at that moment who was taking the lead, for while his legs moved them about the room, steering them hither and yon, her sparkling eyes and soft smile was directing his heart in an altogether different dance. He became aware of her too swiftly, the feel of her hand gripped in his, her soft fingers curling around his skin. Her lush body against his, the curves he examined daily cupped beneath his fingertips, forming hills and valleys of interest, and her smell, a touch of honeysuckle, like her bees, lulling him in with its sweetness. Suddenly she was everywhere, all around him, all at once. Her beauty, her joy, surrounding him, drowning him in the sweetest way.

Phoebe met his gaze, surprise covering her face, and for a moment he wondered if she too felt the shift as he had. A wisp of blonde hair fell in front of her spellbinding eyes, and he lifted his hand from her waist, tucking the strand behind her ear. Her soft intake of breath had his errant thumb brushing against her lips, but before he could make contact, Mildred released a harsh meow, and Phoebe stepped away, turning her attention to the kitten.

"Poor thing, I think I stepped on her tail," she said, kneeling down to the black speck of a kitten on the floor who glared up at them with a look of betrayal.

Harrison's heart, still beating with a tempo, refused to slow as he knelt beside her and inspected the kitten. "She appears all right, and I'm sure your slippers are soft enough to not have harmed her."

Phoebe looked at him and too soon he realized his proximity. Her lips, a soft cherry in the candlelight, were pulled down into a frown from worry, her gray eyes somehow glittering in the dark ballroom. She was beautiful, stunning, this wife of his.

Pushing to stand, he held out his hand to help her up, then took a large step away as she regained her feet. It surely had to be the ambiance that had him feeling enthralled; the candlelight, the proximity, but nothing more.

Clearing his throat, Harrison looked at Phoebe. "Given

the McKinley affair perhaps we should postpone our game tonight."

"I can wait for you to return?"

"I certainly will not have you, or this little mite," he said, scratching at Mildred's ears, "forcing yourself to stay awake on my account. I'll see you tomorrow for breakfast." Bowing to her, her bent down to give Mildred another rough pet. "Have a goodnight, my ladies," he said, with a smile, then left the ballroom.

Upstairs as he readied for the ball, he frowned over the events that occurred.

Phoebe was right. It was too much, all of it. Much too much. The dancing with her as she smiled at him like a dream. Comforting her as she worried over the fate of her precious kitten.

Tucking her into her bed the night before, her face serene as she dreamt.

His mouth tipped into a smile and he caught a glimpse of his face in the mirror. The corners of his mouth slightly upward, not forced but comfortable, a small flash of dimple appearing in his cheek. A true smile, not the one he had spent eons perfecting in his youth.

"Blast," he said with a whisper, uncertain whether the look on his face was a good thing or a bad omen. For surely it must be. Surely, coming to not only feel his heart moved by his wife, but an attraction to her, was nothing but an ill sign of things to come, for that way only led to heartache. It had taken him his entire childhood to learn that you receive love when you are worthy, and as much as he hated to admit it, he was not perfect. And a one-sided love was a worser fate than not being loved at all, and with Phoebe, he was not certain there would be a way back from it.

Inside his carriage, Harrison replayed their dance, his hand on her waist as they spun about the room, her trust in him obvious as she closed her eyes and lost herself in the movements. Her hand had been warm in his as he cradled it, its touch a force that pulled him in, tempted him to linger, even as her softness made him want to cosset her away from the myriad of feelings that threatened to overwhelm them both at every turn. It was baffling. It was frightening.

Once inside the McKinley home, surrounded by the very environment that would send his wife scurrying off to hide, Harrison located Averndale who stood pressed against a wall, his hand tucked in his jacket, no doubt hiding a flask full of scotch. Without a word, Harrison reached inside the man's jacket and confiscated the flask, taking a deep drink, its contents burning a path down his throat and into his stomach.

"Don't drink it all," Averndale said, swiping the thing back and capping it before tucking it away. "I've only been here thirty minutes and you've nearly drained the thing halfway."

Harrison said nothing, turning and copying Averndale's position on the wall, his gaze volleying from couple to couple while he forced his typical grin to his face.

"Everything all right?" Averndale asked.

"Why wouldn't it be?"

"You just drank half of my flask and haven't said a word. Troubles at home?" he asked, a mischievous grin on his face.

"Not at all," Harrison said, wiggling off the frown that had attempted to take over. "I was merely thirsty."

"Mm hmm," Averndale said, his tone clearly calling him a liar.

Harrison cursed under his breath and turned to Averndale. Lowering his voice, he said, "I think I like my wife."

Averndale raised a brow and turned toward him, crossing his arms in front of his chest. "Why does it sound like you think it's a problem?"

"Because it is. Because this was supposed to be an easy marriage. A business agreement."

"What's changed?"

"She's… She's funny, and smart. Caring even though she pretends not to be. And she's—"

"Beautiful?"

"Gorgeous. Her smile is bloody well contagious and her skin is so soft, and she smells like honey and looks like a dream." He groaned.

Averndale chuckled. "I'm not sure what the problem is."

"This isn't what we agreed to. This isn't what she wanted. What I wanted."

With a raised brow, and a quick peek over his shoulder to ensure no one was listening, Averndale said, "How so?"

Harrison sighed and rubbed at his forehead. "We agreed that this was a marriage in name only. No emotional relationship and certainly nothing physical. And—" He paused, terrified of the next words.

"And?"

"And what if that happens and it doesn't work out and ruins the way things are now? We can't undo our marriage." Just the notion had Harrison wanting to run to his familial estate and away from the potential catastrophe.

Averndale shook his head. "Bit cart before the horse, wouldn't you say? You've already deemed the entire thing a tragedy and you haven't even asked Lady Phoebe how she feels. She could have little interest in you."

"At least that would be territory I'd understand," he said, the words low and grumbled. He was well aware of what it was like to not be wanted. What it was like to not be enough. He had loved Meg, and she had chosen another, merely confirming what he already knew. No matter how hard he tried nor how much he gave, he would never be worthy of love.

Averndale pushed away from the wall and slapped him on the shoulder, the resounding clap somehow loud and yet soft in the packed ballroom. "Why not let things happen organically? Who knows, maybe it is all an illusion and you're worrying over all this for nothing. And even if that is the case, you aren't even remotely aware of how she feels in return. No sense in worrying over something that hasn't even occurred yet."

Harrison forced a deep breath out between his lips. "You're right." And he was, blast it. It was typical of him to feel the slightest hint of an interest in someone and spin wildly out of control from the notion before even seeing what it truly was. It could have been a trick of the light, or even sleep deprivation that caused him to look at Phoebe a different way, and as Averndale said, no sense in worrying over something so trifling as that.

"Come along, Romeo. Let's go find my grandmother and let her dote over you now that you're in the state of wedded bliss." Averndale made a look of distaste before making his way through the crowd, and Harrison followed behind, grateful for good friends with solid heads on their shoulders. If not for Averndale, he would have worried he was on his way to falling in love with his wife.

CHAPTER TWELVE

Excitement filled Phee as she checked on the bees the next morning, delighted to find that another swarm had chosen to occupy the other one of her hives. The mingled humming of the different swarms was so like music, she was tempted to spin in circles, dancing to it, but now that she knew what it was like to dance with her husband, doing so alone did not seem as fun. Frowning at the thought, Phee threw it to the wind, instead focusing on the new additions.

The swarm seemed well adjusted, their drones coming and going as they searched for pollen to make food for their queen and hive, and while they appeared content with their new home, there was only one problem. They were cranky. Very cranky.

Every time Phee attempted to move near the hive, bees buzzed angrily, diving to sting her in protection of their home, and it became apparent very quickly that they were going to be trouble. Usually a beekeeper could use smoke to calm a hive so they could extract the honey and honeycomb, but she had begun to worry that this hive, should it continue its volatile ways, would need to be drowned in order to acquire the items inside. And that was something she was not sure she could do.

Standing a few yards away, Phee watched the hive

carry on as if she had not just walked near it, threatening their very existence. Meanwhile, the other hive was so adept at not only caring for themselves, but dealing with her invasive ways, they cared very little as they went about their daily activities. Phee scowled at the new hive, hoping the drones inside felt her disapproval and would decide to change their ways before it came time to acquire the wax inside. It was doubtful.

"You seem perturbed," Harrison said from a distance behind her and a smile tugged at her lips as she went to him, removing her heavy gloves and the hooded veil.

"Yes, we have a new hive," she said, pointing to the new tenants.

He raised a brow. "I thought that was a good thing?" he asked, Mildred curled up in his arms like a babe as he stroked her tummy.

"You would think so, but they are a rather brutish bunch. I barely walked by to inspect them and they sent their squad on the attack."

His eyes widened as he looked her over. "You're not hurt, are you?"

She shook her head. "No, a small sting but nothing concerning for me, although I can't say the same for the bees. The poor things were merely doing their job and died in the process." She sighed. "What I am concerned over is how we're going to extract the items from the hive if we can't get to it." She sighed again. "But that is a worry for another time. We missed you at breakfast this morning, and I didn't get a chance to ask how the ball was."

He smiled, a joyful one as opposed to his usual societal grin. "It was fine. I believe my favorite part was Averndale's grandmother remarking on my marriage every five minutes." He chuckled. "Averndale looked ready to flee as soon as I arrived."

Phee laughed at the image.

"I didn't think I arrived home that late, but when I asked Sterns, he said you two turned in early. Was it another restless night for our little beast?" he asked, tickling Mildred under the chin.

Phee nodded as she looked at the kitten, her amber eyes closed as she purred contently in Harrison's arms. "What if we've damaged her entirely?"

Harrison reached for her hand and gave it a squeeze. "She's content as a plum during the day with us. She'll adjust soon, don't worry."

Phee looked at their interlocked hands, and nodded. "Maybe you were right and we should get her a friend."

Harrison chuckled and Phee moved in closer, delighted by the sound. "Perhaps. Although now that I think on it, this beast is more than enough trouble for us."

Phee smiled as she looked at the pair, enjoying the oddity of what she saw. A grown man holding a kitten like an infant, cradling the tiny thing in his arm as he held hands with her. It was like an odd little family. What a peculiar thought, a family. She shook her head. No, they were friends, and their marriage was a business arrangement, that was all. A family unit was nowhere to be found in their contract.

"Are you off to the conservatory?" she asked, pushing the thoughts away.

"Yes, Mr. Williams is on his way for a lesson. I'm hoping to make a mug today."

"How exciting."

He rolled his eyes. "Yes, I'm aflutter to get started."

"Why so cynical? I thought you were enjoying it."

He sighed and looked at Mildred. "I am, only I'm certain I'll never get any better at this. Every piece I make is flawed. Imperfect. The bowl I crafted shattered in the kiln because there was air in the clay. The cup I thought would surely work is so uneven it barely holds any liquid at all. I'm absolutely terrible at this."

She shook her head and stepped closer once more, putting her hand on the arm that held Mildred. "Sometimes the best pieces are the ones most flawed. So your cup won't hold tea," she said with a shrug, "but it can hold hairpins or cufflinks without issue. It isn't about the product's perfection, Harrison, it's about the joy you find in making it."

He looked at her, his eyes searching and though his gaze was intense, Phee was not sure she could step away, nor that she wanted to. Her hand on his arm tickled and she looked down to find Mildred rubbing her face against it, a heavy purr vibrating her small body.

"My wife is rather adept at giving advice," he said his voice low, and when she looked back up, it was to find his gaze still on her, the intimate touch sending a delicious shiver down her spine. "You should look into writing a book."

Phee scoffed, her fingers dipping into Mildred's soft fur. "I'd be more adept at making someone fall in love with me than writing a book," she said, a smile overtaking her face at her own joke.

She expected him to laugh along with her, or perhaps

even scoff at such a silly notion. Yet he did neither. Possibly it was the sun, or maybe the angle in which she looked at him, but she was certain his lips pursed and his brow furrowed, his gaze flitting away to some expanse beyond the garden, before returning to hers, a soft smile taking over his lips.

"I think you can achieve whatever you set your mind to, Phoebe." The words were said without humor, conflicting with his smile, and she could not be certain the meaning behind them, nor whether to believe them at all. He shook his head and the moment was gone. "Goodness, would you look at us? What a rather melancholy bunch we are, brutish hives and broken ceramics," he said, societal smile back in place.

"More of a tragedy than a comedy," she said, releasing a deep breath. "Shall I take Mildred so you can begin your lesson?"

He nodded, handing over the black furball who meowed in protest at being shifted during her nap. With a final scritch to Mildred's chin, Harrison pulled away. "I shall see you both at dinner," he said, dipping his head to her before departing, leaving Phee and Mildred entirely alone in the garden.

"Do you have any notion of what just happened?" she asked the sleepy kitten in her arms. When the small mite did not respond, Phee sighed and shook her head. "Neither do I, pet, neither do I."

After luncheon, Phee bathed before settling at her desk with her notebook, but no matter how much she tried to focus on the updates of the hives, her mind kept circling back to Harrison.

Her husband made little sense to her, with his interchangeable smiles and kind words which always then would provoke his swift departure. Perhaps it was because she was new at this whole friendship thing, but the entirety of his actions was simply odd. Like having a raging fever and then being dropped into an ice bath, the temperature change so swift, so sudden, one could not brace for it.

Calmly placing the pen back into the ink well, Phee slid her notebook away from her, and let her head fall onto the desktop, her hands cushioning the blow. All of these jumbled moments were turning into a mystery too big for her to understand.

Her mind replayed the night with Mildred, Harrison covering Phee with a blanket before settling down beside her to comfort the kitten. His low and soft words whispered to the inconsolable mite that were so melodious and soothing they had lulled her to sleep as well.

And then there was their dance.

Phee groaned as she rocked her head back and forth across her knuckles, her skin tingling at the memory of his hands holding her close as he guided her around the ballroom, the soft humming of "Greensleeves" filling the air as they twisted and turned about the room. She was free and graceful in his arms, safe and cared for, and the joy had overwhelmed her. Had her looking for more, wanting more. Wondering what his lips would feel like beneath her own. Questioning if he was experiencing the same longing that had taken up residence in her stomach. And as they gazed at one another, Phee almost wondered if she dared to take a chance. If it would truly be that harmful to chase after the feelings Harrison inspired within her.

Thank heavens for Mildred, her timing impeccable, for it would have taken very little for Phee to step closer, to follow the impulse that seemed to be ingrained within her whenever he was near, which would be an absolute disaster for a multitude of reasons, their newly formed friendship merely being one of them.

"Silly, silly man," she whispered. For silly he was. He moved back and forth between friendship and common courtesy with little explanation as to why. If anything, his hot and cold wavering day in and day out firmly under-scored the fact that he was content with the way their arrangement was going.

But that did not stop her heart, her immature, useless heart from pounding resoundingly in her ears when they touched. Nor stop the blasted thing from fluttering when they conversed, his admiration of her filling each sentence.

Phee turned her head to look at Mildred, who decided to settle herself on top of the abandoned notebook, the black minion of darkness grooming herself contentedly as her owner lost her marbles. "You're a fat lot of help," she said, stroking the arrow of white on the kitten's head. "Any chance you can ask him how he feels about me?"

Mildred meowed her disapproval at Phee's cowardice and returned to her grooming session, uncaring of the turmoil before her. It was rude, really, her utter disinterest, but Phee could understand. When your biggest worry is where to take your next nap, the issues of mere peasants seemed trifling.

With a groan, Phee let her head fall back in her hands. If only she had been born a cat.

CHAPTER THIRTEEN

"IT IS TRULY a good start, my lord," Mr. Williams said, his voice soft.

He was lying, of course, but one could not fault his kindness. The vase looked like a vulva. A vulva vase, to be precise. Fitting name if he intended to sell it. He could make a profit selling vulva vases of all sizes and colors, becoming known as the eccentric lord with a peculiar art obsession. His mother, were she still alive, would be horrified at the attention he no doubt would gain, her dismay evident as she would have given him the cut direct, child or not.

With a swift flick of his wrists, the thin metal wire slid through the middle of the vase, the edges deflating with defeat to the tune of Mr. William's soft sigh.

"My lord, you won't produce single piece if you continue to strive for perfection," Mr. William's said, his gaze on the two lumps that now sat dejectedly on the potter's wheel.

Harrison picked up the two folds, dumping them into the metal bin that sat beside his station, the basket overflowing with a multitude of his pieces, their unformed mass a fitting metaphor for not only his hobby, but his marriage. Each of the pieces had been suitable, something to work with if he could merely pick a direction, but none were perfect. All were done with absolute ease from the very beginning but had become a mess the moment he touched them with decision, and like his marriage, he wondered if he was the problem.

In theory, their entire arrangement should have been the perfect execution of a marriage contract, and at the start, it had been. But that was before he had gotten to know his wife. Before he had come to know Phoebe. She was intelligent and thoughtful, particular and resilient, and it had become the most confounding thing, because now, instead of her simply being his wife, she had become his friend. Someone to care for. And that was the damnedest piece of all, because he did care. Deeply. Definitely more than he should. And when she touched his hand, simply graced him with one of her half-upturned smiles, he felt like the sun had come out, its warmth embracing him in the most comforting of ways.

It was confounding. And confusing. And he could not run from it, from her.

Nor was he even certain he wanted to.

No, he wanted to explore the tenderness that overtook his heart when he thought about his wife, search every cavern and crevice of that organ and hold her inside its chambers. Capture the soft giggle that escaped her lips while playing with Mildred. Put a name to the smile that took over her face as she devoured a chocolatey dessert. Cradle her hands in his until he knew every line and dent from wrist to fingertips, could trace them with his eyes closed.

But that was not what they had agreed to. And heaven only knew if she felt the same.

"I think we can be done for the day, Seb," Harrison said, his eyes staring at the pile of scrapped clay. "Head on home. I'll clean up this mess."

"Are you certain, my lord?"

Harrison nodded at the man, forcing his jovial smile to his face. "I'll see you next week."

With a bow, Mr. Williams left, and silence surrounded the conservatory, allowing Harrison's thoughts to fill the void. As he scraped the stone wheel with a wooden scraper, removing the excess clay, his mind replayed the feel of her as they danced, her form so tangible, he swore he was truly holding her. While he wiped the stone, cleaning it with water and a sponge, he heard her soft voice, worrying over the kitten's loneliness. Emptying the bucket of murky water into a flower bed, he sighed as the image of her fiddling with her cards filled his head. She was everywhere, all around him, and he wanted to drown in it, in her.

With a groan, Harrison set the bucket back on the kick wheel, the clang of the metal filling the room with its vibrations, and he thanked his lucky stars Mildred was not present or he would no doubt be calming a startled kitten at that moment. In truth, he was the one who needed calming. He was enthralled with his wife. More than likely slightly infatuated, and was not that the devil of it all? And yet, nothing had happened the way the storybooks say it should have. Not a speck of fireworks at their first meeting nor increased heart palpitations. No blushing debutante or heart-sickened fop. No, his arrival to this point had been methodical, calculated, and cool. Nothing like the bevy of emotions the poets wrote about.

"Right then," he said to the empty conservatory, brushing his muck covered hands against his apron. "That's enough melancholia for one afternoon."

After a hot bath that involved a thorough scrubbing of his hands and arms, Harrison arrived at the library sparkling clean yet irritatingly still perplexed, the feelings only heightening when he spotted his wife. Dressed in an unassuming green gown with her hair haphazardly pinned to her head, Phoebe sat on the floor dragging a piece of red yarn across the Persian rug while Mildred pounced upon it, ensuring its unfortunate demise.

"And how are my ladies this evening?" Harrison asked.

Phoebe looked up at him with a smile, and Mildred took advantage of the moment to wrestle the string from her fingers. With a chuckle, Phoebe returned her focus to the kitten who now had the string wrapped around her like a python, her paws searching for the frayed ends as she valiantly fought for her life.

"We're well," Phoebe said, untangling the string from the kitten and beginning their game again.

"And you, my dear? How were your bees today?"

Phoebe sighed as she trailed the string along the floor, causing Mildred to take a predatory stance, her black bottom wiggling in the air as she eyed her prey. "The malevolent hive is still rather territorial. I merely walked past their boxes today and received an improper hello in return."

Harrison's worried gaze raked over her form. "You weren't hurt?"

Phoebe shook her head. "Just a small poke, nothing

life threatening."

The tightness that had taken occupancy in his throat lessened and he nodded his head. "It worries me that they are giving you such trouble."

She nodded, her fingers stroking the scruff of fur at Mildred's neck while the kitten chewed on the end of the string. "I feel the same. I'm not sure what I'll decide to do when the time comes to harvest, but I'm intent upon not giving up just yet." She giggled as Mildred turned her attention to her fingers, the little mite mouthing the digits. "She's gotten so big, don't you think?"

"How can you say that? It's only been a little more than a week."

Phoebe shook her head with a frown. "I'm sure of it, just look at her ears. If I had a way to document her growth I'd be able to prove it to you." She picked up the tiny ball of fluff, who gave a disconcerted meow in protest, and held her close to her chest. "It's going way too fast. Soon she'll be grown and I'll never be able to recall how tiny she was."

Harrison looked at the pair, his wife's sadness apparent on her face as she held the small kitten to her chest, stroking the white splotch on her forehead. "I may have an idea. That is, if we can get Mildred to cooperate."

"Truly?" Phoebe asked.

Harrison nodded before going to the desk and removing a sharpened pencil from the top drawer. Eyeing the wall of the library, he chose a discreet corner where an armchair sat, blocking the light blue wall behind it. "Do you think you can bring her over here without too much of a fight?" Harrison asked as he wrestled the armchair away from the wall.

Phoebe tucked Mildred against her chest beneath her chin, the kitten settling in with a purr, her paws kneading Phoebe's chest. When she came to stand beside him, Harrison smiled at her as he took the wiggly fluff from his wife and positioned her standing against the wall. "Take the pencil and trace around her as best you can," he said.

Phoebe raised a brow at him but did as he asked while Harrison held Mildred as still as he could, even though the small feline protested.

When the shape of a cat took its place on the wall, Harrison let go of Mildred who gave a disgruntled chirp before coming to sit beside him and groom herself. Taking the pencil from Phoebe, Harrison wrote 25th of June, 1822 beside the wall cat's head, then stood to inspect their work.

"Now what?" Phoebe asked.

"Now we wait, and in a month," he looked down at the cat, "or perhaps a week, we will do it again. Then you'll have a record of her growth and be able to remember how small she was."

Phoebe stood beside him, a smile taking over her lips forcing a small dimple he had never noticed before to appear in her cheek. "It's brilliant."

Harrison shrugged, slightly appalled at how his body warmed at her statement. "It's nothing. A simple thing that will make you happy."

"It does," she said, turning to look at him with a look he could only describe as befuddlement. "It does make me happy. Why do you insist upon doing that?"

"Doing what?" he asked.

"Doing simple things for my happiness. It wasn't part of our agreement. You could just as easily leave it alone but you don't. Why?"

"Because I like knowing that you're happy?" he said, the words coming out like a question. "I like seeing that smile on your face, knowing I put it there." Harrison shrugged, hoping the gesture added a sense of aloofness he did not feel. His hands clenched by his sides, afraid he might do something foolish, like reach for her.

Phoebe wrapped her arms around her waist, lowering her eyes to the carpet beneath their feet. "You should probably stop doing that," she said, the words quiet.

She had given him an out, a chance to remove himself from the spell that she had cast on him, and yet he could not find the want to take it. "Why?"

"Because when you do those things, when you say those things, they make me feel something." Slowly, she raised her head, her beautiful gray eyes awash in uncertainty.

"Something?" he asked, his heart bounding in his chest as he searched her gaze.

"Yes. Warmth and comfort, but also... want. My stomach flips and turns, and my heart races, and it's never behaved like that for another person."

"What... What does that mean?" he asked, his heart pounding its resounding rhythm in his ears. When she said nothing, Harrison took a step toward her, hope filling his person. "Phoebe, what does that mean?"

She looked down at her hands which were clutched before her and sighed. "It means that I like it too much. It means, when you do those things, I want to be near you. I want to hold your hand, or stroke the bristle on your cheek, press my forehead to yours, and I know, I just know that doing so is against what we agreed to. But I can't make myself stop feeling this way, so you have to stop being so kind to me."

"Why?" he asked again, stepping closer to her, hope filling his chest that she could possibly want him as much as he wanted her.

"Because it's the only sane way for me to stop feeling this way about you. I've tried to stop my reaction but it won't go away. You're in my veins, in the air surrounding me and I cannot make this feeling stop." She shook her head. "I'm sorry. I know it's not what we agreed to."

"I feel it too." Harrison placed his fingers beneath her chin, raising it to meet his gaze. "What can I do to fix this?"

Phoebe's teeth worried at her bottom lip; her cheeks flushed with an endearing pink hue. "Maybe not you, but we? Perhaps we approach it from another direction?" she said.

"What did you have in mind?"

"An experiment of sorts," she replied, her eyes assessing him. "One that holds very little sanity."

He frowned. "What sort of experiment?" he asked, his hand cradling her cheek, the smooth skin like velvet in his palm, while his heart pounded a resounding beat in his ears.

"One that will undoubtably make this feeling entirely worse." With a sigh, her hands touched his chest, sliding up to rest on his shoulders. "Should I test my theory?"

"Yes," he said, the word a plea as he lowered his head,

his lips a breath away from Phoebe's delectable cupid bow of a mouth. She pushed onto her tiptoes and brought their lips together, and with that single touch, Harrison's whole world exploded.

CHAPTER FOURTEEN

I T WAS HER first kiss. It was odd and wonderful, strange and extraordinary. The strength of Harrison's body stood before her like a wall, keeping her upright, tempting her to lean against him while his lips pressed against hers, their silken texture alluring and strange.

Phee pulled back, her lips tingling from the contact, and her hand rose to touch them, certain his kiss had altered them in some way.

"Phoebe?" Harrison asked, her name a question. A plead?

Meeting his gaze, his brown eyes hooded, his cheeks slightly flushed, Phee knew she had to know more. "Again," she said, pushing onto her toes to take his lips once more.

It was a fireworks show without the sound, a sonata without the buzz of onlookers. Harrison growled as his fingers delved into her hair, tangling in the strands as they cupped her head, holding her close to him, the few pins that resided there falling to the ground. The pull of the motion heightened the connection, churned the butterflies that fluttered chaotically in her stomach and dampened the space between her legs. It was chaos and comfort, longing and care, battling inside of her as her hands fumbled for purchase, desperate to hold onto something as her husband upended her world with his honeyed lips. Phee flicked her tongue against his lush bottom lip, wanting more, needing a taste of the heaven that was him, and Harrison readily agreed to her request, opening to meet her, tempting her to explore and taste.

It's worse, she thought, as he pulled away, changing the angle of his delicious destruction. Her want of him, as she had suspected, grew much worse. Her heart pounded in her ears, its thumping a sturdy tempo, keeping her aware that she was, indeed, alive. Very much so.

Phee's hands slid up Harrison's jacket, inspecting each dip and pivot of his chest, and instead of soothing the chaos that threatened to overwhelm her, her strokes against his clothed body sent her blood humming as her mind weaved delicious pictures of what the expanse might look like. The images were devastating and she would have bit her lip to stifle the whimper if they were not already entertained. Instead, the noise escaped, the need in it so heavy Phee wondered for a moment if the sound had truly come from her.

It was that noise that seemed to shake Harrison from the moment, and he stepped back from her, his lips parting from hers, leaving only a soft sting. Phee stumbled at the loss of him, her hands gripping the linen of his shirt, and her nails raked his covered skin eliciting a growl.

Taking one of her hands from his chest, Harrison guided her to the white tufted couch, setting her down before kneeling before her. His hand rose to her cheek, the soft tips of his fingers grazing her skin as he cupped her face, his thumb rubbing against her bottom lip as if soothing the tortured skin.

"Phoebe," he said, her name a whisper. "Phoebe, look at me." When she met his gaze, he smiled. His normally neat hair was disheveled, his cravat hanging limp about his neck and his breaths were labored, as if he had just run through London to be by her side. "How do you feel?"

Her brow knit at his question, her mind taking account of each part of her body. Her lips tingled, her skin was warm, her heart raced, and her whole body yearned. It was the yearning that was most disconcerting, a sort of hunger that was unknown and uneasily satiated, and she sighed in frustration at its appearance. "Unfulfilled," she said.

Harrison chuckled at her words, the sound deep and guttural, making her clench with need. What would that sound feel like against her lips? Her skin. What would the hand that so gently cupped her cheek do if the neckline of her day dress were loosened, if she stood before him in nothing but her chemise. Her cheeks heated at her wayward thoughts, but not with embarrassment, no. With need. With need for him.

Leaning forward, Phee cupped his cheek in return, letting her lips brush against his, her sigh foreign to her own ears. He waited not a moment, his lips capturing hers in a devastating kiss that nearly sent her to her knees beside him. There was a power there, a need inside him that was barely contained as his tongue slid against hers, his teeth nibbling on her bottom lip. His hands were gentle, his caresses sweet, but Phee knew the capacity behind that kind of control, had seen him manipulate a block of clay into any shape he wanted. And instead of running from it, she wanted to dive into it, have it surround her like the swarm it no doubt was.

"Phoebe," Harrison said against her lips, before resting his forehead against hers as his strong hands move to her shoulders, effectively holding her still. "Phoebe, this is dangerous. You're dangerous."

"Don't be silly," she said on an exhale. "I'm just me."

He smirked, one corner of his mouth raising in such an alluring way that she had to bite her lip to stop from reaching for him again. "You truly have no understanding what you do to me." He brushed his lips against hers and said on a whisper, "Just you."

"Harrison," she said, hypnotized by the smooth glide of his lips.

"My sweet-honeyed wife," he said, his soft voice velvety smooth. "If only you could hear my heart every time it is in your vicinity, hear how desperately I long for you. The beating alone is so furious I'm certain I'll combust."

Phee pulled back, her eyes shooting to his brown gaze, searching the depths for any sign of insincerity. Instead, she found only honesty as he met her stare. "You can't mean that," she said.

He frowned, his hand reaching for her own and giving it a reassuring squeeze. "I do, Phoebe. I truly do." With a sigh, he pulled back, resting his hands against his thighs. "That, perhaps, is the scariest part."

"Why?

"Because it was not part of our contract," he said. "And not only is it not part, but it was expressly stated that it was unnecessary."

"Our contract," she said, her eyes falling to his disheveled cravat.

He closed his eyes for a pause, then met her gaze. "And if we're both being honest, it is a rather large piece that not only requires thought on both our parts, but a renegotiation if it is something we were to pursue. I don't want to disrupt this friendship we have forged." He took her hand. "I want to do what you want to do, Phoebe. In whatever regard that is. And I'll never pressure you for things you don't want."

Phee remained silent, her eyes fixed on the hand that enveloped her own, its reassuring caresses sending tendrils of warmth along her body, stoking the fire he had already created. Yet, even as her physical self pleaded for her to throw away caution and retake his lips, her mind screamed at her to access the situation. Such a large decision would alter the entire makeup of their arrangement, the comfort she had found in his home and by his side suddenly becoming a rather large gamble to lose should things ever go awry.

Harrison squeezed her hand before leaning forward to press a kiss to her forehead, the action forcing one corner of her mouth to lift in a smile at the loveable act.

"I want to do what you want to do, Phoebe, whatever that is," he said. "Take as much time as you need to think it over. I'll follow your lead either way."

With a gentle brush of his lips against hers, Harrison stood and left the room, the removal of his presence leaving Phee unnervingly empty. Even as a piece of her longed to call him back, to tell him that it mattered not what the effects were of them following that path, she knew that afterward, she would ruminate over it obsessively. No, it was best for them both if she were truly certain that this new facet of their relationship was one she wanted to embark on fully. Because fully it would be.

If his kisses were any indication of the power that he could wield over her, Phee knew that the rest would no doubt be a labyrinth of sinful pleasure and divine delights of which she could only imagine. It was intoxicating, this hold he had over her, and as with any addiction, she would want to drown in its every facet if it meant that Harrison was by her side, conducting the illicit pleasures that only he could arise. But it would change everything.

Standing, Phee let out a long sigh, her shoulders slumping at the motion. The best course of action would be to create a list of pros and cons regarding this new addendum to be sure that she could handle any unforeseen changes. That they both could handle them.

Yet, after three long hours, countless sheets of paper, and several cups of tea, Phee could not seem to find anything positive that might come from beginning a physical relationship with Harrison. Each list of cons grew and grew as she thought on every possibility, every potentiality they might happen upon. Meanwhile, the only positive she could find in the bunch was that she would no longer feel the absurd longing for him that had seemed to overcome her senses making it hard for her to even think without him slipping into her thoughts.

Phee frowned as she stared at the list before her, her writing instrument tapping against her lip as if it were a magic wand merely waiting to change the words before her. But no amount of magic would change the truth of the matter. Their arrangement was solid and unsurprising as it was, any changes to it would remove any stability she might find there. And lack of stability was one thing she did not handle well. It helped when things were certain and surprises were few, and the feelings Harrison elicited were anything but stable. She wanted to crawl inside him, drown in his touch, kiss him whenever the whim demanded, and see how much strength those muscles of his had. It was whimsical, fairy sort of stuff and she had never been one for fairy tales.

Yet, sadness pulled at her. A loss for no doubt what could have been had she made a love match to a dashing man. Instead, she was merely Phee, a spinster engaged in a contract marriage with a remarkably handsome and extremely tender-hearted man who had his own reasons for entering such an agreement.

But he wanted her.

Shaking her head, Phee stood from the chair at her desk and shook out her skirts, the motion eliciting a meow of protest from Mildred who rested on her blanket. This evening would involve the one ball she had agreed to for the month and were she honest with herself, her energy would be better spent preparing for an evening of hell rather than attempting several lists in the hopes that she could continue to kiss her husband.

Her stomach tightened at the thought of the crushing bodies and repulsive smells that she had before her tonight and even if she could will back the bliss she had found that afternoon in the library with Harrison, her nerves would not allow it. The earl and countess would make their first official appearance as a couple, speculation of their quick marriage already filling the gossip pages of the paper, and Phee could not stop the clenching of her shoulders as she imagined the hours of horror before her. If anything, it was another con to add to her list of why she could never follow through with these feelings for Harrison. He seemed to revel in the social aspect of society, longed for it with a frenzy she would never understand.

That in and of itself should be the largest indicator that they should not be together.

CHAPTER FIFTEEN

A S THE CARRIAGE moved toward the Waverly town-home all Harrison could think about was the honey scented woman across from him. Were he another man, he would have convinced her that she belonged in his arms and in his bed, then sequester them away for the foreseeable future where he would do some rather sinful things to her person. Instead, gentleman that he was, his first thought as he saw Phoebe's hooded gaze and rosy cheeks when she pulled back from his kiss was to ensure that she knew exactly what door they had opened. And that it was something she wanted.

The look of befuddlement that overcame her face only certified that she had little inkling of the sensual thoughts that filled his head the moment his lips touched hers. The way his body begged him to touch her, to cup her cheek, and then her breast. To follow the slope of her hips to her delectable backside which he would clasp to bring her closer to him. Heat flooded to his own cheeks as he reviewed the sinful narrative his mind replayed for him, recalled the soft sighs that had escaped her delicious lips as she met his kiss thrust for deadly thrust. The temperature in the carriage was no doubt spiking at his wayward thoughts, and his breeches would be in an unfortunate state were he required to exit any time soon.

Meanwhile, his goddess of a wife sat across from him, quiet as they moved through the darkened streets of Mayfair, unaware of the rather risky thoughts that overtook her husband. Squeezing his eyes closed, Harrison thought of the potter's wheel, the circular motion of the stone moving at a hypnotizing pace. He imagined a lump of clay slapping against the cold stone, his hands moving against the pliable surface, molding it to his whim. A round shape began to form, one much like the delectable figure of his wife, the curves spinning against his hands, giving way to the light but firm pressure he was applying... No.

Eyes flying open, Harrison took in a deep breath, certain there was nowhere safe for him to find salvation. Even the caverns of his mind were intent upon delving into the heaven that no doubt his wife was. It was treason of the brain. Certainly that was an illness that could overtake someone. A brain with, well, with a mind of its own. One corner of his mouth rose in a smile and he must have made a sound because Phoebe's head turned to peer at him through the dim interior.

"Something amusing?" she asked.

"No," he said, clearing his throat. "Merely thinking about an idea for the wheel tomorrow."

"Oh," she said, the words soft.

"How was the rest of your afternoon?" he asked. "Were you with your bees?"

"No," she said. "No, I spent it writing."

"Oh."

Quiet filled the carriage, and Harrison wished he could call back the silly words that had led them to this conversation. But here they were, and, if he were being honest, he wanted to know what she had thought about, whether it be their afternoon kiss or the odd bit of weather they were having. "You sounded troubled when you said that."

"I don't think we should make an addendum to our contract," she said, the words pushed out in a quick rush of breath.

"Oh," Harrison said.

"I enjoyed this afternoon very much. No," she said, a soft laugh accompanying the words, "I enjoyed it immensely. So much so that I would have lost my head in it if not for you. But you were correct. The physical part is not a part of our agreement. And as much as I liked what we did, I can't see it doing anything but ruining what we have found. You're my friend, Harrison, and you've become very dear to me. I can't imagine losing that because of some silly physical nonsense."

Disappointment resounded through his being at her words. While entirely true, her pronouncement was depressing. He would never push her into a situation she did not wish to be in, and he would respect her request that they merely remain friends, but it did not deplete the longing for her that had grown only deeper as their days together progressed, nor did it stop the grief of knowing that once again, he was not worth the price it would take to be with him. But he could have a part of her if they were friends, and maybe, after a time, it would be enough.

Leaning forward, Harrison took her gloved hand in his and gave it a reassuring squeeze. "I enjoyed it too, Phoebe, and as much as I'd love to ask you to reconsider, I also couldn't agree more. I would hate to lose your friendship, especially since I've only just found it."

Phoebe released a loud sigh. "Oh, thank goodness. I was worried you would hate me."

With another squeeze to her hand, Harrison released her and leaned back against the carriage seat. "I could never hate you, Phoebe, especially not over something as important as this."

The carriage slowed to a roll and Harrison looked at his wife, her face alight in the exterior lights of the home. Her lush lips were pressed together in a sour disposition while her eyes shifted back and forth, examining the crush that waited before them. Taking her hand in his, Harrison waited for her to meet his gaze. "We can return home right now," he said. "You don't have to do this."

Phoebe shook her head. "We agreed to it. Plus, it is our first outing as husband and wife. I want to make sure the ton still thinks highly of you given your rushed nuptials."

"I'm not sure how I feel about you doing so to the detriment of yourself." Looking at her, Harrison noted the slight pallor of her face and the way she pinched at the tip of the white gloves that graced her hand. "Run through your checklist with me," he said waiting for her eyes to return to his. "You have your cotton?" She nodded. "And I can already smell your perfume. You have your fan?" She snorted, a corner of her mouth lifting. "Perfect. We'll stay for as long as you want. Whenever you're ready to depart, we will."

She nodded, a smile pushed to her lips, but her hands never loosened from the tight grasp they held on the tip of her gloves. Reaching across the carriage, Harrison cupped her cheek, his thumb rubbing gently at the pair of lines that were forming between her brow. "I'll be with you the whole time."

"That's a comfort." Phoebe swallowed. "All right then. I'm ready. Let's go."

Opening the carriage door, Harrison motioned aside the footman before stepping out and turning to hold his hand out to her. Phoebe's fingers gripped his tightly as if she might fall, but Harrison knew that it had nothing to do with the trip out of the carriage and everything to do with the trip inside. He could already hear the loud voices as they swept out onto the drive, knew that inside the ballroom there would be a crush of bodies, each heavily drenched in perfume water and sweat, their sticky skin pressing up against each other. And while the notion did not in any way unnerve him, the thought of what it might cost Phoebe made his throat tighten and his senses heighten.

He was leading her into the lion's den all because of an item he had added. With a scowl, he looked down at her. Perhaps they needed a contract renegotiation after all.

After giving their greetings to Lord and Lady Waverly, Harrison guided Phoebe down the stairs and into the sweltering ballroom. All of London seemed to be in attendance that night and as they made their way down the final steps and into the fray, he could feel their eyes upon them. Phoebe's hand, which had rested easily on his forearm, now squeezed, clutching at the fabric of his dark blue coat. Leaning down, he said in her ear, "I'm right here."

"Phee, dear," said a voice from crowd, and Harrison spied his mother-in-law making her way toward them. The woman's smile was gentle, her eyes bright as she made her way to her daughter, and the pressure on his sleeve loosened slightly.

"Hello, Mother," Phoebe said, leaning forward and kissing her mother on the cheek.

"Lady Youngly," he said, bowing.

"Nonsense, Everly," Lady Youngly said. "We're family." With a smile, she reached out and took his hand, giving it a squeeze, her eyes investigating with the same curiosity as Phoebe had observing her beehives. Harrison smiled at her in return and bestowed a kiss to her cheek.

With a nod, Lady Youngly turned to her daughter. "Your brother and his wife are already here. Come, I'll escort you to them," she said, taking Phee's arm. "My lord, please feel free to get yourself refreshment and mingle about if you'd like."

Harrison smiled, but stepped closer to Phoebe, his hand resting on top of the one on his forearm. "Thank you, my lady, but I'll stay beside my wife. I'm afraid it is rather hard to be away from her for too long."

Lady Youngly raised a brow at him but said nothing as she released Phoebe's arm. Turning toward the crowded edges of the ballroom, Lady Youngly began to wind her way through the group of attendees. Aware of the swarm of individuals before them, Harrison placed his hand on Phoebe's waist and began to guide her through the crowd.

It was as if they were in the midst of a game of chess, the pieces moving left and right with Harrison ensuring that not a single one captured his queen. A large gentleman made to move from one clutch of people to another and Harrison tightened his grip on Phoebe, shifting her to the side so that it was his body that brushed against the man and not hers. If not for Phoebe bringing his attention to the array of smells at these events, Harrison might never have noticed how the lord's sweat mixed with a cedar smell was slightly nauseating, as was the heat that emanated from his body as it brushed against Harrisons. With a quick glance down at Phoebe, who seemed slightly wide eyed at the sudden block, Harrison took a step forward to keep them moving.

On the other side of the scattering of people, Phoebe's mother stood in her own clutch that included Phoebe's brother, Viscount Hunt, and his wife, Lady Patricia. Phoebe's body relaxed against his hand as they exited the smattering and came to stand within the circle of familiar faces.

"All right, Phee?" Lord Hunt asked.

Phoebe nodded at her brother before looking up at Harrison. A soft smile decorated her lips and she mouthed a quiet, "thank you," before turning back to the group.

"I'm so happy to see you tonight," Lady Hunt said, reaching for Phoebe's hand and squeezing it. "I've missed your presence at these things."

Phoebe smiled at her sister-in-law and with a quick glance to Harrison, moved to the other woman's side where they began chatting quietly between themselves. Harrison watched the pair for a moment, ensuring that Phoebe was all right, before turning to speak with her mother and brother.

"Marriage seems to suit you well," Lord Hunt said, his eyes seeming to have taken note of Harrison's protective regard for Phoebe. "I hope my sister is being kind to you."

"It does and she is," Harrison said. "It isn't a hard thing considering I married the most wonderful woman in England."

Lord Hunt raised a brow at his statement, but Harrison did not care what her brother thought of their situation. Nor did he need to know that his sister truly was the most wonderful woman in England. Were it fate or sheer luck, Harrison was ever grateful that Phoebe Metcalf was his wife.

A waltz began to play and one corner of Harrison's mouth tugged up into a smile. "Excuse me," he said to his in-laws. Stepping toward Phoebe, he watched as she paused in her conversation with Lady Hunt to look at him. "I apologize for my interruption," he said, "but I was hoping to dance with my beautiful wife."

Lady Hunt smiled and looked at Phoebe. Meanwhile, his wife stood still and unmoving.

"Lady Everly, may I have the pleasure of this dance?" he asked, holding his hand out to her.

Phoebe took it, her eyes moving to the mingle of bodies on the dance floor.

"Eyes on me," Harrison said in her ear as he directed her to the floor. Wrapping one hand on her waist, Harrison took her other hand, gloved in long white satin, and kissed her knuckles before holding it out to the side. "You've practiced this."

Meeting her gray gaze, Harrison counted to three, then began to propel them around the dance floor. Phoebe's body remained stiff, the ease and comfort that she had shown in their own ballroom nowhere to be seen, and Harrison wondered if he had made a mistake. "Phoebe?"

Phoebe's eyes slid closed, her body relaxing into his, the tension in her hand loosening against his fingers.

Manners be damned, he rested his cheek against the top of her head. "That's my girl," he said, pulling her closer. "Are you imagining we're in our ballroom dancing? Is Mildred on the couch grooming herself, uncaring that her mama and papa are dancing alone in any empty room like a pair of dolts?"

A soft laugh escaped her lips, the delicate sound meant only for his ears, and he smiled against her hair, humming along to the string quartet that played.

The ton looked on as Lord and Lady Everly swirled about the ballroom, indecently close and yet seemingly uncaring. Many a young girl watched the pair, jealousy and longing battling for a spot in their hearts as they yearned for what the couple no doubt had, while the young bucks wondered at what they could have possibly missed in Lady Phoebe Kent that Lord Everly had no doubt seen.

The pair danced until the music stopped playing, Phoebe's family in a state of stunned bewilderment as Lord Everly kissed his wife's forehead before escorting her from the dance floor. If the ton had any reason to question why the pair married so quickly, the answer was unequivocally found that very night.

Lord and Lady Everly were in love.

CHAPTER SIXTEEN

S NUGGLED UP ON the chair in her bedroom, Mildred by her side, Phee sipped at the mug of hot chocolate her maid, Flora, had brought her after readying her for the night. The gown she had worn to the Waverly ball was finally off her body and put away for another night in the future. Her hair was brushed and plaited, the loose braid falling over one shoulder which had become a toy for Mildred for a good thirty minutes before she finally gave up the game in pursuit of sleep. Yet Phee could not seem to find the want to join her in slumber.

Her mind kept replaying Harrison, shielding her from the crush of bodies at the ball. Dancing with her, soothing her. It was the first time she had ever enjoyed a ball, ever thought that perhaps she had been wrong and there was nothing to worry over. It was nonsense of course, balls were horrendous affairs, but by Harrison's side they were manageable.

Setting the mug aside on the low table beside her, Phee adjusted the blanket eliciting a frustrated mew from the kitten. Rubbing the top of the fluffy head beside her hip, Phee watched as the small dear slipped back into sleep, her soft snores like a soothing melody, and she wished she could curl up right next to her and sleep. But her body would not let her. Could not. For every time she closed her eyes, she could feel Harrison's strong hands guiding her across the dance floor. Feel the press of his lips against her forehead as their dance ended. The comforting scent of citrus that emanated from him in the stifling room as he curled his body around hers, preventing her from even a moment of discomfort. He had listened. He had understood.

And when she had looked at him an hour later, her body already beginning to fade at the onslaught of sounds and smells, he had made their excuses, taken her hand, and left, all without needing a single word from her.

It was as if he were the other part of her, able to sense her moods. Her needs. And where his protective bent should have left her feeling smothered or frustrated, instead, it had been comforting. She knew she was strong, knew she was capable, as did he. But with him there, she did not have to be strong and capable all the time. She could simply be Phee.

Blinking at the pop of a log falling in the fire, Phee sighed. This did not feel right, sitting in her room alone while the thing she wanted, the man she wanted, was in his own room for the night, most likely already in bed. Not near her, soothing her to sleep like she did for Mildred, and she only had herself to blame. Her silly brain with its incessant prattling and nattering on about contracts and comfortability, meanwhile her heart cried out with an entirely different message. And though she knew it had made sense not to change the contract, it seemed that she had failed to factor into account the desire that would come from the care he showed.

She longed for him the way Mildred longed for

warmth and comfort. She yearned for his caresses the way their silly kitten yearned for their pets the moment they came into her sight. And she wanted him beside her after an overwhelming day, holding her close and soothing her to sleep like she did their rat hunter in training. Even more than that, she wanted to be the one he confided in. The first to see his creations after a day at the potter's wheel, the one to calm him when his mercurial moods arose. The one to make him smile over breakfast, a feisty Mildred in tow.

Decision made, Phee picked up Mildred and deposited the kitten on her woolen bed, stroking the small white spot on top of her head until the kitten once more fell into slumber. Then, slipping on her robe, Phee went to the door that adjoined their room. With a deep breath, she raised her hand and knocked softly at the wooden portal. Biting her lip, she leaned forward hoping to hear any sign that he was awake, but all she was met with was quiet.

"Come on, Phoebe. Knock once more. Don't be a ninny," she whispered to herself, raising her hand once again to knock, but the door swung open, revealing a rumpled Harrison. His white linen shirt was opened at the top revealing a sculpted chest, the tan skin there surprising and intriguing, and Phee could not help but stare at the expanse it showed.

"Phoebe?" he asked. "Is everything all right?"

Phee swallowed, her eyes lifting to meet his, but she could not find the words to respond.

He stepped forward into her room and peeked around her. "It's not Mildred, is it?"

The mention of the kitten snapped Phee out of her

trance and she shook her head. "No, Mildred is fine."

"Oh," he said, stepping back and looking at her, his eyes soft from sleep and his usually quaffed hair a bit disheveled. His eyes swept over her, taking her in, but he made no move to touch her even though every modicum of her body wished that he would. But he was not like that. He would respect her wishes, respect her space no matter what, and it only made her want him more.

"I wanted to thank you for tonight," she said.

He shook his head. "It's nothing to be thanked for. I wanted you to be comfortable and feel that you were able to enjoy yourself, that was all."

Phee took a step closer to him, his citrus scent filling her senses. "That's just it," she said. "Not everyone would have done what you did tonight. You soothed in circumstances where I would have been met with frustration."

"Did you have a bit of fun?" he asked.

Phee nodded. "When we danced."

Harrison smiled. "Then I have no need for thanks. I'm glad you enjoyed dancing with me as much as I did dancing with you." He paused and looked at her, his jaw clenched as his hand opened and closed at his side, but he made no attempt to touch her.

Phee opened her mouth, fear and want churning inside her as she looked at the rumpled beauty before her. His bed was no doubt warm from his body and covered in his smell. It would take very little for her to tell him she wanted to be by his side tonight, and she knew he would let her in an instant. But the words remained frozen on the tip of her tongue and she could only look at him.

One corner of his mouth rose in a smile and he nodded. "Well then, goodnight, Phoebe," he said, turning back toward his room and making to shut the door.

It was too late, the moment had passed, but as his frame slowly disappeared behind the door, some secret river of courage spouted up in her, forcing her to take a step forward as she said, "Harrison..."

The door stopped and Phee wasted little time moving around it.

"I—Can I kiss you?" she asked, the question released in a breath.

"Always," he said, his eyes searching hers as she stepped forward and reached for his hand, her fingers gripping his to hold her steady as she pushed onto her toes and let her mouth touch his.

It was a soft kiss, a mere passing of lips, but it was enough. Enough to push her forward against him and slide her hands up his chest and into his hair. Enough to guide his mouth to hers and take his lips in a kiss that would have left Aphrodite weeping. He waited only a moment to respond, to catch up to her and the hands that had momentarily been frozen at his side wrapped around her waist, pulling her closer to him.

Home. She was home in his arms, with her fingers buried in his hair and his body pressed against hers as his lips destroyed her very sanity. Relief filled her as his hand glided to her cheek, caressing the skin there before his fingers delved into the strands of her hair, guiding the angle of their kiss, deepening the caresses of his tongue until Phee was not even certain if they were two or merely one being melded and formed together.

It was bliss.

It was not enough.

"Harrison," she let out in a gasp as he shifted directions, intent on focusing his attention on destroying her sanity. "Harrison, come with me."

Her words seemed to shake him awake from his desires, his body stepping away from her as his hooded gaze took her in. His hair was an utter mess, the disarray charming, and his breaths were erratic, the rise and fall of his beautiful chest creating a peekaboo effect with his shirt, giving slips of skin before they disappeared behind a pool of white linen.

"Phoebe?" he asked, taking a step away from her and running his hands roughly through his hair. "Phoebe, what are we doing?"

"Kissing?" she asked, taking a step toward him. "Maybe more?"

Harrison shook his head as he took another step in reverse, his back pressing up against the door. "Earlier this evening, you said you didn't want this."

Phee nodded her head. "I know what I said, but I was wrong," she said. Stopping in front of him, Phee kept her hands to herself even though she desperately wanted to stroke the skin that shown between the parted folds of his shirt. "Harrison, I don't know that a half marriage is something I'm capable of doing. Not when I care for you this much. Not when I want you this badly. I want to know that my nights will end with you by my side and that my days will begin with your beautiful smile being the first thing I see. I want to know that if I long to touch you I am freely allowed to, that I am as much yours as you are mine. Contracts can be changed, but I don't foresee me ever changing the way I feel about you right now."

Harrison swallowed, and Phee watched his Adam's apple bob up and down at the motion. "Phoebe, you have no idea how much I want you."

Phee reached her hand up and cupped Harrison's cheek.

"I want you so desperately," he said with a whisper, his eyes closed as he rubbed his stubbled skin against the palm of her hand. "I can't even begin to describe the things I want to do with you."

"Maybe not, but I would like to find out." Phee smiled. "Can you show me?"

Harrison opened his eyes and looked at her, his brown gaze touching on every speck of her person, and Phee forced herself to stand still and meet his gaze. Whatever it was he was looking for seemed to be found as he stepped forward and closed the door that connected their rooms, sequestering them together in his.

Within a breath, Harrison had taken ahold of her, his hands cupping her arse and lifting her up. Her legs wrapped around his hips of their own inclination, and he smoothly pressed her against the shut door as his mouth returned to hers in a kiss so all-consuming it was a wonder they did not catch fire. But burn for him she did. Every cell of her being longed to meld itself to him, to wrap around his luscious shape and become one. To disappear into the chaos and craving he created.

The hands cupping her arse squeezed her cheeks, massaging the mounds, and between his hands and his mouth it became an overload of want and need. She wanted to drown in his smell, to swim in his kiss. To bury her fingers into the silky strands of his hair to keep him close as she sank into him. Hands on his shoulders, Phee held on, uncertain where this ride was going but unwilling to let go and make it stop. Slipping one hand up into the strands of his hair, Phee scratched her nails against his scalp and Harrison growled in response, his kiss turning deadly as his tongue stole the very breath from her lungs.

Harrison ripped his mouth from hers, his breath leaving his chest in gasps as he rested his forehead against hers. "What are you doing to me?" he asked, his lips falling to her shoulder. "I want to dissolve into you."

The giggle that escaped her lips even left Phee stunned. She was intoxicated, from power or possession she did not know nor did she care. The only thought that ran on repeat in her mind was *more*. More Harrison, more fire, more want, more everything. For even if everything burned down around them, she had little doubt that they would still be left standing.

The open gap of his shirt drew her gaze and Phee took the hand resting on his shoulder and stroked the exposed skin, its warmth only giving more merit to the notion that they were ablaze.

"God, yes," Harrison said, his lips falling to her neck where he bestowed a kiss of teeth and tongue that made heat pool between her legs.

Phee let her head fall back, its thud against the door a boom in the quiet room.

"Is it good, Phoebe?" he asked, dropping a final kiss on her neck. "Do you want more?"

More. There was that word again, trying to prove that she would never have enough of him. Cupping his jaw, Phee looked at him, her body in flames, burning for him. "I want everything."

CHAPTER SEVENTEEN

Her words were the gunshot at the start of a race, the bell in the theatre as the show was set to begin. His lips collided with hers with a tender fierceness as he pulled them away from the door and began walking toward the bed. Excitement coursed through Phee's veins but a small thread of anxiety tugged, demanding its presence be known. Harrison stopped at the foot of the bed and let her legs slide down his until her feet rested once again on the floor. With a final scorching kiss, he stepped away from her.

"Tell me to stop, Phoebe," he said as he whipped the linen shirt over his head and stood before her in only his trousers. His chest was smooth with only a simple line of hair trailing down from his bellybutton and into his trousers, each divot and dip illuminated by the dim light of the fire that burned in the fireplace. Swallowing, Phee drank him in, his beauty so surreal she was certain she was imagining the whole thing. If not, then perhaps he had been molded by human hands, his perfection so unbearably beautiful that it was the only way she could conceive his existence. "If you're unsure you can tell me you've changed your mind and you must go."

Phee shook her head and reached for the ties of her wrapper, pulling at the string until the fabric gave way. "I don't want to stop. I don't want to leave. I want you. I want this." Removing it, Phee threw it to the floor, aware she stood before him in a cotton nightgown and nothing more. "What do you want?"

Harrison fell to his knees before her, his eyes drinking her in. "You," he said, the word choked. "You're stunning, Phoebe. So fucking lush and lovely." He shook his head as he ran a hand across his mouth. "And mine. All mine." There was no scrutiny in his eyes, no judgement. Only pure need as he rested back on his heels to look at her. With a groan, he pulled himself toward her, his head low as if he were meant to serve only her, and Phee released a gasp at the power that coursed through her as this giant of a man bowed at her feet.

With a deep breath, he raised his head to look at her, pushing the strands of his hair out of his eyes with his fingers. "I want to kiss every inch of you. To love you until you scream from pleasure, and then when you're spent, I want to do it all again," he said, and she could feel the heat from his words across the tops of her thighs. "Do I have your permission, Phoebe?"

"Yes," she said, the words a whisper. A prayer.

Harrison sighed as he leaned forward, his lips falling to her stomach still covered by her nightdress. It should have impeded his touch, should have felt ridiculous, but it did neither. Instead, his warm breath and damp mouth wreaked havoc as the fabric created a partition, a damnable screen that separated her skin from the ultimate wickedness. It was bliss and punishment rolled into one as he kissed his way down her stomach toward her sex, never fully touching, never fully kissing, but killing her anyway.

As his breath fanned over her quim, Phee groaned as her knees shook with need.

"Grab the bedpost," Harrison said, his voice low as his hands skimmed up her calves, pulling the nightdress with them.

Phee clutched at the wooden post behind her, leaning against it as if it would be her salvation from the velvety caresses of the man before her. His lips brushed back and forth at the top of her quim, smooth strokes and wet heat, that only rivaled his skilled hands that now stroked the back of her thighs, his deft fingers nearing her core, tempting her with destruction.

"Harrison," she said, his name a plea.

"Rest your foot on my shoulder." It was a command; one Phee would happily comply with.

Resting one foot on his rounded shoulder, Phee became aware of how exposed she was. Open to his wandering mouth and pliable fingers, she was overwhelmed by it all. The sensuality of the moment, the sheer boldness of it as the air of the room brushed against her hidden parts, nearly pulling her out of the haze he had so expertly directed her through, but when his tongue touched the swollen lips of her sex, his fingers gliding between her thighs to her core, she could not seem to care any longer. His torturous mouth unleashed chaos as he found the swollen nub at the top of her sex that longed for his touch, licking it with a persistence one would eat their favorite treat, swirling and gliding against it, all while his fingers slid and skated through the swollen folds, massaging her sex but never penetrating, never giving what she needed.

It was exquisite.

It was hell. To be so close to the oblivion of pleasure and never be thrown over its edges. Her legs began to shake, need so potent it left her begging, words of desperation slipping between her lips as she moved against him, aching with need. For him. For release. For salvation. "Please," she cried.

Harrison shook his head, his warm breath an agonizing addition that only heightened the ache. "Not yet, love. Soon."

"I can't take much more."

A husky laugh escaped his lips. "You can and you will, love," he said, his tongue soothing her while his hands created mayhem of another kind, weaving against the swollen lips of her sex but never truly touching where she wished.

"What can I say?" she asked, her body moving against his mouth, searching for salvation. Her hands gripped the wooden bedpost behind her with such force she was certain she would break it as she hung on, her entire being shaking with need.

"There's no magic words, Phoebe."

"Please," she gasped as his teeth joined the game, their soft nip at her bud nearly pitching her off the edge. "I'll touch you anywhere. I'll kiss you everywhere. I'll love you for always."

Harrison growled, her words releasing his control. He pulled her closer, her foot falling from his shoulder, pushing her forward into his waiting mouth which had become a labyrinth of sensuality, tongue and teeth, lips and skin set on a path of destruction at the engorged bud while his fingers slipped inside her core, stroking and rubbing until she could take no more.

Phee screamed as her climax crashed over her, her hand falling to Harrison's head, to hold him still or push him away, she was not sure. Her core clenched his fingers, greedy, desperately seeking out every last ounce of pleasure they could provide. And he hung on, one hand on her waist ensuring she remain upright, his shoulders strong and sturdy beneath her leg, bracing her as the storm swelled, then finally passed. He brought her back down with soft kisses, and tender swirls, with smooth caresses and loving words, and when she was certain her body would give out, he stood and lifted her, wrapping her legs around his waist as he carried her to the bed.

Laying her down on the rumpled quilt, then taking the space beside her, Harrison rubbed his nose against hers, before reaching for her hand and lacing his fingers through it. The silence stretched between them, a soothing quiet as she returned to earth. His scent covered the sheets that surrounded her creating a cavern of comfort as she turned toward him and buried her face in his neck. When his arm snaked out around her waist and he pulled her onto his chest, Phee sighed, the action so easy and yet so full of meaning.

"How are you, love?"

Phee smiled against his neck. "I've been through battle."

His husky chuckle warmed something inside her and Phee wished she could get closer, wished she could envelope herself in him, never to be separated again.

"A battle, was it? Did you win?"

She snorted. "Absolutely not. I caved fairly quickly.

You'd be disappointed."

"I'm not so sure about that," he said, rolling them over so she was on her back. Her hair fell in her face at the motion and his strong fingers pushed it aside so he could see her, tucking it gently behind her ear. "I thought you conceded masterfully."

"I shall win the next round," she said, her fingers tracing the outline of one bicep.

"You know how competitive I am, Phoebe. Snap isn't the only game I'm a master of."

Phee laughed, turning her head to his arm and kissing the bare skin there, its warmth an odd juxtaposition of calming and exciting. "Yes, but I've beaten you in Snap before. I think you're underestimating me."

Harrison's chuckle was smooth velvet against her skin, his lips falling to her neck to minister attention to the skin she had exposed. "You seem comfortable like this," he said, kissing the sensitive area where neck and shoulder met. "You seem comfortable with me like this. No hesitation or fear. Even your climax seemed welcome." He pulled back and looked at her.

Phee shrugged, heat flushing her cheeks. "I was curious and explored."

His groan as his head fell forward filled the quiet room. "Are you saying you've touched yourself?" He growled as his head rocked back and forth across her chest. "I can only imagine how beautiful that was."

"Beautiful?"

He pulled back, his pupils large and his breath rough as he looked at her. "Yes, beautiful. Your lush body open and inviting," he said, his mouth falling to bestow a soft kiss on her lips. "Your hands wandering your warm skin, touching, stroking." He kissed her again, his tongue slipping between her lips to tangle with her own. "Did you bring yourself to climax? Did you do it over and over again just to be sure it was real?" His hand fell to her side, stroking the outer cusp of one breast, then skating down to her hip and back again. "What did you think of? Who did you imagine?"

"Harrison…" Her breathing was rough as his heady questions and sinful hands worked in tandem to destroy what little sanity she had regained.

"Will you show me? Show me how you touch yourself? Show me what you like."

Phee's cheeks heated and she turned her head into his chest to hide the blush that no doubt took over her face. "I don't know if I can," she said.

"Can I?" he asked, his hand sliding down her thigh to grip the edge of nightgown.

Phee nodded and the fabric began to rise, Harrison's hand slipping beneath its edge and making its way to the part of her that was once more eager for him. His fingers dipped into her heat and Phee squirmed against him, her quim sensitive and needy.

"What do I do, Phoebe?" he asked.

"Play with the seam," she said, her face muffled against his chest.

"Like this?" His devilish fingers stroked the seam of her sex like an artist applying their brush for the very first time, his smooth digits gliding up and down, soft but sure, teasing the swollen lips beneath to come and play. Phee could only mumble a reply as her knees fell apart to give him more space to explore.

"Then what?" His voice was dark, heavy with need.

"Dip," she said.

He kissed her neck before whispering in her ear. "Dip where?"

Biting her lip, Phee said, "Dip your fingers inside me. Get them really wet."

Harrison chuckled, the sound guttural. "Happily." His naughty hand slipped between the swollen lips, swirling in the heat and desire that he had created and Phee groaned, her hips raising to meet him. His fingers slipped and slid in the moisture, working the sensitive bit at the top into a frenzy and Phee could not help the undulation that her hips had taken on, dancing to the unheard music that Harrison played. It was torturous. He was torturous, playing with her again, bringing her close to ecstasy before slowing and Phee thought she might explode. Her own hands gripped the fabric of her nightgown, squeezing and twisting the cotton until she was certain she could split it in two.

When his hand slipped away from the bud that craved him a second time, Phee moaned, her hand rising of its own accord to join the play. To show him exactly what she needed. And when her fingers bumped into his, he growled, removing his own hand from her needy quim.

"Yes, love. Just like that," he said, the words dark and sultry, and she knew she was about to perish.

CHAPTER EIGHTEEN

HE WAS SO hard he truly thought he might burst, but it did not matter. Not when Phoebe was laid out like a feast before him. Not when she had her head buried against his chest, her nightgown around her hips and her hand stroking her quim so that she could bring about the pleasure he had been denying her. It was the most sensuous thing he had ever seen, and given that he was no young lad quick to spend at the first delectable sight, all he knew was that he wanted to make the moment last for as long as possible.

Taking his free hand, Harrison stroked the swell of Phoebe's breast as he looked at her. Her cheeks were flushed, her breaths rapid as she looked back at him, her teeth worrying her bottom lip.

"I'm close," she said, shaking her head. "Harrison…"

"Not yet, Phoebe. Wait for me," he said, taking her hand and licking the fingers that had been swirling in her heat. "Stay right here, no moving, and no touching."

She jerked her head in agreement and Harrison slipped off the bed and removed his linen pants that he had changed into for bed. Phoebe's eyes froze on the space where his sex jutted out and she swallowed, her eyes pinned to him. In any other circumstance, he would bask in her admiration, stand like David and let her feast her eyes upon every inch of him, but in this moment, all he wanted to do was lose himself in his wife.

Walking back toward the bed, Harrison grabbed his sex and cupped the tip, stroking the length with the moisture he had found there. "All right?" he asked.

She nodded her head, her gray gaze taking him in from top to bottom, and Harrison stroked himself again as his eyes locked onto hers. She swallowed, then lowered her eyes to where his hand rubbed against his cock, her rapid breaths returning. Her hand began to move, lowering itself to her quim and Harrison stopped and stepped forward, taking the hand and placing a kiss on it before sliding back into the bed beside her. "You promised, love."

She shook her head. "I can't. I want…"

"I know," he said, bringing her into the cradle of his body, his cock sandwiched between her arse cheeks. Taking his thumb, Harrison pushed his penis down to the notch between her thighs, the warm heat and damp moisture of her cunny so intoxicating he nearly spent himself then. Sliding one hand down her thigh, he brought her top leg over his hip, opening her to him while his cock sat contentedly between the swollen outer lips of her sex. "Like this," he said.

"How?" she asked.

"Just like you want, love. Touch yourself exactly like you want." Dropping a kiss to her shoulder, Harrison propped himself up so he could see. "Let me watch you play."

His words lit the fuse and her hand fell to her quim with speed. Gripping the thigh that rode his hip, Harrison watched as Phoebe touched herself, her fingers dipping and sliding against her sex in a familiar rhythm. It was erotic, it was exquisite. It was heaven on earth watching his wife play with herself while his cock was nestled between the panting lips of her sex, feeling every squeeze and sigh as she touched her quim.

It was too much, this erotic picture before him, and Harrison shifted his hips, his cock sliding back and forth against the outer lips of her sex, the friction and heat against his cock intoxicating as he watched Phoebe. His hips picked up speed and Harrison gritted his teeth against the pull of his own climax, but his wife's warm quim and his exquisite view did little to help, each one set upon making him spill his speed. A growl left his throat and Harrison leaned forward, his mouth falling to Phoebe's shoulder. Biting softly, Harrison began to suck and kiss the skin he had captured as his hips pistoled back and forth erratically, gaining speed as his climax coaxed him to surrender.

And Phoebe, with her luscious thigh wrapped over his hip, needed little enticing to join him, his unplanned bite spurring her own pleasure to throw her off its edge. Head back, Phoebe's breathing became ragged as she shook beside him, the lips of her sex quaking around his hard cock, urging him to join her in heaven. Seed spilled from him in spurts as he held onto her thigh, grinding his cock against her quim, ensuring that every last ounce of delight was given to them both. And when they settled back on earth, Harrison kissed the spot he had assaulted, letting his tongue soothe the tender skin.

Rubbing the thigh that still rode his hip, Harrison chuckled against Phoebe's shoulder. "We're making quite the mess, aren't we?" he asked, his voice hoarse.

Phoebe smiled, rolling her head back to look at him. "It's a good thing we have two beds."

He made a noise of agreement. "We'll muddle that one up in a bit. Just give me a moment to collect my sanity."

"You seem to be conversing just fine."

"Yes," he said, lowering her leg before stroking her hair, "but my bones feel like mush as does my brain." She laughed, the sound soft. "How are you, love?"

"The mush comment sounds right." With a groan, Phoebe stretched beside him, her marvelous backside rubbing against his length. The confounded instrument perked up at the brush and Harrison groaned, his head falling onto her shoulder.

"Heaven help us," he said against her nightgown.

"We'll both be unresponsive if we keep us this pace," Phoebe said.

"Have no fear, love." Kissing her shoulder, Harrison pushed up to sitting. "It'll pass."

Cleaning himself with a cloth from the wash stand, Harrison rinsed the towel, then returned to Phoebe and performed the same actions to her person, mopping up the remnants of his pleasure that coated her thighs.

Picking Phoebe up off the soiled linens, Harrison strode to the door that connected their rooms and opened it. A discontented yowl from Mildred had him looking down in surprise. "Sorry, pet. I didn't know you were trapped in here," he said, depositing Phoebe on her own bed. Kissing his wife on her forehead, Harrison stood. "Where are your clean nightgowns?" he asked.

Phoebe looked at him quizzically but pointed to the

dressing room. After retrieving a clean gown for Phoebe and a fresh pair of linen pants for himself, Harrison returned to the room and helped Phoebe change. Ensconced in their clean clothes, Harrison pulled aside the covers and joined Phoebe in the bed. Mildred, who seemed to be one to hold grudges, commandeered a spot at the foot of the bed, presenting them with her back in a sign of disgruntlement.

"I forgot she was in here," Phoebe said with a whisper, wrapping herself around Harrison's torso and resting her head on his shoulder.

"Why are you whispering?" Harrison asked.

"Because," she said, "if she finds out that I forgot about her she'll no doubt hate me for the rest of her life. I'm a terrible cat parent."

Harrison chuckled and kissed the top of Phoebe's head. "You are no such thing. She had no need to be involved in the business that was going on in there, and if I were her, I'd be grateful for the innocence that was spared."

Phoebe rubbed her nose against his chest, a smile at her lips. "I didn't think of that."

"She'll forgive us for the slight soon enough, but just to be safe, we'll give her an extra helping of cod with her breakfast."

"You're spoiling her," Phoebe said, her hand reaching up to brush the strand of hair out of his face.

"I'm allowed to care for my girls in whatever form I'm inclined to, thank you very much. If that means extra fish for breakfast," he leaned down and kissed Phoebe on the nose, "or several climaxes, I will do so."

"Is that all I get?"

He frowned at her. "Of course not." Rolling onto his side, he shifted Phoebe so that she lay facing him. "What would you like, love? More bees? Another kitten friend for Mildred?"

She wrinkled her nose. "Don't be silly."

"Ask and it's yours, Phoebe. Whatever it is."

"An answer to a question and your promise not to laugh?"

Harrison propped his head up with an arm and looked at her. Crossing his heart, he held his hand up. "I swear it."

"I thought sex required a man to put his penis inside a woman."

The sentences was said in a flat and even tone with nary a sign of jesting. It was an honest question, and one she felt comfortable asking him without any shame. Pausing, Harrison assessed his response before saying carefully, "It can be, but there are many ways to have sex. The way we did was to ensure that you do not become pregnant."

Phoebe's brow crinkled. "Oh." She remained silent for a short amount of time before asking, "Is there a way to do it with you inside me that would not get me pregnant?"

Harrison smiled, taking his thumb and rubbing at the divots that had formed in between his wife's eyebrows. "Yes, but it can take a lot of preparation and I don't want to make any decisions about that because it is your body and only you have the right to it."

"Surely you can't mean to never have penetrative sex with me. Do you even find pleasure in the other options?"

Kissing her forehead, Harrison wrapped his arms around her. "I find pleasure in any and everything we do, love. Just now with your sweet thighs clutching me, drowning me in your heat, was no doubt the closest to heaven I'll ever be, and if we were only to ever do it that way for the rest of our lives, I'll die a happy man."

"Truly?" she asked, leaning back to look at him.

Harrison nodded. "I want to do what you want to do, Phoebe. In whatever regard that is. And I'll never pressure you for things you don't want."

She grew quiet, resting her head on his chest, and Harrison stroked her hair, wondering if she had fallen asleep. After a moment, she shifted, placing a soft kiss on his chest. "I like being your wife," she said.

The absolute joy that he found at her words made him pause, but Harrison shook his head. Whatever it was, those were worries for another time. He had a sleepy wife in his arms and a grumpy cat whose favor he must win back. All of those things were priority. Closing his eyes, Harrison felt the corners of his mouth pull up into a smile, the words she had said so simple and yet so much.

"I like that you're my wife," he said, closing his eyes.

*   *   *

A SOFT BRUSH against his cheek woke Harrison. Opening one eye, he looked around the unfamiliar bedroom before spotting the urchin that had awoken him. Mildred sat on his pillow, one paw raised as if to stroke his cheek again should he decide to go back to sleep. "Good morning, little miss," he said, snaking his hand out to scratch the white spot on her head. "I see you've forgiven me for last night."

Her responding meow seemed to indicate that all was forgiven as she leaned into his hand, eyes closed in happiness at his attention.

A peek at Phoebe proved that she still slept. Harrison quietly left the bed and headed to his bedroom, the furry miscreant on his tail. Scooping up the little one, Harrison handed her off to a footman with orders to feed her breakfast with an extra helping of fish on the side. When the demanding princess left, Harrison shut the door to his room, completed his ablutions, then returned to Phoebe's bedroom.

His wife was buried in the covers, only her blonde hair peeking out. Sliding back between the sheets, Harrison scooted closer to her, pulling her body into the cradle of his. Her hands reached for him, gripping his arm and using it as a pillow as she wiggled in next to him, her legs coiling around his like a snake. A smile tugged at Harrison's mouth and he kissed her head which elicited a soft sigh.

"I need to feed Mildred," she mumbled, her eyes shut tight in opposition.

"It's been done," he said, stroking her hair. "Sleep. Our little tyrant will return after her breakfast."

"I promised her extra fish."

Harrison chuckled softly. "I made sure she got her offering for last night's treatment."

"Do you think she'll forgive us?"

Kissing her cheek, Harrison stroked her arm, captivated by his lush wife. "If we play with her, I'm sure all will be well. Our darling girl is rather easy to please."

She sighed in agreement.

"And what does my darling wife need this morning? More sleep? Some tea and breakfast in bed?" he asked.

Shaking her head, Phoebe pushed up to sitting and

looked at him. "We should probably eat in the breakfast room."

"And after? What are your plans?"

"Tend to the bees and journal my observations."

Harrison smiled. "Is it too late to see about adding in an outing with your husband?"

Phoebe paused, and for a moment he wondered if he had made a mistake. Slowly, she looked up at him and said, "I think I might be up for a schedule adjustment. What did you have in mind?"

"We could go to the bookstore and browse the shelves. Then to Gunter's for ice?" Scooting closer to her, Harrison tucked a strand of hair behind her ear. "Or we could wander the park? I'm available however you would like," he said. Kissing her cheek, he whispered, "So, Phoebe, how would you like me?"

Her breath grew heavy. "The- the bookstore sounds lovely," she said, meeting his gaze.

"And then ices?" he asked, smiling at her.

Nodding she returned his look. "And then ices." She smiled, pushing back the covers. "Best get my day started then. We wouldn't want the staff gossiping."

Harrison wrapped his hands around her waist and pulled her into his lap. "Let them gossip that we lazed about in bed all morning. Let them tell all of London that Lord Everly is fond of his wife."

"You are?" she asked her head resting on his shoulder.

"Very much so."

Raising her head to look at him, Phoebe smiled, a gorgeous blush covering her cheeks. "Me too."

CHAPTER NINETEEN

FTER A SCRUMPTIOUS breakfast, which was had in bed, Harrison took his leave and Phee readied for the day. As she dressed, she found herself humming the tune of the waltz that they had danced to the night before, and while gathering her things to inspect the hives, a smile pulled at her lips as she recalled every touch and word from their evening. Joy filled every reservoir of her body, buzzing through her veins like the bees in her hives.

The skirts of her blue gown swished as she walked to the hives, their bounce joyful against the walking path. Mildred followed behind, stopping every few steps to inspect a fallen leaf or blade of grass before scurrying to catch up. The dear had forgiven her after only five minutes of playing fetch with her stuffed rat, and relief had filled Phee. Perhaps, if she and Harrison were to continue their nightly shenanigans, they should find a better occupation for the kitten.

The hives were abuzz when she arrived, even the angry one busily working away as bees flew in and out gathering pollen. When the cold eventually began to creep into London, Phee would have to worry about whether their honey production would be enough to get them through the winter, but with the warm summer days ahead, they needed little help from her in fortifying their reserves.

"Good morning, bees," Phee said, pulling on her padded gloves and adjusting the mesh cloth to cover around her head and neck. "I hope you all had a lovely evening."

The bees buzzed, their response undecipherable, but Phee continued on. "The ball last evening was crowded and stuffy, but Lord Everly and I danced a most beautiful waltz and when I had reached the limit of my interaction, we returned home with him giving little fuss about leaving the event early. My mother used to prattle on about what the ton would think were we to exit an engagement to soon, but Harrison seemed to understand."

Leaning forward to inspect for rat droppings, Phee smiled as she remembered Harrison's insistence that she tell him if she had even a moment of discomfort.

"Let's see, what other gossip do I have for you?" she asked, her brow furrowing. The gossip sheets had been rather sparse that morning with only insinuations into the ongoings of the ton, and whether the bees cared for the current scuttlebutt or not, Phee had read that telling the bees the happenings of the world was a sure way to have a healthy hive. Considering there was no downside to the tip, she did not see any harm in following it.

Biting her lip, Phee moved onto the next hive, examining the ground around it. While it was true that there was little ton gossip, it could not be said that there was not gossip going on within her own home. Looking around the garden, Phee sighed when she found it empty. Turning back to the hive before her, she took a deep breath. "Lord Everly and I consummated our marriage last night."

Heat rushed to her cheeks and a smile took over her lips. "Twice," she said.

The bees continued their busy buzzing, uncaring of her admission, but once the words had begun there was very little use in stopping. "He was so caring and thoughtful. And captivating," she said. "Utterly captivating and alluring. His hands were masterful and skilled and his mouth was sensuous and soft and so intoxicating that I thought I'd perish. If that is what the physical aspect of a marriage is like, then I now truly understand why ladies marry. Surely if not for every day societal requirements they would be engaging in the activity constantly. I know I would."

Phee paused before a lavender bush as her mind replayed the gentleness Harrison had shown after. He had cleaned her of his seed, carried her to a fresh bed and helped her to dress in a new nightgown without her having to say a word. It was such a fascinating facet of the man who only moments before had brought her to such exquisite pleasure, her body shaking with release. And then, as if he were caring for Mildred or a small bird, he had switched into a gentle role, tucking her into the covers and pulling her close to keep her warm. He was an enigma in the best way and it only made her long to be around him more.

She smiled. He had said he was fond of his wife as if it were the simplest thing, knowledge that was readily known and available to those who asked.

A multifaceted man was this husband of hers.

"I like him a lot," Phee said to the bees, her admission floating over their buzzing and filling the air around her as her eyes caught sight of the very man she talked about.

Removing one of her padded gloves, Phee walked to

him, the tether that linked them pulling her toward him even as her mind questioned at her stability. "Hello," she said over the buzz of her bees.

Harrison raised a brow at her and took a step closer, lifting her veil and bestowing a soft kiss on her lips that left her insides clenching. "Hello," he said, the word low and sultry.

"Careful," Phee said, pushing him back a few steps. "I don't want you to be stung."

Harrison lowered her veil and smiled at her. "Lady Everly, are you worried for me?"

Phee wrinkled her brow. "No, I'm worried over my bees. They die if they sting you, and I think that is a waste."

Harrison raised his hand to his heart as if he had been stung through the chest. "You wound me," he said, dramatically staggering back.

"You'll recover." Following him, Phee stopped at the steps that led to the upper portion of the garden, grabbing Harrison's hand and pulling him to a stop. "I thought you were to have another lesson with Mr. Williams."

Harrison shook his head, his hand gripping hers through the monstrous glove that covered her fingers. "I paid him for his visit and then informed him he had the afternoon off."

"Just like that?"

Stepping closer to her, he pulled the glove from her hand and placed it on his cheek, the bristle of his beard growth tickling her palm. "Just like that. I'm much too excited to spend this time with my wife."

"Truly?" she asked.

"Is there anything I can help with?" he asked, kissing her wrist, and her eyes closed at the press of his mouth.

The question went unanswered as he placed another kiss on her wrist before moving his lips higher up the inside of her arm and bestowing another, then another.

"Phoebe?"

"Hmm?"

"Is there anything you need help with?" he asked, a mischievous smile taking over his lips.

"Oh," she said, her brow furrowing. "I- I don't think so. I've already played with Mildred, and the bees are sorted." She looked around the garden.

"Well then, since your daily chores are finished, perhaps I can tempt you to other diversions."

Phee swallowed, the heat his words stoked relighting the fire that had burned so brazenly the night before. She wanted to race him to the house and strip herself of her clothes, repeat everything they had done and then do some more. But if they were to do so, they would no doubt never leave, and the idea of browsing a bookstore tickled a very different part of her brain. The part where she wanted to spend the entire day with him talking and laughing. The part where she could pretend they had courted and fallen in love instead of marrying as a business arrangement.

Removing the hat from her head, Phee slipped into his arms and wrapping her own about his waist. Pushing onto her toes, she kissed his jaw. "Outing first and then diversions."

Harrison chuckled, his lips falling to the top of her head.

Taking her hand in his, Harrison intertwined his fingers with hers. Following behind him, Phee looked back to the hives and the sleeping cat who lounged in a sunny spot on a nearby bench.

"Mildred, come along, pet," she said, calling to the kitten who had once again become a side character in their story.

Harrison stopped at her words and spun around, walking them to the bench where the sleepy Mildred sat yawning. Scooping her into his free arm, Harrison rubbed his nose against her fur, turned, and began walking once more to the house.

It was that simple. That easy.

Phee smiled as she happily trailed behind the pair, delight coursing through her veins. This man was a treasure and he was all hers.

Well, hers and Mildred's.

Phee giggled at the thought before picking up her skirts and quickening her steps to keep pace with them. She should not doddle, after all. She had an afternoon to spend with her husband.

CHAPTER TWENTY

HIS WIFE LOOKED rather stunning in the dappled sunlight that slipped through the window of the bookshop, highlighting the delicate blush at her cheek and ensuring he saw every fleck of gold in her eyes that he may have otherwise missed. A smile pulled at one corner of his lips as he made a mental note to himself to remedy that problem this evening. He would kiss every delicate inch of skin around her luminous gaze, ensuring to pay homage to whatever God had created the gorgeous creature before him. It would take hours, surely. He could not wait.

"What are you smiling about?" Phoebe asked in a hushed tone, her finger holding her place in the book she perused.

"You're beautiful," he said simply, the truth falling from his lips with ease.

She scowled at him. "You're smiling because I'm beautiful?" She shook her head and returned her attention to the book she held. "You're full of nonsense today."

Harrison's smile grew wider and he stepped closer to Phoebe, his chest brushing against her arm. Leaning down to whisper in her ear, he said, "I'm filled with you, not nonsense. Your smile, your scent. The way you scowl at the book as you read it. It's left me overflowing with want of you, Phoebe. Greedy to soak up every sun-soaked inch of you, to gather every laugh that escapes your lips so that I might save them for a cloudy day. To return to our bed so that I may continue to hold you in my arms as you sleep, your breathing soft against my neck, your thigh wrapped around my hips."

The blush on Phoebe's cheeks darkened at his words. "We're in a public space. Surely you shouldn't talk to me like this. What if someone hears you?"

Harrison kissed her cheek, the sweet honeyed scent of her filling his senses. "They'll no doubt be jealous that the phenomenal creature I whisper to is mine and mine alone."

Stepping away from her, Harrison leaned his forearm against the bookcase beside them. "Is this the book of your choice, love, or shall we make our way to another aisle to peruse its offerings?"

Phoebe shook her head at him as she put the book she held back on the shelf. "I've already read this one. I just wanted to look at it again."

Harrison picked the book up off the shelf and looked at the cover. The green leather and gold writing were smooth beneath his hand, the words *Ivanhoe* written in flowy script. "Do we have it at home?"

She shook her head, reaching for the book. "No. My parents have a copy at their country estate. I read it last summer at least a dozen times."

"You must have enjoyed it."

She nodded. "I did. I think that's why it was so lovely to see it here on their shelves."

With the nod of his head, Harrison removed the book from Phoebe's hands. "Well then, we shall purchase it and have our very own copy as well."

Phoebe reached for it but Harrison grabbed her hand, placing a soft kiss on her palm before resting it on his chest. "No arguing. It's coming with us," he said.

With a kiss on her cheek, Harrison took her hand and began to lead her down what remained of the aisle they were in. "Shall we head to the next row?" he asked.

"All right," she said, smiling at him, her hand tightening in his.

At the end of their endeavor, which took two hours of perusing each book lining the shelves of the bookstore, Harrison carried a stack of four books in one hand while the other held tightly to Phoebe, leading her to the counter.

"Did you find everything you were looking for, my lord?" asked the saleswoman behind the counter as she rang up his purchases.

"I believe we did although I'm sure there was more we could have found," Harrison said, smiling at the older woman. "My wife and I could have whiled away the day in here."

The woman smiled at his comment. "If my lady is interested, we do have a backroom. The books there are in rather poor condition but we're selling them for a farthing a piece, and I've seen some rather unique titles when I've looked myself."

Harrison looked down at Phoebe whose eyes seemed to have brightened at the woman's comment, and he laughed, nodding his head. "We'd love to look at the treasures you no doubt have."

Phoebe put her hand on his forearm and looked at

him. "As much as I'd love to spend the rest of the day here, I'm feeling a bit famished."

Harrison felt his eyes widen. "Darling, you should have told me. Let's get you some food before you waste away."

Phoebe rolled her eyes at him before turning back to the saleswoman. "I'll most certainly return another day to browse the back room. Thank you for thinking of it."

The woman nodded. "Of course, my lady. I know the looks of someone who is as enthralled with literary works as myself."

Pushing the books across the counter to them, the woman said. "Do you need help out with your purchases?"

Harrison smiled at her, tucking the books under one arm as he reached for Phoebe's hand with the other. "Thank you, no. We've got it covered. We shall see you again soon."

Looking at Phoebe, he winked at her. "Come, love, let's get you something to eat."

Outside the bookstore, Harrison handed the books to the waiting footman, then helped Phoebe inside the carriage before following behind her. The serene smile upon his wife's lips was too much to resist. Taking the seat beside her, Harrison pulled his wife into his lap and kissed her. Her soft gasp was adorable and he could not resist letting his tongue trace the seam of her lips before she willingly parted them for him. His tongue dove inside the warm place, tanging with hers in a dance as old as time as his hands cupped her waist, caressing the expanse that was so rudely covered by fabric. Phoebe was soft in his arms, her fingers clutched in his hair to hold him close as she kissed him back with a fervor. The silly woman, as if he had any intention of leaving her side. He smiled as he changed the angle of his attack, his hands stroking their way along her spine.

A soft gurgle interrupted their kiss and Phoebe groaned as she pressed her face to his neck. "I'm sorry," she said against his skin.

Harrison chuckled, the sound low in his throat as he lowered his head to her shoulder and kissed along the collar of her day dress. "My poor love. Don't worry, I'll feed you."

Pulling back, Harrison slid his finger beneath her chin and lifted her head so her eyes met his. "What an unfortunate time to be hungry," she said.

Kissing her forehead, then her cheek, Harrison rubbed his nose against hers, unable to wipe the smile away that seemed to have taken over his face. "We'll get you fed and then continue what we were doing if you'd like? What are you hungry for?"

Phoebe shook her head. "Anything? Everything?"

"Everything it will be."

Peeking out the carriage window, Harrison knocked on the roof. As the carriage slowed, he picked up Phoebe and set her down on the bench beside him before opening the door and jumping from the conveyance. A vender stood several paces away, the scent of the meat pies he was selling filling the air.

"I'll take two of your best," Harrison said, tossing a shilling at the vendor. The man handed him two meat pies, and Harrison nodded at him before heading back to the carriage.

Inside, he handed Phoebe one of the tasty treats. "Careful, love. It's hot."

Phoebe nodded as she broke off a piece of the crust and popped it in her mouth, her eyes closing, a noise of contentment escaping her body. Removing his handkerchief, Harrison opened the cloth and set it across Phoebe's lap, ensuring that not a drop of the food fell onto her dress.

She ate the pie at an impressive pace, and, when it was finished, she brushed at her mouth before wiping her hands on the handkerchief. Harrison shook his head and handed her the second pie, taking the cloth from her hands, and shaking the excess crumbs outside the carriage window before placing it back over her lap. "Both are for you."

She frowned at him. "Nonsense. I'm fine."

Harrison merely shook his head at her. "Eat. We'll be at Gunter's soon but this should tide you over until then."

"Harrison…"

Holding up a hand, Harrison watched Phoebe's mouth snap closed. "You are hungry and I shall feed you."

Phoebe huffed at his comment, but broke off a piece of the golden crust and placed it in her mouth, a small wiggle of excitement escaping from her body as she took a bite of the stuffed pie.

"Good?" he asked.

"So good," she said.

"My chef at the estate in Dorset makes wonderful steak and kidney pies," he said, smiling, and a brilliant idea lit up in his mind. "What do you say to going on a trip to see it? We never did get to have a honeymoon after all."

Phoebe smiled. "A honeymoon in Dorset?"

"If you're up for it. I have a home in Poole that is near the ocean and it's fully staffed."

"I don't know," she said. "What about Mildred? What about the bees?"

"We can ask Mr. Drake to care for the bees while we're away. You can leave him very detailed instructions so nothing goes amiss." He took the forgotten pie in her hands and set it on the seat across from them. "Sterns and Mrs. Beatley can care for Mildred, unless you'd like to bring her with us."

"It would be such a long journey for a small kitten," Phoebe said. "She'd hate it."

"Why don't you and I spend the next few days planning so that all is in order before we depart? I truly think you'd love the home in Dorset, but I want to make sure you're comfortable before we go."

Phoebe nodded, a soft smile on her lips. "All right. It really does sounds lovely."

As they neared Berkeley Square, Harrison watched Phoebe decimate the second pie, nothing remaining but a few specks of crust. A pleased smile took over his face, so he looked out the window, certain that if she saw his enjoyment of her eating the food he had procured for her, she would have questions.

It was not that he had a thing for feeding women. It was that he had a thing for feeding Phoebe. He enjoyed watching her enthusiasm as she tried each dish and dessert. The excited wiggle that took over her as she ate something she truly enjoyed, as if the bliss she found in the item was too much for her to keep in. He would supply her in all of her favorite dishes for the rest of her life if it would guarantee that he would be allowed to witness her innocent display of pleasure.

Harrison chuckled.

"Are you laughing?" she asked.

Clearing his throat, Harrison looked at Phoebe and shook his head, unable to make the smile that sat on his face disappear. "Swallowed wrong."

She gave a noise of disbelief before folding up the handkerchief on her lap and placing it into her reticule. "I'll have Flora launder this and return it to you."

"All right," he said as the carriage slowed. "Do you know what you'd like from the shoppe?"

"A violet ice, please."

Nodding, he opened the carriage door to flag down one of the waiters from Gunters who stood outside.

"A violet ice, a slice of whatever cake is available, and an elderflower ice," he said to the young lad who pulled alongside his carriage.

"Right away, my lord," the boy said, before scurrying across the street, dodging a black phaeton that had no inclination of slowing.

"I'm not eating all of that," Phoebe said across the carriage from him.

"Eat however much you'd like from all of the treats and I'll finish the rest. We'll make it our goal to always leave empty plates."

Her brow furrowed but Harrison suspected he could see one side of her mouth lifted as if fighting a smile.

Moving across the carriage, Harrison sat next to Phoebe, taking her hand in his. "I'm your husband," he said, kissing her knuckles. "It is my job to take care of you. To ensure you are never hungry, never without flowers for your bees, and never without your favorite books."

"That wasn't in the contract," Phoebe said, her fingers curling around his.

"Perhaps we should renegotiate the contract. Or hang the whole thing," he said, shrugging his shoulders, hoping the motion minimized the honesty of his words. The contract had been their outline, the rules that they had played by. With it gone, so to was the safety of the game.

Phoebe looked at him, her brow furrowed. "Without a contract what will our marriage look like?"

"It shall look however we want it to. One ball a month or even none at all. Evenings spent with your husband, card games optional, or quiet nights to yourself. All the bees and flowers you want, Mildred and any other animal companions you foresee yourself getting." He placed the hand he held against his cheek, and sighed as the familiar honey scent filled his senses. "Whatever we'd like, Phoebe."

"And what if there's something we dislike? Or don't agree on?"

"Then we talk it over. We're good at talking with each other. How about," he said, kissing her palm, "if you're uncomfortable with scrapping the contract indefinitely, we just remove it for the rest of the day? We are simply Harrison and Phoebe, husband and wife, spending time together."

Phoebe looked at him, her gray gaze examining every

inch of his face as if searching for the right answer there. After a pause, a soft smile graced her lips and she nodded her head. "Harrison and Phoebe."

CHAPTER TWENTY-ONE

AFTER FINISHING THEIR treats from Gunters inside the carriage, Phee and Harrison returned home. Harrison carried in her books, the stack appearing unassuming in his hands, and yet the joy she felt at the sight was large. It had been a near perfect day spent in his company, doing things she very much loved, and she was certain that at any moment she would awaken to realize that it all was just a dream.

Harrison deposited the books on Phee's nightstand, adjusting the titles so that they could be seen from the bed and easily reached.

Phee looked away at the sight, her gaze falling to Mildred who blinked up at her from the plush chair she had been napping in. "Hello, pet," she said, scratching the white spot on the kitten's head. "Did you have a lovely afternoon?"

"It appears she had a long slumber while we were away, didn't you, my darling?" Harrison said from behind her, his hand reaching around her to scratch under Mildred's chin. "She looks like she could use a run about, don't you think?"

Harrison sidestepped around Phee and picked up the kitten, moving them toward a small wicker basket beside the fireplace that held her toys. Grabbing a piece of yarn from the pile, Harrison set Mildred down before sitting on the ground beside her, his back leaning against the couch. It was ludicrous, this large man dressed in his tailored jacket and trousers, Hessians polished to a shine, sitting upon the floor taunting a kitten with a piece of string. And yet, there he was, uncaring of how it appeared. More focused on giving the small dear the attention she no doubt required after a day of being cooped up in her mistress's room.

Sliding her feet out from her slippers, Phee grabbed one of the books that Harrison had so delicately stacked, then settled into the chair that Mildred had vacated.

Opening the cover to the first page, she tried to allow the words before her to pull her in, but her eyes kept sliding to the pair on the floor. It was a lovely image they painted. Harrison's gruff laugh as Mildred executed a flip in the air in her attempt to capture the string sent a pin prick near the vicinity of her heart, an ache so joyful she was certain she was imagining it. The scene was so homely, so wholly warm and wonderful that she blinked, waiting for it to disappear before her. But when her eyes opened, it was to see Mildred climbing the arm of Harrison's black coat, her attention focused on a speck on sunlight that danced upon his face.

"Oh, Mildred. You'll ruin his coat," she said, snapping closed the book and leaning forward to retrieve the kitten.

Harrison grabbed her hand, kissing the back of it before interlacing his fingers with hers. "She is no bother, Phoebe," he said. "She's merely being an inquisitive kitten."

"But your coat," Phee said, her eyes falling to where

their hands were linked.

Harrison laughed and gave a gentle tug, moving her to the floor with him. "I have many coats, but not very many moments with our dear girl. Let her play, love."

Phee looked at him then, his words of affection softly dancing about in her head. He had spent the entire day entertaining her, caring for her every whim and desire without asking for anything in return, and now, as their kitten sunk her sharp nails into the threads of his expensively tailored coat, he welcomed it. He encouraged it, even, dragging the thread up his arm so she climbed him as a child would a tree. How on earth had she found this man to be her husband?

"You're wonderful," she said, raising her free hand to cup his jaw, the scruff there itching her palm. Her thumb traced over his lips where a smile played, a small dimple appearing as an indent in his cheek, but as her words registered the smile fell, his faux one taking its place.

Harrison swallowed, his Adam's apple bobbing, before he looked away from her, returning his attention to Mildred. "Such lovely praise from my wife," he said, lifting the kitten from his shoulder where she had begun to knead her small claws into the fabric to kiss her on the nose.

Phee's lips pursed as she watched him stand. "I'll see you both tonight," he said, heading to the door that connected their rooms, closing it behind him with a snick.

Her mind tumbled over what she had said, examining each word with care, and yet she could not find what it was that had sent him scurrying from the room. Her praise, as he had called it, had been little more than her speaking the truth, and he had responded with near terror at her words.

Frowning, Phee retrieved the string that Harrison had abandoned and began to drag it across the floor, gaining Mildred's attention. The kitten did not show an ounce of concern at the removal of Harrison, and taking her cue from the cat, Phee decided she would do the same. Whatever had sent him from the room likely had nothing to do with her, and her time would be spent uselessly if she tried to analyze it. If his sour mood persisted into dinner, then she would ask him about it. Instead, for now, she would ring for Flora and have a relaxing bath before readying herself for dinner.

An hour and a half later, Phee left her bedroom with Mildred at her heels, her bath reviving her senses from the day she had spent out. Mildred's small meow as she followed Phee down the hall sent a smile to her face as she glanced down at the kitten. "I know you're hungry, pet. Let's see what magnificent meal Cook has prepared for us, shall we?"

Mildred meowed, in agreement or discontent, Phee would never know, but continued to follow her into the parlor where they found Harrison nursing a glass of scotch before a roaring fire. The kitten seemed unconcerned of his previous disposition, and made her way to him, rubbing herself against his bootleg as if he were the most prized possession in the room.

"Good evening, my ladies," Harrison said, bending down to pick up Mildred and placing her against his chest. The small dear nudged her head against his jaw, happily reminding him of the attention she required and Harrison laughed at her antics, his fingers scratching her cheek as he settled her into his arms. Looking up, he met her gaze. "Did you have a good rest?"

Phee nodded, moving to one of the sofas that bracketed the fireplace. "I did. You?"

He nodded his head, a corner of his mouth raising in a smile. "It was relaxing to wash the day off of me before dinner."

She gave a soft sound of agreement but said nothing further. She longed to go to him, to kiss his jaw and tell him she missed him, to pout because they never got to the diverting part of the day, but instead she just watched him, once again unsure of the ground they stood on.

"I heard Cook made a chocolate soufflé for dessert," he said, moving to sit on the sofa opposite of hers.

Her stomach growled in anticipation and she raised a hand to cover it. "That sounds delicious."

Harrison smiled at her, his mouth opening as if to say more, but Sterns entered the room.

"Dinner is ready, my lord," Sterns said.

Harrison's mouth closed, whatever he had been on the cusp of saying disappearing in the large room. A practiced smile fell on his lips and he stood, holding his arm out to Phee. "Lady Everly?"

Phee took his hand and stood, his skin warm in hers and as she followed beside him to the dining room, his thumb rubbed softly against her hand, its motion soothing, as if all were suddenly right in the world once more.

Once seated, the footmen began to place plates before them, the smell of each dish divine as their scent filled the room. Mildred occupied her usual seat at the table, a small dish of tuna already before her and the kitten wasted little time, her face disappearing into the dish as she consumed her dinner with enthusiasm.

Taking up her own fork, Phee paused as Harrison's voice filled the room.

"You're dismissed," he told the footmen, who each looked puzzled at the pronouncement but left without a word.

When the room was empty, and the doors firmly closed, Harrison looked at Phee and smiled. "I wanted to apologize for my mood earlier." He picked up his wine glass and took a sip, setting it back down on the table. "I have no excuse, but I promise it will not happen again."

Phee nodded, her fork still poised over a portion of chicken breast on her plate. Nudging it, she said, "Did I say something wrong?"

He shook his head. "No. No, I just—" He sighed. "I'm not used to praise, is all."

Phee's mouth dropped. "Surely that cannot be true? You must have had praise from someone in your life."

He nodded, his focus on his plate where his knife shifted about a couple of peas. "Certainly. Just not—" He cleared his throat. "Not in the manner that I have from you. There was sincerity in it, and if I'm being honest, I haven't been surrounded by many individuals who did so. You didn't simply say what you did because I had earned it after treating you to a delightful outing, but because it was truthfully how you felt and it left me feeling... Well, unsteady."

Phee pushed back her chair and stood, moving to where he sat at the head of the table. She paused for a moment, uncertain whether to listen to her heart's persistent nudging instead of reason, but the look of sadness on his face made the decision for her. Kneeling beside Harrison's chair, Phee set her hand on his forearm, the muscles beneath flexing at her touch.

"Harrison," she said, waiting for his gaze to meet hers. "You are wonderful. I mean it truly and honestly, without expectation of excessive outings or societal dictates. I mean it because you spend every effort ensuring that my day is pleasant, and you do so because you want to. And this afternoon when we returned home, you could have simply dismissed yourself to partake in activities that brought you joy, but instead you played with a kitten and let her destroy a jacket you looked very handsome in. If my proclamations make you feel uncomfortable, I shall endeavor to keep them to myself, but please believe me when I tell you that I mean every word. You are wonderful, Harrison Metcalf. And I'm glad to be your wife."

The fork and knife fell to his plate in a clatter as he pushed his chair back from the table and bent down, grasping her arms, guiding her to sit on his lap. His arm wrapped around her waist, securing her to him, while the other hand delved into her hair, the few pins there falling to the floor as he guided her lips to his. It was a heartbreaking, soul shattering kiss. The earth shifted as his tongue tangled with hers, dancing with a melody of fire and greed as he devoured her whole. The hand at her waist clutched her closer to him, and she happily gave in to its demands and leaned against him as the heat he concocted grew, want pooling in her belly as she melted into him, close as she could be, but somehow not close enough.

He pulled away gently, his kisses softening even as the arm at her waist held firm. "Finish your meal, darling. It's nearly time for our game."

Phee swallowed at the husky growl of his voice, his lips like silk against her own. "What about dessert?" she asked, her mind recalling the soufflé he had mentioned moments before.

Harrison groaned against her mouth, his hand gripping the fabric of her dress tightly in its grasp. "You'll have dessert, love," he said, taking her mouth once more in a kiss that lit her aflame. "I guarantee it."

He lifted her from his lap where the evidence of his desires sat apparent. With a nod to her chair, Harrison placed his napkin on the table, then leaned forward as she resumed her seat, her legs shaking with need.

"Eat, Phoebe. You're going to need your strength," he said with a growl as his eyes raked over her body and a smile pulled at his lips.

Heaven help her.

CHAPTER TWENTY-TWO

D INNER WENT QUICKLY, mostly due to the fact that Harrison sat in his chair, his brown eyes gleaming as he watched her attempt to eat the food before her. Phee squirmed in her chair, excitement and want urging her to throw her fork aside and follow Harrison wherever he longed to go. But he had said to eat, and surely she would need sustenance for whatever delight he was conjuring in his mind as he watched her.

"I'm done," she said, setting her fork aside.

He raised a brow. "You're certain?"

Phee nodded, placing her napkin on the table. "Are we to play Snap tonight?"

Harrison chuckled before standing and holding out his hand to her. "Yes and no," he said. "We'll play our normal hand, but instead of sharing a secret," he smiled at her, his gaze flicking from one part of her body to another, "we'll remove a piece of clothing. Does that sound all right with you?"

Phee nodded a smile tugging at her lips. Taking his hand, his strong fingers sliding against hers sending a tingling down her arm, she followed him. Mildred hopped up from the chair she occupied and followed them out of the dining room and up the stairs to the bedrooms.

Harrison stopped in front of Phee's door, his hand

raising to tuck a piece of her hair behind her ear as he leaned forward, his breath warm against her skin. "Tuck Mildred in, then meet me in my room," he said, the words a whisper. "And send Flora away. I'll be your lady's maid for the night."

Kissing her softly on the neck, Harrison opened the door to her bedroom, guided her and Mildred inside, then shut the door behind them. Phee stood in the stillness of her room, uncertain what to do next, but Mildred's soft meow brought her back to reality. Adjusting the fluffy blanket that resided on the end of the bed, Phee lifted Mildred onto it, watching as the kitten fluffed and fixed the linen to her liking before collapsing on the soft mound, her small paws kneading the cloth as she nursed on the fabric. Phee stood and watched her small amber eyes slowly closing as she soothed herself to sleep.

With soft steps and a large breath, Phee opened the door that connected their bedroom and went inside. Candles lit every surface, their glow brightening the room to an almost stage like quality. The two chairs that normally bracketed the fireplace were pushed to one side, the coverlet of the bed covering the floor before the roaring fire. In its center, a deck sat, unambiguous and ominous all the same.

"That was fast," Harrison said, rising from one of the chairs.

Phee nodded, her eyes feasting on the man before her who wore only his linen shirt and the tan trousers that he wore to dinner, and nothing more. His bare feet sunk into the plush rug on the floor. "She loves the blanket you brought her, so I'm sure that helped."

Harrison held out his hand to her. "Shall we play?"

The words were simple, childlike, and yet, somehow Phee knew that this game would not be like any of the others they had enjoyed. Taking his hand, she allowed him to lead her to the blanket. He knelt before her, removing first one, then the other slipper that graced her feet. His hands slid up her calves, his fingers dancing along the ties that held her stockings up. With deft movements, he undid both the ribbons, then pulled the fabric to the floor. With her stockings pooled around her feet, Phee stood rooted to the spot, her awareness heightened as his devilish hands slid up the now bare skin, coasting and sliding along the tops of her thighs. Her legs parted, making space for him at the place she desired him most, but he simply chuckled, his hands cascading over her linen drawers and back down to her feet, pulling the stockings from her.

"Soon," he said, before standing once more. "Turn around, Phoebe."

Phee presented him with her back and the buttons of her dress loosened as his crafty fingers worked their way down her spine. Deft motions slid the dress from her shoulders, down her arms, the fabric catching at her hips. His thumbs slipped into her petticoat and he pushed both pieces to the floor where they collapsed in a puddle of blue and white around her feet. The heat of his mouth danced across her neck as his hands wrapped around her waist, spanning the front of her stays before stopping at the ties that held them together. "We'll leave this for now," he said against her neck. "Come with me."

His hand grabbed hers and he had her sit on one side of the deck of cards before taking the side opposite of her.

"We're to play like this?" she asked, uncomfortably aware of the heat the pooled at her sex.

"If you're up for it."

"Oh," she said, her eyes falling to the pieces of clothing that covered his body. "I'm not sure that it's a fair game."

Harrison smiled at her. "We both have on drawers which would put each of us at an even three items of clothing. A perfectly reasonable number."

Phee swallowed. "What do you mean?"

Harrison smiled at her, taking the cards from the center of the blanket and shuffling the deck like a professional. "Not too little and not too many. Just the right amount to ensure that soon, one of us is going to be naked, and I can't wait to see which of us it is." He winked at her, the motion doing something funny to her breathing. "Should I deal?"

Harrison dealt out the cards, one after another flicking back and forth between them, the motion of his fingers simple, smooth, and captivating. Swallowing, Phee looked at the man across from her. The light from the fire lit his golden locks into shiny strands that fell around his face, his brown eyes shining from the dancing flames. One corner of his mouth was raised in a smirk, as if he had already won the game before they had even played it. Perhaps he had. Perhaps she had, too.

Taking up her pile of cards, Phee pushed them into a stack, their weight a reminder that this game would quite possibly be the death of her.

Harrison smiled at her and motioned to her deck. "You draw first."

Licking her lips, Phee nodded, watching as his eyes fell to her mouth, the feral want that filled his face sending her blood rushing. Taking the first card off the top of her deck, Phee flipped it over, and placed it on the blanket. A two of spades. Looking to Harrison's pile she spotted a ten of hearts.

"Again," he said, the word husky. Goosebumps rose on her flesh as she pulled her next card, laying it on top of the one before it. A seven and a queen lay face up, challenging them to pull a match.

"Again."

Phee wriggled, the spot between her legs aching, already anticipating his touch and they had only just started. With a deep breath, she reached for the next card and flipped it, the kings jovial smile filling her gaze as she placed him down. Her eyes slid to Harrison's pile where a one sat atop his pile taunting her and she swallowed, uncertain how much longer this could go on before she broke.

"Again," she said, looking at Harrison, his eyes pinned to her hands where she held the deck. Her breasts tightened at the look, her mind chanting, torn between paying attention to the game and deciding which item of his clothing would go first.

Phee flipped over the five of hearts, setting it down on the pile with a simple motion, then looked to his.

A five sat face up on his side of the blanket.

"Snap," they said in tandem, and Phee looked at him, her cheeks warming.

"How do you feel about each of us sacrificing an item?" he asked, his eyes pinned on her stays. "For fairness's sake."

Phee nodded, coming onto her knees and reaching for the ties, but stopped as his hands covered hers. "Allow me."

Moving behind her, Harrison's hands took their time unlacing the strings of her stays. His warm breath danced across her shoulder and she shuddered, tempted to lean against him as he worked. The strings fell against her shift, loosened of their tight embrace, but instead of removing himself back to his side, Harrison's hands slid down to her still-covered hips, his fingers sinking into the flesh he felt there, while his mouth fell to her shoulder, bestowing a kiss upon the exposed skin.

A soft gasp escaped her lips as his teeth nipped at her shoulder, the sting captivating, but no less more than when his tongue followed over the spot, soothing the tender skin. The cards fell from her hand as she gave into the temptation and finally allowed herself to lean into him, her arm coming up to wrap around his neck as she leaned her head to the side and granted him more room. Her fingers dug into his hair, holding him in place as he waged war on the strip of territory he had found, his hands sliding forward to meet at her stomach before rising, making their way to her breasts. The fabric of her stays fell to the floor while his hands soothed the confined skin, stroking away at the tender places where the whale bone had marred.

"Better?" he asked.

Phee whimpered as his fingers circled her nipples, the points tightening at the attention, determined to make their presence known. "No," she said, moving against him. "Worse, actually."

He laughed against her skin, the chuffs of air chilling the spot where his mouth had been. With a final kiss, he pulled back and Phee squeezed her eyes shut, her body mutinous at the notion of playing the game any longer.

"My turn?" she asked, turning back toward him, her tongue gliding over her lips as she raised her hands to the hem of his shirt, her fingers slipping beneath to slide over his skin. Harrison growled as she traced along the edge of his trousers with her pointer finger, the sound animalistic and all together delicious. Pulling the linen up toward his shoulders, Phee leaned forward, kissing his newly exposed chest, a hiss escaping his lips as she traced one nipple with her tongue. After a gentle nibble to the tender spot, Phee pulled the shirt over his head and let it fall to the floor before smiling at Harrison whose breaths had grown ragged, his pupils large as he gazed down at her.

Sitting back down at her spot, Phee's quim wept with need and she shifted, trying to find any sort of pressure that would ease the ache there. This game they were playing was dangerous.

"Take off your drawers and pull up your chemise," Harrison said, the smoky request making her lips part as she looked at him.

"What?"

He nodded to her shift. "I see you trying to soothe yourself, love. The least you could do is let me see."

Phee swallowed. "See what?"

He smirked. "See that delicious spot where you need me."

The air rushed from her lips at his words, the request

so dark, so carnal that part of her wanted to squeeze her legs tighter to ease the ache while another part wanted to follow commands. Pulling in a breath, she met his gaze. "Take off your trousers."

Harrison smiled. "Done." In a swift motion, he flicked the front closure of his trousers and stood, pushing the fabric to the floor revealing the outline of his swollen sex. Nodding at her, he licked his lips. "Show me."

Phee wriggled her hips, lifting the hem of her chemise. Pulling down her drawers and letting the excess fabric of her chemise fall behind her, she leaned back. Widening her knees, she shivered as the spot that ached for his touch met the cool air of the room and the soft scratch of the blanket. Looking at Harrison, she froze, want filling her at the abject need written across his face as he took her in. His brown gaze bore into her, his teeth worrying his bottom lip while his hands gripped his deck of cards tightly, nearly folding them in half.

"Should we continue?" she asked, the words choppy.

He nodded his head, his eyes pinned to her quim. "Draw."

Phee flipped over her top card, a queen smiling gracefully up at her. Before she could look at Harrison's pile, his soft exclamation of "snap" filled the room, his body lunging forward toward her as she raised her hands to wrap them around his neck.

Fingers delved in her hair as his lips met hers, his mouth soft even as he bestowed punishing kisses. His tongue swirled and stroked, devouring every inch of expanse it could find while his free hand pulled her chemise up over her breasts before falling to the swollen buds, torturing the pointed tips endlessly. She was engulfed, aflame, drowning in him and the only thing she wanted to do was surround herself in it. In him. In his citrus scent and unyielding grasp until she exploded from the delight of it all.

Her hands traced the expanse of his chest, sliding around to his back and holding on as he consumed her. It was too much. It was not enough.

"I want you, Phoebe" he said with a moan.

"I want you too."

Harrison pushed away from her and stood. He held out his hand to her, and she took it, his strength pulling her to standing as if she were a feather. Her chemise was whipped over her head in sure motions before he picked her up and carried her to his bed, depositing her in the middle of it.

With cat like moves, he stalked her across the bed, his lips dancing up the outside of her thigh. "So beautiful," he said as he kissed her skin. "So fucking beautiful." His lips trailed up her side, his hands stroking every inch of exposed skin they could find.

When his lips reached her ear, he kissed the shell, his teeth tormenting and soothing. "You need to grab the headboard."

"What?" she asked, the words a gasp.

Laying down beside her, his hand slid between her thighs, the delectable torment forcing her to separate them so he could reach his goal. Instead, he shifted the leg, moving her to straddle his chest, and she placed her hands on his chest to righten herself. He made a tsking noise at her before taking both her hands, kissing their palms, and lifting them to the wooden headboard before her. "Grab the headboard."

"I don't understand," she said as Harrison shifted his body so that his shoulders were between her thighs. Her hands tightened their grasp and she looked down, her cheeks heating at the image of her quim sitting poised before Harrison's mouth. "Harrison…"

He turned his head to the side, kissing the inside of one thigh before bestowing the same gift on the other. "You are my dessert. I am going to devour you like the sweet morsel you are, and you, my love, are going to enjoy every minute of it. Think of yourself as my own personal chocolate soufflé."

"I—" she said, shaking her head. "Like this—"

His mouth lifted, his tongue stroking her sex with a divine lick of wet and heat, and Phee choked on her words, her thighs shaking at the contact. Instead of pulling back, of trying to convince her with words, Harrison kissed her quim again, the firm stroke sending a moan of need between her parted lips as all thoughts fled, the chant of pure need pulsing through her brain as his hands gripped her arse and lowered the feast to his waiting mouth.

Sensation reigned as he ate to his content, his greedy tongue devouring every bit of her, coaxing and consoling the swollen nub at the top of her sex before eating her up again. His hands held her firm, one on each globe while his thumbs played in her heat, swirling and baiting the entrance of her cunny with attention, but never enough.

Phee's thighs shook. Each time her pleasure lured her closer, her brain nagged that she would smother him, kill him with her quim, and her desire fled only to be rekindled again. It was torturous to be pleasured this way, her body buzzing like her bees, with unfulfilled need and a touch of fear. A whimper escaped her lips as she pulled herself up again, her climax so close and yet so far out of reach.

Harrison shifted her, setting her on his chest as his hands cupped her hips. His lips glistened with her desire and he licked them greedily as he looked at her. "What is it?" he asked.

She shook her head, her body pulsing with want. "I'm scared I'll crush you."

The smile that overtook his face was beautiful, and were the situation not so utterly preposterous, she would have stopped a moment to take it in. But worry ate at her and desire squirmed through her, and she was not certain if she should scream or cry.

He squeezed her hips. "Phoebe, you will not hurt me," he said, a smile in his words, "And if I do die, I can't think of a more pleasurable way to go."

Phee frowned at him. "This is serious."

He nodded. "Very. Since we're being serious, I must say, that I seriously want you to sit on my mouth. To cover my tongue in your honey, to drown me in your thighs as you come. I will have you this way every moment of everyday until it becomes your most favorite spot to sit."

"Harrison—"

"I want you to ride my mouth like a jockey at the Ascot. I want your thighs to warm my ears in the coldest of winters."

Phee laughed.

"I want you screaming my name as you take your pleasure from me, and then, Phoebe," he said, his hands squeezing her hips. "I want to do it again."

"All right," she said with a whisper.

"That's my girl," he said, nodding to the headboard. "Your saddle awaits, my lady."

A corner of her mouth rose and she shook her head before shifting again, her quim poised over his mouth., her hands holding onto the ornate headboard of his fourposter bed. "What do I do?" she asked.

He smiled as his hands gripped her arse firmly, pulling her in place. "My darling, you just enjoy."

He lifted his head, his tongue delving into the place that longed for his touch and her body needed little coaxing, his attention most assuredly missed. His thumbs traced the entrance of her sex, the sensitive skin there aching for his touch while his tongue danced across her nub bewitching and beguiling the pleasure point.

Strong hands pulled her down to him and with very little resistance, she sat, and he dined like a starving man. He wasted not a moment, annihilating her senses while his thumbs carved out an ache so sharp she could feel it in her heart. Her hands clutched at the headboard, nails digging into the wood as she ground herself against him searching for the pleasure only he could provide. And when the peak claimed her, her body quivering as he absorbed every ounce of pleasure inside her, she screamed his name until her strength left her.

Leaning against the headboard, Phee shook her head, a soft giggle escaping her lips as she looked down at her husband who in truth seemed the happiest man alive. Smiling wide, he licked his lips before kissing the inside of her thigh. "I knew you'd like it."

CHAPTER TWENTY-THREE

For as long as Harrison could remember, the trip to Dorset had taken three arduous days, but inside the carriage with Phoebe, they passed in a besotted blur. If Harrison was not coaxing his wife to new heights, he was sitting beside her as they read *Ivanhoe*, or holding her close while they dozed. In any other circumstance, the long trip would have been unbearable, boring and monotonous, but with Phoebe by his side, he had found that time held little sway over him. He found himself looking forward to their carriage ride each morning nearly as much as he enjoyed their nights at the inns, excited to see what the days adventure would bring them to.

When the carriage finally drew to a stop at the Everly estate in Poole, Harrison mourned the loss of their quiet retreat, a small haven where only the two of them existed, but Phoebe's excitement lessened the sting. As soon as she exited the carriage, a smile graced her beautiful mouth as she took in the whitewashed manor before her. Cunston Gap had been in the Everly estate for nearly a century, the home acting as a refuge for generations of earls and their families. Hot London summers were but a distant memory as soon as one stepped out into the salty sea air, the lush green fields and copse of trees appearing like something out of a fairy tale, sans nymphs and sprites. The look of joy on Phoebe's face only further proved that his choice of destination was not only ideal, but exemplary.

"Do you like it?" he asked, taking her hand and placing it on his forearm.

"Very much." She looked around, her eyes scanning the landscape before her. "I wonder what the gardens look like."

Harrison smiled, rubbing his hand against hers. "I thought you might be interested. Would you like to freshen up or would you rather go on an exploration now?"

Phoebe smiled at him, her joy contagious. He had little care for the gardens of the property, nor the insects that buzzed around, choosing to make it their home, but the knowledge that it would make Phoebe smile, her eyes alight with wonder... Well, he very much cared about that.

"Let's freshen up first and then explore," she said.

After washing off the dirt and dust of their travel, Harrison dressed in a simple pair of trousers and cotton shirt sleeves, choosing to forgo a jacket and tie. An old pair of boots covered his feet, ones he did not worry about sullying, and a simple straw hat that he borrowed from the stable master sat atop his head. To the London set he would no doubt look ridiculous, but he knew Phoebe would care very little on his appearance. And when she met him in the hallway, a simple blue striped dress and straw bonnet gracing her person, he knew he had the right of it.

"Ready, love?" he asked.

She paused, her eyes moving from the boots on his feet

to the hat on his head. "You look like a farmer," she said with a smile.

Harrison raised a brow and stepped toward her, one side of his mouth lifted in a smirk. "A farmer, am I?" Taking her hand, he placed it on his chest, her fingers gripping at him as soon as she touched fabric.

She laughed. "If a farmer wore a pair of scuffed Hessians and some very well-made trousers, then yes, you're a farmer."

Harrison took off his hat, doffing it as he dropped into a low bow. "Well then, if my lady will have me, I'd be honored to show her about my land."

Phoebe took the hat from his hand and placed it back on his head, tilting it upward so she could see his face. "If you'd be so kind," she said, kissing his cheek before taking his hand and leading them to the outside.

Harrison had never paid much attention to the gardens. Until observing them with Phoebe, he had never noticed how the back portion of the home appeared more forest than well-manicured garden, the shrubs and trees not so much overgrown, but lush and full, wild in their appearance. Birds chirped a happy song from somewhere while a few fluffy bees dipped from flower to flower in a search for pollen.

Phoebe squeezed his hand, and Harrison released her from his grasp, slowing his pace as he watched her buzz from one spot to another inspecting the greenery, her smile wide as she followed one bee and then another to different areas of the garden, her leather boots scurrying this way and that. He watched as she gave attention to a collection of blooming Dorset heath, then skipped to a vine of honeysuckle, her finger brushing at a pink petal. She slowed as she spied a small bird bath, a starling perched on its edge taking a drink, and with quiet steps, she walked around past it, determined to let the bird have its peace.

On her face he saw the same expression she had exhibited at the bookstore, a beautiful combination of joy and wonder as she attempted to take it all in. As if a clock were ticking somewhere in the distance, counting down the minutes until she would be removed from a place she could no doubt stay at forever. Here there were no crush of bodies, no boisterous noise. There were no rules or regulations determining the amount of emotion she could display. Here in the garden, with him, she was free to be Phoebe. Able to enjoy each moment, to chase each thrill to her hearts content.

Swallowing, Harrison looked away from the sight, pulling the brim of his hat lower to shield his gaze. What must it be like to be so free with yourself. To embrace who you are fully, without fear or worry that you would become a disappointment. Without anxiety plaguing you that you are not doing enough.

"There must be a hive nearby," Phoebe said, calling from several beds away. "There are so many at this one patch."

Harrison turned to her, his practiced smile at the ready on his face, but the sight of his wife sitting in a patch of orchids sent the false attempt away with speed, a smile of genuine delight taking over. In a puddle of flowers, Phoebe smiled as she watched bees buzz around her, a cabbage moth flying with effort over her head. Dappled sunlight fell across her hat, its beams of light casting a heady glow on her as she sat in splendor.

At that moment, he wished he were an artist, able to capture the beauty of the moment before him. Wished he were a composer, capable of compounding the heartbeats and serenity that flowed through him as he watched her. His lack of skill was so glaringly apparent in that moment, when all he wanted to do was form a memory of it so detailed, so finite, that he could take it out and look at it whenever he liked. This woman was becoming home for him, a safe place filled with honest joy and warm comfort. A place where he could simply be Harrison, as he was meant to be.

"How are you not afraid?" he asked, walking toward her.

His wife, sitting like the queen of the forest, smiled at him as if he were a dolt. "Don't be silly. They can sense I'm not a threat just as I know they are not one."

"If only that were true," he said, the words softly floating away on the wind.

"Hmm?"

Harrison shook his head. "Come along, Titania. We have more to see."

"More?" she asked, taking his proffered hand.

Harrison pulled her to standing, guiding her out of the garden bed and back to the stone path. "More," he said, lacing his fingers with hers. "You don't think I brought you out to Dorset for meat pies, do you?"

She frowned at him. "Honestly, yes."

He laughed, kissing the back of her hand. "Oh, ye of little faith. You shall think me a knight in shining armor after today."

Guiding her down the path, they strolled following the trail as they weaved in and out of the grounds, the melody of the birds filling the comfortable silence. After a time, they came to a gate. A low ivy wall in the shape of a rectangle shot out at either end, enclosing the space and the items inside, which just so happened to be hives. A small shed stood guard in one corner, filled with the required gear for the estate's beekeeper.

"You have bees?" she said, the words whispered as she leaned over the wall, peaking at the four Huber hives that sat inside.

"We do," he said with a smile. "Do you like your surprise?"

Phoebe nodded enthusiastically.

"We also have a beekeeper who ensures the hives are well taken care of. He renders the old wax which is used to make candles for the estate, and the honey that he does gather is either stored in the cellars or shared with the community."

She pushed up onto her toes as if the added height would allow her to see more. "How long has the estate done this?"

"As long as I can remember. I'm fairly certain the family decided to follow in the regents' footsteps and adopt every aristocratic notion that they have. Hence the bees."

Phoebe nodded. "That makes perfect sense." Dropping back down to her heels, she turned to face him. "I'd love to speak with your beekeeper if he has a free moment."

Harrison smiled at her, tucking a strand of hair the blew across her lips behind her ear. "I sent a missive to

Mrs. Kenneths weeks ago and she has already set up a time for you within the coming days so that you may pick Mr. Cole's brain with any bee related questions you might have. I've also informed him about the feisty hive and it would seem he has some rather interesting insight into what can be done."

She smiled at him. "You knew I'd want to talk to him?"

Bending his knees, Harrison lowered to Phee's eye level. "I did. It wasn't just the steak and kidney pies of Dorset that made me think you'd love this place." Cupping her cheek, Harrison rubbed his thumb along her lips. "I knew you'd fall in love with the estate which is why I suggested it. Knew you'd see that gardens and the hives and suddenly begin to make plans for your own in London. I knew your eyes would light up the minute you saw this place, knew your mind would race with future plans." He leaned forward, brushing his lips across the space his thumb had just occupied. "Knew you'd be so eternally grateful to your husband that in the time you weren't scheming and planning that I'd be able to convince you to be naughty with me."

She sighed against his lips. "How devious," she said, pressing her mouth against his.

"Always when it comes to you."

Wrapping his arm around her waist, Harrison pulled Phoebe in close, his tongue slipping along the seam of her lips. It was all the invitation she needed as she opened to him, her tongue meeting his in a dance as her hands rose to his hair, knocking the hat from his head. They were in a public space, person or animal free to view them as they wrapped themselves around one another. He should be more circumspect, at the very least slightly ashamed at how brazenly he flaunted the physical relationship with his wife. His mother would have had fits if she were to learn that he was seen pawing the newly appointed countess in the open for all to see, unthinking and uncaring about what someone passing by might think. But with Phee's lush body pressed to his, her sighs of contentment filling his ears with its beautiful sound, he cared if neither bird nor beast saw them at that moment. Let them look. Let them gaze at the earl with envy. For in that moment, everything was right. And he was damned well going to enjoy it.

CHAPTER TWENTY-FOUR

THE REMAINDER OF the week was filled with long discussions with the beekeeper and quaint outings with Harrison. When they were not exploring the beach or visiting the shops in Poole, the pair secluding themselves to the primary apartments. Dinner was typically served on trays in their room, a simple meal of soup and bread and wine before the fire as the sun disappeared from the sky, giving way to its dark mistress. Something about ending their evenings wrapped up together in their own little world felt special. After eating, they would sit side by side and read, or talk, or play Dirty Snap.

Rubbing at a knot in her shoulder, Phee sighed. Her body ached, no doubt a lingering consequence of their journey along with the more physical aspects of their time in Dorset, and she groaned as the knot rolled beneath her fingers, persistent in inducing an annoying pain.

"Are you all right?" Harrison asked, brushing her hand aside and nimbly inspecting the tender spot. At her wince, he used his thumb to rub at it.

"A bit sore, is all."

Placing a soft kiss to her neck, he stood and went to the bell pull, giving it a swift tug.

"What are you doing?" she asked.

"Calling for a bath. Nothing helps sore muscles more

than disappearing in warm water up to your chin and letting it soothe the ache. Afterward, I can massage it if you'd like."

"Oh, that sounds nice. Have them bring some lavender oil, as well. I've read it can help in relieving the soreness."

Harrison gave orders to the waiting footman and in very little time at all, the bath was filled with pots of warm water and Harrison was escorting her to the door. Phee peeked into the room, the heat from the water falling across her face. Linking her hands together before her, she turned to Harrison who stood next to her with a smile. "What about you?"

He squeezed her shoulder before kissing her forehead. "This is for you. I can't have my countess out of sorts on our honeymoon."

Phee smiled, looking back at the tub that sat in the room.

Nudging her inside, Harrison smiled at her before closing the door. Phee turned, looking at the bath once again.

"Is everything all right? Is it too hot?" Harrison asked from the other side of the door.

With a smile, Phee opened the door to find a stunned Harrison on the other side.

"Are you all right?" he asked, peeking around her into the bathing room.

"Yes. Are you all right?"

Harrison looked back at her, his eyes searching her face.

"It's lonely out here without you," he said, closing her eyes.

Cupping his cheek, Phee waited for him to open his

eyes and look at her, a smile at her lips. "It's lonely in here without you."

"Really?" he asked.

Phee laughed. "Yes, really."

Kissing her forehead, Harrison smiled. "Get in the tub, Phoebe. I'll grab my book and come right back."

"All right," she said, a smile pulling at her lips. Pushing onto her tip toes, Phee kissed his cheek then dropped back down and went to the tub where she removed her robe. She slipped into the water, the warmth wrapping around her like a blanket.

Within minutes, Harrison returned to the bathing room, his book tucked beneath one arm while in his hands he held her wine glass, refilled with the delicious brew that she had sipped on at dinner, and a pillow from the bed.

"You look as if you're preparing a picnic," Phee said with a smile as he handed her the glass.

Harrison sent her a heated look, his gaze raking over every bit of skin exposed to his wandering eyes. With a wink, he set the pillow against the wall before sitting on the floor, leaning against it. "Drink your wine and relax, love."

"All right," she said, sipping from the glass in her hand.

Harrison leaned forward and took it from her when she was finished, taking a sip himself before setting it down on the floor beside him. Opening his book, he looked at her and smiled before turning his attention to the words before him.

Phee leaned herself against the wall of the tub, the water sliding over her at the movements. With a smile, she rested her head against the cushioned lip, her eyes never leaving Harrison. His golden locks glinted in the candlelight, the red of his banyan turning a dark crimson in the dimly lit room. His beard had begun to look shaggy again and her hand itched to rub against it and feel the hairs tickle her palm.

The quiet of the room wrapped around her, the gentle quality of it soothing, as if the quiet knew that there were two hearts in that room, even if they did not speak a word.

It was nice, this feeling.

Closing her eyes, Phee let herself relax into the water's warm embrace. Harrison's soft breaths and the occasional turning of the page were the only things to be heard in the room, yet she was beginning to think that there were other things being spoken. There was a fullness to her time with him, a comfort in his quiet presence, and care in his thoughtful gestures. The way he surrounded her with his whole self, granting her the safety to simply be Phee and nothing more.

Just like the quiet of the room, she knew she did not have to say it, but it was there nonetheless.

Love.

Somehow, there was love. She had not planned for it. Had never agreed to it, but it was there just the same. In his loving gestures toward Mildred, in his forehead kisses and hand squeezes. In his chocolate desserts and midnight dances.

Bit by bit he had pulled her in until she could do nothing but want him. Want his hand around hers. Want his kiss on her lips. Want the smile she was becoming certain was only meant for her.

So no, she had not said it, but the quiet knew. And, perhaps, he did as well.

Soft lips pressed to Phee's forehead and she opened her eyes to see Harrison smiling at her. "The water is turning cold, love. Let's get you warm and in bed," he said.

Standing, Phee let Harrison wrap a towel around her before helping her step out of the tub and onto the plush rug on the floor. Strong, sure hands rubbed the cotton against her skin, covering every millimeter until she was once more warm and dry.

Harrison wrapped her robe back around her body, tying the string at her waist securely before scooping her up in his arms. Phee left out a soft shriek and wrapped her arms around his neck. "I can walk," she said as he set her down on the full mattress.

"I'm aware," he said, crawling onto the bed next to her.

"And?"

"And you think I'm going to pass up the chance to hold you after watching you get all pink and soft in the bathtub?"

"Harrison," she said, her breaths short at the look of want in his eyes.

He took her mouth in his, his kiss bold like the wine they had drank, his lips reheating her until she was inflamed. Pulling away from her, he said, "Phoebe, I'm not sure I'll ever have my fill of you." Cupping her face, he kissed her lips, her cheeks. "Tell me to stop. To go to bed," he said between kisses.

"No."

"I'm going to make you scream, Phoebe. I'll make you scream my name until you're hoarse. Do you understand?" he asked with a growl.

She whimpered at his words, her core already clenching at the thought of such ecstasy.

"You're so fucking beautiful," he said as he undid the ties of her robe. "So beautiful. Laying in that tub, pink and flushed, the water cupping every bit of skin like a lover should." His words were strained as he pulled apart the sides of her robe, exposing her to his gaze. "Imagine, being jealous of water. Jealous that it gets to embrace you the way I do, to bring a flush to your cheeks and make your eyes flutter in bliss." His hands fell to her breasts, cupping the orbs as his fingers toyed with her nipples. "I'll make the soreness go away. I'll make you feel so eased you'll never want to be without me."

Phee arched into his hands with a whimper, his words so raw she was not sure which one of them was more exposed. "Harrison..."

"Shh," he said, lowering his mouth to hers. "I'll make it better, love."

His kiss was rough even as his hands were gentle, the two at such odds but still lighting a fire within her that burned so hot, so fast, that she would surely go up in flames. Her hands flew to his shoulders, her nails sinking into the flesh there as she lost herself to his kiss. He pulled back only briefly to remove his banyan, and when he returned, it was in all his glory. Skin on skin as he covered her.

Phee's hands roamed every exposed bit of him, greedy as he consumed her whole, her body shaking with need. "I want…" she said, the words a pant.

"I know, love." He grabbed both of her hands, pinning them above her head as his knee moved up to the juncture of her quim, pushing against the needy spot. Phee cried out at the pressure, her senses aflame as she ground herself against his leg, searching for relief.

"You're so wet already," he said in her ear as she pressed herself against his leg. "Wet for me?"

Phee squeezed her hands, her fingers twisting with his as she rubbed her quim against his leg, her climax just out of reach.

"Are you wet for me, Phoebe?" he asked as he kissed up her neck, his teeth scouring her skin. "Are you flushed for me?" Lowering his head he took her nipple in his mouth, sucking and teasing the tip, driving her mad as she pleasured herself on his leg.

"Are you nearing your bliss as you rub your cunny against my leg?"

Phee whimpered, her need so heavy she was shaking. It wasn't enough. She needed more.

"Are you imagining my mouth on your quim, Phoebe? My cock?" His hand fell to her arse, his fingers gripping one cheek as he ground his thigh against her. "Will you scream my name as you come for me?"

"Harrison," she chanted, his name like a prayer.

"Scream it, Phoebe."

"I can't…"

"Yes, you can. Come for me. Make my name ring off the rafters." His mouth fell to her shoulder, his teeth scraping against the spot where neck and shoulder met before he sucked at the skin.

"Harrison!" she screamed as her climax took her, the waves crashing over her with such force that she could only hold on for the ride.

"That's my girl," he said in her ear, his voice a growl. "Fuck my leg as hard as you want. Rub your cunny on me. Let me feel your pleasure."

Phee whimpered, her body shaking as she ground herself against him, moisture pooling from her quim. As the quakes subsided, Phee turned her face toward Harrison's chest, her breath releasing in pants against his skin.

Harrison pulled her close before rolling onto his back, pulling her on top of him. His hard length lay against her stomach, and Phee raised her head to look at Harrison, want still pulsing through her at the touch of him. Longing poured through her at the want to feel the hard length of him inside her, but she could not find the words to voice it.

"Did you think we were done, Phoebe? We're only just getting started."

CHAPTER TWENTY-FIVE

THEIR FINAL DAY in Dorset was met with thunderstorms, and Harrison scowled at the sky as if in doing so it would change the clouds' minds. The deluge had removed the potential for what would no doubt have been a perfect day, the crack of thunder only deepening the lines of his furrowed brow.

"What a vicious storm," Phoebe said, her fingers laced with his as she peered out the window of the library at the menacing clouds. Streams of water spilled down the pane as if one were pouring a watering can along it creating a hazy view before them.

Forcing a smile to his face, Harrison turned to Phoebe. "I'm sorry we have such a horrendous end to our trip."

She shook her head at him. "Don't be silly. You couldn't have known it was going to rain. And as endings go, it's kind of romantic."

Harrison turned back to the window where water sliced down the pane like a waterfall. "How so? It's abominably gray and horrendously wet. Romantic would be a light sprinkle of a shower or better yet, a sunny day where one could go to the beach for a picnic."

Stepping in front of him, Phoebe wrapped her hands around his waist and rested her head on his chest. "A beach picnic is very romantic, but so is staying inside and snuggling in close while the world appears to fall apart outside." She placed her chin on his chest and looked up at him. "I'm sorry your plans didn't happen the way you wanted but that doesn't mean we cannot make the situation what we want it."

Wrapping his arms around her, Harrison kissed her forehead. "How so?"

"A picnic indoors?"

"How is that any different than what we already do?" He frowned at her, aware of how childish he sounded. "I was going to surprise you with a dandy horse."

She smiled at him. "We'll ride in the ballroom then."

"Phoebe ..."

"What? I don't care what we do." Pushing onto her tiptoes, she kissed his lips, quieting all other protests. "A perfect day for me is simply one I get to spend with you."

The words sounded so simple, so obvious, but part of Harrison rebelled against them. He wanted to spoil her with his attention, lavish her with gifts and treats. Create days so perfectly spectacular that she would never want to be far from his side, yet all she wanted was him. Just him. Harrison Metcalf, as he was. It was preposterous.

"Harrison?" she asked. "What do you want to do today?"

His brow furrowed at her question. "What do you mean?"

With a smile, she cupped his face, forcing him to meet her gaze. "What do you want to do today? Laze about and read? Play a game? Go back to bed with your wife?" She kissed his lips with the softest touch, a fairy kiss, before whispering, "What is your ideal rainy day?"

"I don't–I don't know."

"No?"

"I–I've never thought of it." He shook his head, puzzled. "I'm not sure I've ever been asked by anyone what I'd like to do on a rainy day."

"Surely that can't be true. What did you do as a child on rainy days?"

He scowled, attempting to think back but his memories proved fruitless. It was as if his brain had drawn a shroud over that time, covering every event with a black veil, hiding them from him. "I don't remember."

Phoebe smiled softly at him. There was no judgement in the movement, no pity, just understanding.

"Come with me," she said, taking his hands and guiding him from the room.

In their apartments upstairs, she motioned for him to sit on the bed before dropping to her knees before him. It was a position of subjection and yet the power was all hers. She tugged at one boot, then the other, then pushed onto her feet and began unbuttoning his coat and waistcoat. The motions were efficient and yet the consideration that came with them left his throat tight with each tug and pull she made. When he was left in nothing but his trousers and shirt, she turned around presenting him her back. Moving her hair to the side, she said, "Would you untie me?"

The laces ran through his fingers as he dragged them loose, freeing her from the purple day dress, his heart beating in his ears. She stepped away from him and removed everything but her chemise and stockings before turning around to face him. With a nod of her chin, she said, "Get in the covers," before retrieving the heavy blanket and book that sat on the armchair by the fire.

The blanket was quickly spread over the top of him before Phoebe crawled across him and wiggled into the covers beside him. Her hand slid out from beneath the quilt to cup his neck as she guided him to rest on her chest, her bosom a soft pillow beneath his head. It was too much. Too soft, too sweet, too caring. His brain urged him to move, yelled at him to stop being so selfish, so spoiled, but when she dropped a kiss to the top of his head, he forced his eyes closed and his breaths to slow.

With a sigh, she opened *Ivanhoe* to the very beginning and with a soft voice, began to read.

> *"...having once seen him put forth his strength in battle, methinks I could know him again among a thousand warriors. He rushes into the fray as if he were summoned to a banquet. There is more than mere strength—there seems as if the whole soul and spirit of the champion were given to every blow which he deals upon his enemies. God assoilzie him of the sin of bloodshed! It is fearful, yet magnificent, to behold how the arm and heart of one man can triumph over hundreds."*

Her melodic voice echoed beneath his ear as he lay on her chest, the warmth from her body and the quilt soothing him from the chilly air of the room.

It was an intimacy he had never experienced, a sort of gentleness he had never known. Her free hand brushed through his hair as she read, the curls twisting about her fingers like clinging vines. When she turned the page, her lips fell to his head, kissing him softly before she began to read once more, as if reassuring him that she was still there. Still by his side. It was a small gesture, not one he was certain she even noticed, but it sent his heart racing nevertheless.

He must have dozed off for when he awoke the rain had become a soft sprinkle and the sun attempted to make its presence known. He lay on his stomach, his head resting on Phoebe's chest, her arms wrapped around his shoulders holding him close, her soft snores indicating that the quiet moment had claimed her as well. Pushing off of her, she mumbled her frustration as her arms fell from him and Harrison smiled, shifting onto his side before pulling her into the cavern of his body.

"What have you done to me?" he whispered as he tucked her against his chest, her body fitting like a missing piece of a puzzle.

It had not been some extraordinary feat. There had been no dragons slain, no ogres fought, and yet she had taken a rather ordinary day and made it into something peaceful. A safe space where he could simply be.

Her question had provoked him, stirring his memories, or at least, what little ones he had. His childhood seemed like a blank slate, something anyone could fill in with stories as he had no memory of it. Surely there must have been rainy days when he was a child. Surely he must have done something with his time when the sun was covered in gray and the clouds had opened their fury on the world. But if he had, he could not recall. The few things he did remember were memories that filled him with pain. Chasing after his mother, wanting to show her something he had made and her look of disdain when she finally stopped to listen to him, as if he were a nuisance she was forced to deal with. The ever pressing need to fit the mold and make her proud, to prove he was worthy of her love, even if it meant a time away from her under the tutelage of tutors hired by his uncle. Standing before the mirror in his room practicing his smile, his bow. Tying his cravat and adjusting his hair over and over again so that not a speck of his person would cause her irritation. If he were perfect, she would love him. If he were perfect then he would be worthy of her love.

When she died, it was as if everything he had worked for, all the modifications and labor he had made were for naught, for now she would never love him. Now things would never change.

Shaking his head, Harrison attempted to push away the memories, tuck them back into the box so carefully hidden in the recesses of his mind, but Phoebe's simple question still lingered. What did he like to do on a rainy day?

Better yet, what did he like to do?

He thought through the options she had suggested; dandy horses in the ballroom, a picnic indoors. Reading before a cozy fire or playing a game. Looking down at the woman in his arms, he smiled. On a rainy day he liked to lay in bed with his wife. He liked to slip in and out of consciousness in the safety and warmth of her arms, to listen to her melodic voice as she read to him from the latest book that caught her attention. To play with his clay in the conservatory while drops tinkled against the glass, a cat sitting nearby on a chair, her purr filling the room.

And when the rain stopped, he wanted to bundle his beautiful bride up in a blanket and explore the changes that occurred outside from the deluge. He wanted to see her cheeks pinken in the chill, to brush at the errant rain drop that chose to fall on her cheek. To pull her close as she inspected every flower and bud to ensure there was enough food for her bees.

Harrison's chest tightened and he shook his head. How ludicrous he sounded. How wistful and childlike, as if any of those things were options for an earl. Had his mother heard a single one of his thoughts she would have furrowed her brow and frowned at him, her mouth turned down in disdain that her son would do something so capricious without thought for what others might require of him.

Phoebe stirred beside him and he tightened his grasp on her, his hand falling to her head where it stroked at the strands of hair that had come free from her chignon. Kissing her head, Harrison pushed the nonsensical thoughts away and forced a smile to his lips. He would not sully a day that Phoebe had tried so hard to recover.

"Hello, love," he said when she raised her head to look at him.

"You're awake?" she asked, rocking her head against his chest.

"And now, so are you."

She shook her head. "I wasn't sleeping, just resting my eyes while I waited for you to wake up."

"Is that so?" Harrison asked, rolling her onto her back.

She made a noise of agreement before pushing her arms

over her head, her body undulating as she stretched beneath him. Her soft moan as she did so sent longing through his veins and he let his head fall to her neck to drop kisses along the skin.

"The sun has come out," he said the words vibrating against her neck.

"Has it?" She cupped his cheek, forcing him to meet her gaze. "Shall we go see?"

Harrison paused, his eyes searching her face, certain she has heard his thoughts from mere moments before. "Should we?"

She nodded, a smile pulling at her lips. "Who knows, you might get your dandy horse after all."

With a kiss to his lips, Phoebe pushed up from the bed and scurried over the covers to the bell pull. "I'll ring for Flora to help me to dress," she said.

"May I help you instead?" he asked.

Nodding, Phoebe picked up her discarded garments, and Harrison helped her lace and tie the items before putting himself back to rights. After a quick inspection of his hair, and a few adjusted pins for Phoebe, they made their way downstairs and outside to the garden. The air was crisp, the smell of rain tinging the air as they walked the dirt path. Small puddles splashed beneath their feet and Phoebe laughed when one exceptional puddle splashed against his boots.

"Find it entertaining, do you?" he asked.

"A bit," she said with a smile. "What are your thoughts on finishing out the day as you had planned?"

He pulled her close, his arms wrapping around her shoulders to keep her warm, and he cursed at himself for not grabbing a blanket for her. "A bit too damp, I'm afraid. But what do you say to a stroll along the beach instead?"

Phoebe leaned against him, her back nestled against his chest. "I say it sounds lovely, especially if it means that I'm with you."

Harrison's throat tightened as he pulled Phoebe closer. He knew she meant what she said. Knew with every fiber of his being that her only requirement was to be sincere, but he could not help but hear the voice of his mother in the back of his mind that warned him. What if he failed? What if she left? If he did not ensure that Phoebe was utterly infatuated with their life, if he was not the best husband possible, she would leave and he would be all alone again.

CHAPTER TWENTY-SIX

With shoulders tensed and a pleasant smile plastered to her face, Phee stood beside her mother, greeting the attendants of their ball. With each curtsey, Phee wished she were back at the estate in Poole, ensconced with Harrison as they had been a month ago. Even with him by her side now, his support comforting, she could not help the buzzing that vibrated through her as she dipped curtsey after curtsey and made small talk while the temperature of the room rose and the cotton in her ears fought against the noise that threatened to bombard her.

She loved her mother, truly she did, but she could not ascertain how the woman found such joy hosting these productions every year. The stress that plagued her mother during the planning of their yearly ball, combined with the monotonous duties of hosting, left Lady Youngly a shell by the end of the night and yet each year she dutifully sent out invitations and repeated the occasion as if the previous one never happened.

Lady Tabitha Grayson came to stand before her, her husband Sir Reginald Grayson beside her, and Phee dropped another curtsey before meeting the abominable woman's gaze. "Lady Grayson, it's lovely to see you this evening."

"Yes," Lady Grayson said, her smile artificial, her gaze calculated as she took in Phee's pink ball gown, which held nary a ruffle of itchy lace, and simple coiffeur that required few of the uncomfortable pins to keep her hair off the back of her neck. "So glad we could attend. Sir Reginald wasn't certain we'd be able to come. After all, we only just returned from our honeymoon."

"How wonderful," Harrison said, stepping into the conversation. "As did we. Where abouts did you journey to?"

Lady Grayson batted her eyes at Harrison, her smile gentling in a peculiar way as she titled her head toward him. "We were in Rye. Sir Reginald has his estate there and wanted to show me the manor as the new lady of the house." She shook her head. "It's more of a castle than a manor, honestly, but castle sounds so dreary."

"Yes," Harrison said, placing his arm on Phee's back. "We visited our estate in Dorset. While it is no castle, it was rather nice to spend the days at the beach with my beautiful bride." With a smile to Sir Grayson he said, "No doubt you understand, Grayson."

Sir Grayson nodded at him, a pleasant smile on his face before he turned his attention to Lady Sundry who made her way past, her crimson dress cut daringly close to her bosom.

"Well, it's lovely to see you both. Please enjoy yourself," Harrison said, bowing to the couple before turning to Phee. Leaning down, he said in her ear, "Come with me?"

Phee nodded, relief pouring over her.

Taking her hand, he gave their excuses to her mother

before leading her away from the receiving line and down the hallway to her parents' library. Inside, Phee took a breath, her shoulders loosening as the quiet of the room washed over her, the buzz of people dissipating as Harrison closed the door.

Coming to stand before her, he took her chin in his hand, tilting her face toward his. "That was a lot of people you spoke to. All right, love?"

"Better now," she said.

Stooping to her height, his brow furrowed. "You look like you need a hug."

Laughing softly, Phee nodded her head before stepping into his open arms, his familiar scent filling her senses. His arms wrapped around her shoulders squeezing her tightly, willing away the overwhelming sensations of the receiving line. With his strong grasp and citrus smell, the tension eased from her shoulders and neck, her breaths becoming shallow as tranquility flowed over her.

"Can't we just stay like this?" she asked, pulling back to look up at him. "I know it's my mother's ball, but I'm sure no one would notice if we didn't return."

A corner of his mouth rose in a smile and he kissed her forehead. "The idea has merit, but I'm sure your mother would come searching for us. And if I'm being honest, I'd like to not be in her bad graces."

Blowing a puff of air through her lips, Phee leaned against his chest. "You act as if she will bite you."

"Angering your mother terrifies me." Harrison rested his chin on her head. "You've practiced for this, love, and I'll stay by your side like a sentinel, ready to take on anything that comes."

Phee groaned.

"I know, love, but you can do this. I'll be by your side the entire time."

With a sigh, Phee pulled herself away from Harrison's arms. Shaking out her soft pink skirts, she looked at her husband in his navy coat with tails and white breeches, his black slippers polished to a shine and his golden locks brushed handsomely away from his face. "I've begun to think we should make an addendum to the contract. I should receive a prize every instance I put myself through one these things," she said, taking his proffered arm and following him from the library.

"What would you like, love?" he asked.

"A day with you," she said. "Like we did at the bookstore."

"Phoebe, I'll happily give you that anytime you'd like. Choose something outrageous."

Pausing before the ballroom where couples swirled and matrons cloistered in groups no doubt gossiping, Phee turned to look at him a smile on her lips as she shook her head. "There's something special about knowing that I get to have a full day of you all to myself. And perhaps, if I spend my time thinking about what adventure we'll find instead of how overwhelming this event is, I'll be able to get through it easier."

"We could always change that part of the agreement entirely. I don't want you to suffer through something that makes you uncomfortable."

Smiling at him, she said, "Yes, but then I won't get to dance with you." Taking a deep breath, she squeezed his arm. "Ready?"

A quizzical look overtook his face, but instead of continuing their conversation, he merely nodded and led them into the fray. The scent of sweat and perfume filled the air, chasing away Harrison's clean smell and sending her stomach roiling. She desperately wanted to cover her nose or bury it in the folds of his cravat, but Phee merely squeezed Harrison's arm, holding on as he guided her to the circle of people that included her parents and her brother and sister-in-law, all the while her fan moved at a constant pace, wafting the scent of honeysuckle to her nose.

"Better, dear?" her mother asked, her eyes scanning Phee's face for any sign of distress.

Phee smiled and nodded her head, certain if she opened her mouth, she would be able to taste the hideous odors.

Harrison placed his hand on the small of her back, navigating her toward the side where the wall of windows stood open, the breeze giving her some relief. "You're wrinkling your nose," he said in her ear.

"Thank you," she said.

As the strains of "The Earl of Mansfield" began to play, Harrison held out his hand to her, sending her a wink. "Come along, Lady Everly. I believe this is our dance."

Lady Hunt smiled at them as they made their way to the edge of the line to dance the Scottish reel. Taking their place on either side, Phee looked at Harrison who quickly puckered his lips in a kissing motion before turning his attention back to the music.

Harrison bowed before her and Phee dropped into a curtsey before they picked up the moves of the dance. Eyes glued to Harrison, Phee imagined they were at home in their own ballroom and the noise around her dimmed. Whether it was the cotton in her ears or her imagination, she did not know, but a smile pulled at her lips as she watched her husband skip and hop before her, his eyes bright and his face jovial.

"I had forgotten how physical this dance was," he said as he drew closer, taking her hand as they spun in a circle.

Phee laughed. "It does seem rather excessive, doesn't it?"

Harrison chuckled as they separated and returned to their lines while the other couples danced before them.

In little time, the song ended and Harrison made his way to Phee, his cheeks red and his breath choppy from the exercise. "That was tiring," he said, placing his hand on the small of her back to guide her off the dance floor.

"Poor dear," Phee said, taking his hand and patting it. "Shall we get you home for a nap? I know how cranky the elderly can get when they're tired."

Harrison leaned forward, his hooded gaze no doubt a sign that whatever he planned to say would be rather witty, but whatever he intended was cut short as a shoulder bumped into Phee hard, the shove sending her a few steps forward. Harrison caught her deftly, pulling her to his side as he turned to confront the villain.

"Oh, how clumsy of me," Lady Grayson said as she moved forward flanked by Lady Minerva. "I'm ever so sorry, Lady Everly. I didn't see you there."

"No apology necessary," Phee said as the woman's cloying cinnamon scent nearly overwhelmed her before Harrison stepped in front of her, a scowl on his beautiful face. "I'm sure it was an accident."

"Of course it was," Lady Grayson said. "You looked to have been enjoying yourself on the dance floor." She looked to Harrison, her eyes raking over him. "You have a wonderful dance form, my lord."

"What a tasteless thing to comment on, Lady Grayson," Harrison said, his eyes dark as he pulled Phee close.

Lady Grayson tittered, no doubt unaware of just how unwelcome her advances were. "A mere flirtatious comment, my lord. It doesn't harm anyone. The ton is filled with inappropriate innuendoes and illicit affairs. After all, what is one to expect with marriages such as ours?" she said, looking to Lady Minerva with a catlike smile.

Phee's stomach dropped at Lady Grayson's words.

"Marriages such as ours?" Harrison asked, the words low.

She smiled what she must think a coquettish grin. "Yes, my lord. Marriages like ours. Ones made for the betterment of business or finances." She glanced to Phee. "Or for the procurement of a title for those who would no doubt see the spinster shelf."

Harrison glared fiercely at Lady Grayson. "Surely you're talking about yourself, my lady?"

Lady Grayson frowned. "Don't be silly. I married Sir Grayson because it was what my father wanted and they came to an agreement. Isn't that what all marriages end up being? An agreement?"

Harrison looked at Phee, a softness taking over his face. What Lady Grayson said was true, truer than she would ever know to be. Their marriage had been an agreement. A contract between two people who were desperate to free themselves from the paths they were forced upon, just as Lady Grayson's marriage no doubt was. Unlike theirs, however, their contract had changed, and so had the motive for such a marriage. Now, she could not fathom a day where she did not wake up beside Harrison, her arms wrapped around his waist, her head on his shoulder while Mildred sat contentedly at the bottom of the bed awaiting her breakfast. No, their marriage was not like that of Lady Grayson. It was something more.

Lady Grayson moved closer to Harrison, dropping her voice so only they could hear her. "I know the boredom of such a marriage."

Harrison raised a brow at Lady Grayson, his mouth set in a firm line. Raising his voice, he said, "My wife fills every need I could ever have and unlike your marriage made of contractual agreements, ours was made of love. This beautiful woman chose me to be her husband, and I'll count myself lucky every day that she told the minister yes." Stepping closer to Lady Grayson, his eyes bore into her as he lowered his voice so only they could hear him. "If I ever hear that you've dared to sully my wife's name, I'll ensure that not only your husband, but the ton, learn how truly ill-mannered and disgraceful you are."

Bowing to Lady Grayson, Harrison placed his hand on Phee's lower back and guided her away from the pair.

"That was rude, Harrison," she said.

"Me or her?"

Phee bit her lip to hide her smile. The man was trouble, but she could not contain her glee at knowing that he would gallantly fight for her no matter the monster. She recalled every small moment where he had stood beside her as she pushed herself through a hard encounter. Every moment of interest when he asked after her bees or Mildred. Every gentle touch and soft kiss that was done without thought or request.

Perhaps, for others, such declarations of love would be required as soon as they were felt. Demanded, even, but if she could see the love so clearly, then surely there was no need for pronouncements, no suffering speeches where they confessed their undying love. Perhaps, like they had started, their love was simply an understanding. A gentle acknowledgement between them merely seen through their actions.

But, if he were to ever say the words, even in the simplest of ways, then she would answer him truthfully. She loved him too, ardently, desperately, wholly. She loved Harrison Metcalf, the Earl of Everly. Phoebe Metcalf loved her husband.

CHAPTER TWENTY-SEVEN

WRAPPED IN HER robe and nightgown, Phee sat on Harrison's bed, watching him undress. The actions were provocative, yes, but they were also familiar. There was a comfort between them as he undid the buttons of his waistcoat, his hands moving to untie the intricate knot at his neck, his bare feet sinking into the plush carpet on the bedroom floor. It was all so cozy, these actions reserved for the private moments of one's life.

"Your mother seemed pleased with the turnout this evening," he said, throwing his cravat on a chair that held the remains of his jacket and stockings.

Phee smiled, recalling the joy that had filled her mother's face as she had gazed upon the ballroom, the attendees swarming and swirling in their finest. "I think even given the stress that plagues her year after year, when she sees the results, it merely gives her more reason to host another the next season."

"It's obviously something she enjoys even given the stress it brings. Like you and your bees," he said, unbuttoning the top buttons of his shirtsleeves and rolling up the cuffs as he walked toward her.

Phee nodded. "I hadn't thought of it like that, but you're right. The product of her hard work brings her joy, just like my bees do for me. Or your pottery does for you."

Harrison frowned. "No, my pottery is an absolute mess that brings me little joy and only frustration."

"Why is that?"

"There is nothing I produce that leaves me feeling like my work was worthwhile. Each piece is a disaster. It'd have been better as a hunk of clay than whatever monstrosity I've attempted to form it into."

Phee shook her head, holding out her hand to him. "I don't believe that. I've watched you work on your pieces. You find peace in it even if you do not see it, and your pieces are a sign of growth and change. Of betterment."

He shook his head as he took her hand, one knee coming down to rest on the mattress before her. "It's just a silly hobby. Something to waste my time."

Phee frowned at his words. He gave himself such little credit for the many wonderful attributes he contained. She could not fathom how he did not see what a phenomenal contribution he was, could not see what value he held and brought to those around him. Pulling him to her, Phee rose onto her knees, her free hand sliding up his chest and into his hair. She could spend a lifetime pronouncing the amazing values of her husband, but knew it would fall on deaf ears, so instead, she would show him. Show him just how much he gave to her. Show him just how much value he had.

Lowering his head to hers, Phee touched her lips against his cheek. It was a fairy kiss, so soft she was not certain he would even feel it, but something urged her to be gentle with him. To kiss and caress with such care that he would surely feel her love and devotion.

She trailed kisses along his jaw, across his chin, pouring as much love as she could into each press of her lips. And with each kiss, Harrison squeezed the hand she still held, his breath pausing with each touch before starting again. Phee's heart ached, the overwhelming need to protect this man at all cost firming her resolve and propelling her motions.

"Phoebe," he whispered.

Pulling back, Phee cupped his cheek, meeting his gaze. "Silly man. Do you have any idea how wonderful you are?"

Harrison's brow furrowed and he opened his mouth, no doubt ready to argue with her statement, but before he could utter a word, Phee leaned forward and kissed him, her lips a whisper against his. "You are wonderful and I'll never believe anything else," she said, kissing him once more. "Wonderful and mine."

At her words, Harrison's free hand rose, sliding into her hair as his lips crashed against hers. He was a tempest as his tongue tormented her, sliding and savoring every morsel it found, his hand directing the kiss like a conductor guiding an orchestra to its crescendo. Like a ship at sea, she was tempted to release the wheel, to allow the waves of his want to steer the moment, but something called to her, begged her to love him just as ardently as he did her.

Placing her hand on his chest, Phee gently pushed him away. His brown eyes were hooded as he stared at her, his lips swollen and pink from the pressure of his kiss. With a smile, Phee pulled the hand at her hair away, kissing the palm of his hand before placing it at her breast. His fingers curved around the globe as a soft groan escaped his lips.

Removing her robe, Phee moved closer to Harrison and pulled his shirtsleeves from his trousers, guiding the fabric over his head. Harrison growled as his hand left her breast and Phee could not help but smile at the emphatic response, nor could she help the small giggle as his hand returned to its prize after she freed him from the linen.

As his hand cupped and molded her, tweaking her nipple into a stiff point, Phee's hands fell to the placket of his trousers. There, his length pressed against the fabric, making its presence known, and she rubbed her hand against the front of him. Harrison's breathing grew sharp at her touch, the hand at her breast stilling as if afraid any sudden movement would scare her off. Instead, it only emboldened her further. For weeks, uncertainty had kept her frozen, unsure and timid to explore the dips and lines of his body, but courage surged through her now and she felt emboldened by the power.

Guiding her finger in a swirling motion, Phee drew hearts and stars against the raised flesh like a schoolgirl did in the margins of her notebook. She wrote her name, her title, her birthdate, until the length had become so hard beneath her finger it was more rock than phallus and Harrison's breathing had turned to ragged pants before her. Given his apparent desire it was little wonder that the folds of her sex ached, moisture pooling as she tormented him with her touch.

"Phoebe, I will give you a minute more of your torment before I lay you down and make you pay for this agony," Harrison said, the words a growl as the hand at her breast began its own expedition, sliding its way down her belly as his fingers pulled up the hem of her night-gown.

Phee smiled, even as her breaths came in pants at the motion of his hand. "Agony? Torment? Are you not enjoying yourself?"

Harrison chuckled, the sound devilish. "I will be soon," he said. "Thirty seconds."

Her heart raced as her hand picked up its speed, draw-ing flowers and bees and flightpaths against the fabric covering his length. "Wait. I'm not done."

The hem of her nightgown rested upon his wrist as his hand slipped beneath, his fingers finding where she was warm and wanting. "Yes, you are," he said with a growl as he spread the lips of her sex, the pad of his finger brushing against the aching bud of her sex.

"Harrison," she said, her hand wrapping around his bulge, squeezing and massaging him even as she quivered from his touch.

"Christ." With speed, her pulled the nightgown over her head and laid her down on the bed, his mouth falling to her breast, his devilish tongue making short work of first one and then the other while his fingers returned to her heat, rubbing and circling the place where she needed him most.

A small semblance of sanity remained, nudging her, reminding her that she had started this for him. Fisting his hair, Phee pushed him away. "You. What about you?" she asked, the words escaping her in a breathless gasp.

"This is for me," he said, kissing her lips, her chin, her cheek. "Hearing you scream my name. Feeling you come because of me. Knowing that you're experiencing the best pleasure of your life because I'm giving it to you."

"Harrison…"

"This gives me pleasure, Phoebe." Dropping his head on her chest he traced his lips across her collarbone. "You give me pleasure."

Phee tugged at his hair, forcing him to look at her. "I want to feel you inside me."

His gaze narrowed, his pupils black in the firelight. "You're sure?"

"More than anything," she said, her throat constricting at the look of want in his eyes.

"I'll take care of everything," he said, rising to kiss her on the mouth before leaving the bed to remove his trousers. When he returned, he pulled her into his arms. "You won't feel any pain, I'll make it so good for you."

Phee kissed him attempting to pour every bit of love into the action, every iota of trust into each touch. "I trust you," she said against his lips.

Harrison laughed, the sound harsh. "I'm shaking," he said with a dark chuckle. "You have me shaking, Phoebe."

Pushing his hair out of his eyes, Phee lifted her head, kissing his cheek. "I love you, Harrison."

He froze under her hands, his eyes blinking as he stared at her.

She smiled softly, cupping his cheek. "I love you."

His head dropped, his lips capturing hers in a kiss so tender, so deadly, Phee was not certain she would survive it. Her heart burst with joy as she wrapped her arms around his neck, pulling him closer as he destroyed her senses, his hands pulling her in close until their bodies aligned.

He was everywhere. His mouth on hers, his hands lighting a fire within her that burned so bright it would surely never be put out. All she could do was hang on as he touched and swirled, kissed and rubbed until she writhed beneath him, a touch, a spark, away from combustion.

"Harrison," she said, his name a cry, a plea.

"Yes, love?"

"Please…"

His mouth captured her nipple while his fingers tormented her sex. "Please what?"

"I want you. Please, I want you."

"Since you asked so nicely," he said.

Spreading her legs, he took the place between them, his hard sex nudging against hers, and Phee swiveled her hips, aching to feel his long length inside her. Instead of pushing it in, however, Harrison circled the bulbous head around the outside of her opening, the movement, combined with his nimble fingers playing at the bud at the top of her sex, took little to bring about her pleasure. Wave after wave of warmth flew through her as her body convulsed, but Harrison merely continued his ministrations, ensuring that every drop of pleasure was pulled from her.

As she began to settle, Harrison kissed her chest, the head of his penis pressing against the opening of her core while his hand circled the hills and valleys of her quim. "Again," he said.

Shaking her head, Phee bit her lip as her body tingled, her hips rising and falling against the pressure at her center. "It's too much."

Harrison kissed his way to her neck, his tongue swirling at the tender spot where it connected to her shoulder. "Take me inside you and come on my cock, Phoebe. Squeeze me until I see stars." His teeth pulled at the lobe of her ear as his length pressed inside her, stretching her aching core. "Love me, Phoebe."

Phee wrapped her leg around his hip and undulated, taking him deep inside her. There was no pain as she stretched to accommodate his length, only a sense of fulness, as if a piece of her that had been missing was finally returned.

"Sweet Christ," Harrison whispered in her ear, his body like stone beneath her hands. "So good, love. You feel so good."

Pushing onto his forearms, he kissed her face, his stubble scratchy against her skin. "All right?" he asked, the words soft.

Phee nodded, kissing the underside of his chin.

With a piston like motion of his hips, Harrison withdrew his cock from her core before pushing himself back into her depths, the motion sending Phee's eyes closed as the intoxicating feel of him filled her. "Good?" he asked.

"Yes," she said, the word a moan as his hips pistoled forward, his cock strumming against a place that felt like heaven. "Don't stop."

"Never," he said against her ear as he rocked against her, the fire he had started rekindling with ease at the motions.

Lifting her hips, Phee moved with him, her body accepting him with each thrust of his cock. Taking her hands in his, Harrison placed them above her head, his fingers lacing with hers as his mouth crashed down on hers, his tongue tangling with hers, luring her to pleasure again as his sex took her to new heights.

Fire pooled in her belly as her climax built and Phee clung to Harrison, his sturdy presence reassuring as she was thrown from the cliff once more, her body convulsing beneath his. With a groan, Harrison pulled himself from her and thrust once, twice against her quim before streams of seed spilled on her stomach.

Phee held onto him as he shook in her arms, her body pulsating as she came down from her climb. When he finally pulled back to look at her, she smiled at him, eliciting a chuckle to fall from his lips.

"You're amazing," he said, kissing her lips before pushing himself off of her. He moved across the room and cleaned himself with a cloth and water from the washstand before returning to the bed and wiping down her stomach and thighs. Throwing the rag to the floor, Harrison climbed back up into the bed, wrapping his arms around Phee and pulling her into his chest before covering them both with the coverlet.

"Is that what it will always be like?" she asked, her fingers dancing along the skin of his chest.

He shrugged, kissing the top of her head. "Maybe. I don't know."

"I guess we've got forever to find out," she said, wrapping her arm around his waist and wiggling her head against his shoulder. With a sigh, she closed her eyes. "I love you, Harrison."

He tensed against her before saying, "I love you, too."

As Phee drifted off to sleep, a notion niggled at her, pleading for her to notice that even as he said the words back to her, there was a sense of reservation in his tone. How odd.

CHAPTER TWENTY-EIGHT

"MY LADY," STERNS said from the doorway of the sitting room. "The Marchioness of Greenwood is here. I've placed her in the front parlor."

Phee's brow furrowed at the name. The widow of the former earl had been rumored to be close with Harrison, but when she failed to make it to the wedding, Phee wondered at her absence.

"Very good," she said. "Please send tea and refreshments."

"Yes, my lady," Sterns said.

Standing, Phee brushed at her blush skirts. The garments, while not out of style, were a season or two old. Shrugging, she decided to forgo changing since she planned to return to the hives later that afternoon.

With a deep breath, Phee entered the sitting room where Margaret Ludlow, the Marchioness of Greenwood, sat, her brown hair in a simple chignon and her plum day dress fitting her lush figure with gracefulness.

Phee curtsied. "Lady Greenwood, it is lovely to finally make your acquaintance."

Lady Greenwood stood, and hurried to Phee, taking her hands in her own and squeezing them as one would an old friend. "Forget decorum, we're family. It's so lovely to finally meet you, Phoebe."

Phee smiled. "Please, call me Phee.

"Only if you promise to call me Meg," Lady Greenwood said.

"It's lovely to meet you, Meg," Phee said, motioning for her to sit. "I've called for some refreshments."

"That sounds wonderful," Meg said, setting aside her reticule and taking off her gloves. "I'm so sorry I wasn't able to make it to the nuptials. We had a bit of an emergency at Baron and given how fast you and Harry wed, I just knew that there would be a much better time to finally meet you."

"Harry?" Phee asked.

Meg looked at her, her brow furrowed over her brown gaze. "Harry? Lord Harrison?"

Phee smiled, a soft chuckle escaping. "I didn't know he had a nickname."

Meg smiled, nodding. "I've called him Harry for as long as I've known him."

"Does he like it?"

Meg blinked at her. "You know, I've never asked him."

It was such a simple question and yet the surprise on Meg's face as she answered left Phee biting her lip. Why had he never been asked what he wanted to be called? Why had he asked Phee to call him Harrison, but said nothing regarding Meg's nickname? It was as if they were speaking of two different people, and Phee's throat knotted at the notion that perhaps she did not know her husband at all.

Meg waved off the topic. "Enough about Harry, tell me about you. When he wrote to say he was marrying quickly I had to assume it was for love. Harry never does anything irrationally."

Phee forced a smile to her lips even as her heart skipped at Meg's question. "We met and simply could not imagine a better union than one with each other," she said. Not a lie, but not the truth. "He's a phenomenal man. I'm so lucky to have found him."

Meg nodded. "That sounds like Harry. He's always so cooperative. I remember when I was restoring Baron, he would send letter after letter asking what he could do to help. He's always been so ready to care for others."

Phee smiled. "I'm terribly sorry, but you've mentioned Baron several times and I'm not sure I know what it is."

Meg smacked her forehead with her hand. "What a dolt I am. I'm so sorry. Baron is my home. It's a manor in Brighton that I've turned into a sort of home for wayward souls."

Phee leaned closer. "Really?"

Meg nodded. "Yes. We've a Romani encampment that has settled in the sheep pasture, and my gardener and his family live in a cottage not far from the manor. There's a community garden and a stable as well."

"How wonderful," Phee said. "You mentioned an emergency? I do hope everything is all right?"

Meg smiled. "Yes. We had a young woman who was rather far along in her pregnancy arrive. Her parents wanted to send her to a nunnery to have the baby, but she insisted upon raising it herself so she came to Baron. It just happened that when she arrived, she went into labor which made for a rather eventful night for us all."

"Goodness! It sounds as though things are quite a

commotion there."

"Yes, but I love it."

A knock at the door indicated that a maid had arrived with refreshments. Once the items were delivered and they both had a cup of tea, Phee turned her attention back to Meg. "Does Baron have bee hives? Harrison just took me to the estate in Dorset and they had four hives on the property and used the wax and honey for all sorts of purposes."

"I hadn't thought of hives. How ingenious," Meg said. "We don't have any, and in truth, I wouldn't even know where to start."

"Starting isn't very hard once you establish the hives," Phee said, sipping at her tea.

"Do you know a lot about bees?"

Phee nodded. "I do. I have two hives out back and just acquired a cat to help with the rat problem." She laughed softly. "Although I'm afraid she's more of a pet than a worker."

With a laugh, Meg set down her teacup. "How wonderful. I did not think Harry was a fan of bugs or cats, but I'm not surprised he gave such permission given how much he obviously adores you."

Phee set her cup in her saucer, the porcelain clinking as she stared at it. "I wasn't aware he disliked them." Her mind replayed images of him with Mildred, holding her as one did a child. How he said he had longed for a dog when he was a boy. None of those seemed in line with the man Meg was describing.

Meg set her cup on the low table then placed her hand on Phee's arm. "I wouldn't say dislike, just neutral. I'm so sorry if I said something I shouldn't have."

Phee forced a smile to her lips and turned back to Meg. "Not at all. It seems we're still learning about one another."

"I'm afraid that will never stop no matter how long you are married."

"Truly?"

With a smile, Meg nodded and picked back up her tea. "Oliver, my husband, is so multifaceted I'm not sure I'll ever learn all of his quirks. He's like one of those telescopes with the broken glass at the end, each time you turn it there's a brand-new picture."

"A kaleidoscope."

Meg nodded. "Exactly." Taking a sip of tea, Meg lowered her cup, her brow furrowed. "Now that I think on it, having hives would be extremely beneficial to Baron." She placed her cup in its saucer and set it back on the table before reaching for her reticule and removing a small notebook and pencil. "You said the estate in Dorset used the wax and the honey for the property?"

"Yes. The beekeeper, Mr. Cole, said he renders the old wax and uses it to make candles for the manor and that the housekeeper uses some of the renderings to create furniture polish and other cleaning items. The honey that isn't used by the bees can easily be harvested and used for so many things in the kitchen."

Meg scribbled furiously on the notepad, flipping page after page as she filled it with notes. "And you said you know how to start hives?" Meg asked.

Phee pursed her lips. "I've had some luck with the ones here, yes, but I don't know how helpful I'll be in theory elsewhere."

Meg waved her statement off. "Nonsense. If you've accomplished it here, you no doubt can accomplish the same feat anywhere. You're obviously knowledgeable and talented in this field, far more so than someone like me." She set down the pad and paper and looked at Phee before smiling. "Would you have any interest in coming to Baron to help me set up hives for the estate?"

"What?"

"That is, if Harry can spare you." She laughed. "What am I talking about? You both should come to Baron. I know Oliver would love the additional set of hands, and we can make a party of it. Work during the day and then have dinner and socializing at night. It'll be like a holiday."

Phee smiled at Meg even as her head shouted that it was new. It was different. A home full of people she did not know and a setting she had never been in. Would the rules of polite society pertain at Baron as they did in the social setting? And what of Mildred? The sweet dear had become a sort of comfort, a fluffy and persistent reminder to remain focused on the things she knew to do.

"I'll have to talk with Harrison, but I don't see any reason we should not be able to attend," Phee said.

"Wonderful!" Meg said, clapping her hands together.

"Phoebe, Sterns said we have company," Harrison said as he walked into the parlor, his steps slowing to a sudden stop when he spotted Meg.

"Harry!" Meg said, jumping to her feet and hurrying to him where she wrapped him in an effusive hug.

The look of shock on Harrison's face quickly disappeared and a graceful smile took over as he returned her hug. "Hello, Meg" he said. "You look well."

"I am," Meg said. "I was just talking with your wonderful wife and telling her how sorry Oliver and I were to not make it to the wedding."

"You're a newlywed, Meg, it's understandable."

Meg shook her head. "Nonsense." She pulled back to look at him. "But look at you, you're married. I never thought I'd see the day."

Harrison laughed, an odd chuckling sound that was nothing like his true laugh. "After meeting Phee, I just couldn't help myself." He looked at her, the fake smile peculiar on his face. "Isn't that right, my lady?"

"Yes," Phee said.

Harrison looked at Meg. "I hate to cut this short but I have an appointment Is must get to which is why I was searching for the countess."

Meg placed her hand on her chest. "Blast. I'll leave you both to it then." Picking up her reticule from the couch, Meg hugged Phee, her hands clasping Phee's in a warm embrace. "Don't forget to tell Harry about our plans. I can't wait to show you both Baron. We'll have dinner soon and make all the plans."

Phee nodded, squeezing Meg's hands in return. "I can't wait."

With a quick kiss to Harrison's cheek, Meg departed, and Phee watched the mask slip from Harrison's face, the faux smile evaporating as he turned to look at her.

"Our trip to Baron?" he asked.

Phee nodded, uncertain of Harrison's change in demeanor. "She's asked for my help in setting up hives for

Baron and thought it would make a lovely holiday if we both went."

"A holiday?"

"Yes." Wringing her hands, Phee stepped closer to Harrison, her eyes scanning his face. "She said her husband would love another set of hands and we'd have dinner parties at night."

Harrison swallowed before lifting his hand to cup her cheek. "That's–that's a lot."

"I want to help, especially because she is your friend, but a trip to Brighton is..." Phee paused, closing her eyes as she rested her cheek against his hand. "I've never been to Brighton."

"Neither have I," he said. "It could be romantic, the two of us in Brighton together for the first time. We could go on walks in the afternoon, maybe explore the town?"

"It's new."

"It is." He tipped her chin up and Phee opened her eyes to look at him. "The decision is yours. I want to do what you want to do."

Nodding her head in determination, Phee firmed her brow. "It's just like Dorset. I've done this before."

He smiled. "You have."

"Can we bring Mildred?"

"I'm sure there won't be a problem in doing so. Can't have the little mite angry with us."

Phee nodded, a soft smile pulling at her lips. "Then it's settled. I'll send a message to Meg and let her know that we'd be happy to join them at Baron."

Harrison's smile was tight as he looked at her. Stepping closer, Phee set her hand on his forearm. "What's wrong?" she asked.

He shook his head. "Just making a list of what will need to be done for the trip." Kissing her forehead, he said, "I've some estate matters to look at. I'll see you for dinner?"

Without waiting for her reply, Harrison left the parlor. Phee's brow furrowed as she watched him depart, his change in demeanor its familiar peculiarity.

With a sigh and a troubled heart, Phee walked the hallway to the garden, her mind twisting and turning as she analyzed her husband's odd mood. She would not let it suffocate the happiness they had just started to build with one another. After all, a queen never loses her composure, not even when the hive is in danger, for a hive without a queen will fail.

CHAPTER TWENTY-NINE

THEY HAD DEPARTED for Baron the following week in the early hours of the morning, arriving in the small town of Woodingdean after a three-day journey. Mildred, not one to hide her disdain, had become phenomenally vocal during the hours that she was awake, her displeasure at the travel arrangements obvious to everyone including the horses. It was as if she could sense that their destination was going to be no doubt uncomfortable in its unfamiliarity and she felt the need to ensure that her disapproval was heard. Averndale, having joined their traveling caravan as he had promised Oliver he would come and see the estate, had threatened to throw Mildred from the carriage on more than one occasion.

As much as Harrison loved the little mite, he could relate.

After three weeks of acclimating to Baron and its small passel of guests, Phoebe had thrown herself into her work, determined to have thriving hives at the manor that would be capable of actively providing for the visitors that passed through its doors. From the early hours of the morning until dinner time, Phoebe was out at the old gamekeeper hut with Meg, directing which field to clear and what walls to build. Where the tables were to be laid out for the hives, or in the greenhouse with Oliver Ludlow, Meg's husband, discussing the type of vegetation that should be placed around the area.

Now that the primary parent was no longer present, Mildred was forced to settle in with Harrison who she viewed as the interloper, and while her presence was comforting during the day, it hurt his pride to know he was second place for her affection.

In the morning, the room would be empty of Phoebe's presence, the only remanence that she had been there the smell of her on the sheets. Mildred would curl into a ball on her pillow, surrounding herself in the honeysuckle scent.

The action had triggered a memory the very first night, him as a young boy sneaking into his mother's room and falling asleep on her bed as he waited for her to return from her night's events, her lilac perfume filling the air, soothing whatever nightmare had woken him. He had woken the next morning in his bed and had been scolded firmly by his nurse. He had never seen his mother, not even for a reprimand on escaping the nursery. She merely pretended it never happened just as she pretended he did not exist.

Perhaps that was the start of his demise, the learned notion that he mattered very little to the people he cared for most. Good or bad, he could do nothing to elicit a response. Nothing to earn him the affection he so greatly desired. It was not until his uncle had not produced an heir that he began to hold value to his mother, and only as it pertained to the title. Only then did she become focused on his mannerisms, mostly the bad ones.

She had become determined he resemble a noble peer

of the realm, requiring weekly updates from his tutors, commenting on his posture, his smile, his laugh. And he had become determined to pass every one of her tests. To prove that he held value. That he was worthy of her love. But each test led to new ones, each focused on what a disappointment he was in her eyes. With each criticism she had molded him like clay until he was no longer able to recognize himself.

It had not been until Eton that he had finally found himself once more.

With Averndale he had found such ease as himself. No weekly check-ins. No criticisms. Just two boys gadding about, being lads with little mind for what was required for their future. It was the first time that he begun to understand that there was something terribly isolating about the way he had been raised and that love was not meant to be a scale. But habits are hard to break when they have been ingrained in you for that long.

It took very little for him to revert back when he had returned home. Back in place was the practiced smile, the stiff posture. The inauthentic laugh as he met with his uncle and other peers, danced with debutants and charmed matrons. A mask was in place that he could not seem to remove, glued to his face no matter the hour of the day, and even if he wanted to, he could not find the means to take it off. And then he met Meg.

In her he saw his reflection, someone required to fit into a mold that did not fit. It mattered little that she was older than him and mattered not at all that she was married to his uncle. She was the same as him, her struggle just as demeaning and isolating as his own. And in that similarity, he found love. Surely just like him, she wore a mask, and he found comfort in that.

When his uncle passed and Meg was finally free, instead of remaining in that mask, however, she had ripped it off and ran, and Harrison, with all his knowledge of even tallies and fear of being a disappointment, could not follow. What would the ton think if the newly appointed earl disappeared into the countryside after his dead uncle's wife, giving little care for the management of the title? It was safer to stand on the side, ready if Meg ever said she needed him. But she never did. Instead, she built Baron off her own merit and found the love of someone willing to take the risk because it meant he would be with her. And Harrison had simply watched.

Watched as they were married. Watched as the ton came to adore the new Earl of Everly without ever really knowing him. Watched as he was alone again in a big house with his mask firmly in place.

And then Phoebe had arrived with her bees and her kitten and her dislike for blueberries and love for chocolate. And even with the darn mask still on she somehow saw him. Saw every piece of him that was broken and damaged and instead of criticizing, instead of dismissing, loved him because of it. And while part of him longed to lean into the love that she offered, another part, the scared little boy part, wondered when it would all change. Wondered when the other shoe would drop and she would leave him just like everyone else had.

What if she came to hate him? What if his laugh was grating and his smile was crooked? What if his hobbies irritated her or she came to hate playing games with him each night? What if she took her love away because he did something wrong?

No, he thought, as he fluffed the pillow beneath his head, releasing her honey scent into the air. No, it was better that he just try to be the best version of himself, that he do everything in his power to earn her love. Should she ever leave he was quite certain he would not overcome it.

He chuckled, the sound dark.

Who was he kidding? He was barely surviving things now.

When the sun rose in the sky, Harrison sat tired eyed, staring out the window. Mildred slept peacefully at his side, her soft snores soothing but doing very little to lull him to sleep.

He wanted to be with Phoebe, but what if she left him as well?

Attempting to not awaken the cat, Harrison crawled from the bed and went into the bathing room. After a quick scrub of his face, his growth scratching the palms of his hands, he left the room. Notifying a waiting footman that Mildred would need her breakfast, Harrison took his leave of the manor.

Woodingdean was quiet in the early hours, its residents slowly wakening to begin their daily routines, the bustle of the manor not yet happening. It should have been settling, the lack of noise, but it merely gave his mind more ability to ruminate. Even the chirping birds in the trees did little to quiet his meandering thoughts.

"Everly," a voice said as a large body sidled up beside him.

Harrison scowled. "Averndale."

"Early morning exercise?" Averndale asked, his cravat untied and his jacket unbuttoned. The man wreaked of alcohol and cigar smoke, but the jaunty smile on his lips said that he had enjoyed wherever he was returning from.

"It's reportedly highly recommended. You?"

Averndale raised a brow at him. "I'm was on my way back to the manor." Averndale continued to walk beside him, the scrape of his sword cane irritating. "Are we to continue in silence or shall we discuss what has you out exercising at such an ungodly hour?"

Harrison scowled. "You're more than welcome to leave at any time."

"Yes, but I have a feeling that I might enjoy whatever it is that has caused such disruption," Averndale said with a smile. "You aren't normally one for walking about. Decidedly more so since you've taken a wife."

With a sigh, Harrison looked at the ground. "That's the problem."

"Your wife?"

"Yes," Harrison said. "No. Maybe I'm the problem."

"Why?" Averndale asked.

"I love her, and she loves me. It should be simple, just two people who care for one another, but I'm terrified it's not that at all. One part of me knows that our love is good, healthy even, but another part of me worries that I'm not good enough. That I'll displease her. That she'll leave."

Averndale stopped, his hand pulling at Harrison's arm. "Tell me you're joking."

Harrison groaned, his hand running through his hair.

"Shit," Averndale said, shaking his head. "You're a

ninny."

With a frown, Harrison turned and started his walk once more. Averndale kept pace beside him as he picked up speed. "How? My mother required perfection, my uncle could barely stand me. Even with Meg I tried to be perfect, tried to please her in any way she wanted, and she left me and fell in love with another man."

"None of those relationships were healthy," Averndale said, his breathing harsh.

"What on earth are you talking about?"

"Every relationship you just used as an example isn't how love is supposed to be. Love is not a scale, Everly. There isn't a balance that needs to be evened out or sacrifices you are forced to make."

Harrison pulled to a stop and Averndale followed suit, folding in half and resting his hands on his knees as he caught his breath.

"What do you mean?" Harrison asked.

"I mean," Averndale said between breaths, "that when you love someone you are thoughtful and supportive and caring because you love them. Not because you have to be to make them love you in return."

"I don't–I don't deserve to be loved like that."

Averndale shook his head and took a deep breath. "Why on earth do you think that?"

Harrison shrugged. "I'm not enough. I'm flawed."

"So is she."

"Don't you dare—"

Averndale held up a hand, stopping his words. "Keep your self-righteous indignation quiet for a moment. She is flawed too. She is obsessed with bees, hates balls for whatever reason. Dislikes blueberries, which in my opinion is egregious, and yet you still love her. Would you remove your love because of those things?"

Harrison's brow furrowed. "Of course not."

"Then why do you think the rules don't apply to you?"

"I—"

Shaking his head, Averndale adjusted his waistcoat. "We live in a world where everything we do is judged and evaluated, so I've tried to understand why you adopted this persona of the affable earl, but the people who really know you and really care about you don't give a fig that you're flawed, don't care about your imperfections. We love you just the same." With a sad smile, Averndale looked at him. "Don't you think it's time you start loving yourself that way?"

The words were stiff, a punch to the gut and a blow to the head, which would take any man down but for Harrison it was as if some piece had shaken free. Yet, the quick grip of a fist around his throat at what he may have left unsaid stole the brilliance of the moment.

"Fuck."

Averndale smiled, his head crooking to one side. "Absolutely right." With a nod, he turned around and walked back toward the manor. "Best of luck in finding your wife. Do let me know when you are planning to return to London for I should very much like to join you. Something about this place has become rather disagreeable with my constitution."

CHAPTER THIRTY

THUNDER CRASHED SHAKING the panes of the windows. Meg called the place Bitch Manor, glee surrounding the words each time she said it, but Phee could not fathom calling such a wonderful place such a horrid name. Baron was the epitome of a magical place one found in storybooks, the warm interior as welcoming as a small cottage in the woods while the exterior looked as if nymphs and fairies lingered in the garden which grew lush with vegetation. Bird baths dotted the landscape as did benches and footpaths turning each exploration into its own adventure.

It was a place of mythical proportions, but no matter how many trails she could walk nor books she read on cozy arm chairs and sofas, Phee missed her home. She missed spending her days with Mildred and the bees, and she missed the quiet nights alone with her husband.

Her sleep had become atrocious as she tossed and turned each night, the bed unfamiliar and uncomfortable while her mind rambled over her husband's continuingly odd behavior. As soon as they had departed the carriage in Woodingdean, her husband's sociable smile had returned to his face like a jester's mask, his faux joy beginning to grate on her. It was as if a lever had been pulled into place forcing him to step back into the role of Lord Everly, leaving Harrison Metcalf, the man she loved, well behind.

Instead of filling her days troubled with her husband's moods, Phee threw herself into work at the Baron estate. The old gamekeeper's cottage that was still in good shape sat beside an old grazing field on the south end of the property which would work perfectly for housing several hives as well as a beekeeper.

As Meg had yet to find one suitable for the property, Phee had taken it upon herself to fill the vacant position, moving her books and journals to the cottage for the time being to be closer to the hives during the day. At night, she returned to Baron for dinner with Harrison, thankfully more comfortable with the intimate setting of Meg's dinner guests as compared to the atrocities of events in London.

Currently, the guests of Baron comprised of a young woman of nobility named Felicia who was unwed and pregnant, a second son who had no interest in the church or military and dreamed instead of painting, and Mr. Howell and his young ward, Felix. They formed a motley crew, the lot of them, with Meg and Oliver as their fearless leaders. It mattered not their backgrounds or trials of life, only the friendship they had found in the walls of Baron.

As the rain poured outside the groundskeeper's cottage, Phee sat at the small desk near the window, her books and journal laid out before her. A fire roared in the hearth, thankfully driving away the chill of the unexpected morning storm, but she wished she had asked Felix to bring her a pot of tea. Instead, like a dolt, she had dismissed the child so he could return to the stables, certain he would be less bored there than with her while she gallivanted around the grounds.

When the dark clouds had begun to rumble in the sky, Phee chose to make her way to the cottage thinking it would simply be a storm that passed swiftly, but after what had to be nearly an hour, she had begun to think it would have been a better idea to have returned to the manor. Now, she was either trapped in the cottage until the torrent cleared or forced to make a run for the manor and become soaked in the process. Neither sounded like an acceptable choice.

Thunder clapped once more, and Phee looked nervously to the fire as it flickered in the hearth. She had never had to build one and while she had watched people light the thing, she was not certain she could direct anyone on how to do it properly. If the blasted thing went out, she would have no choice but to run into the downpour for fear of freezing. Eyes pinned to the fire, Phee cared very little when she heard a pounding at the door to the cottage. Surely, no one would be out in this torrent and the wind had simply blown something against the door and it would roll away soon. When the knocking sounded again, she sighed. Perhaps Harrison had sent a footman to help retrieve her?

Yet, when she opened the door, she saw none other than her husband on the other side, soaked from head to toe.

"Have you gone mad?" she asked, reaching for his sleeve and pulling him inside, closing the door with a harsh crash behind him. "What on earth could you have been thinking going out in this?"

"I was thinking," Harrison said as he shivered, "that my wife was trapped in the gamekeeper's cottage and that I had to get to her as quickly as possible."

Phee rushed to the closet that held the linens for the bed as well as some towels. Thrusting one at Harrison, she threw the other over his head and stood on her tiptoes as she rubbed the cloth back and forth over his hair. Cold water seeped into the towel in her hands but she continued to dry his hair and face as he shivered beneath her.

"Phoebe," he said, the words muffled by the towel.

Phee ignored him and dropped the towel in her hands to the floor before snatching the one he held. "You're completely soaked through. I helped Meg clear out the house and clean it so all the clothes that were left have been handed off to Flora for mending so we can give them to guests in need."

"Phoebe."

"Perhaps you can stay warm in the quilt while we wait for the fire to dry your things," she said, the words less a question and more her thinking aloud.

"Phoebe Metcalf, will you stop a moment?" Harrison asked, throwing the final towel aside and cupping her cheek. His hands were icy against her skin and she raised her own, covering it, rubbing at the skin to put some warmth back into him.

"You're in sopping wet clothes in the cold," she said.

"Does that worry you?"

"Yes."

"If I change out of them and put on the quilt will that make you feel better?" he asked, already removing his jacket.

"Yes." Going to the bed, Phee removed the quilt that lay draped over the top, bringing it back to Harrison who stood naked in front of the fireplace, his clothing laid out to dry. Swallowing at the sight of him, Phee took a deep breath, then walked to him, handing him the blanket. Once the quilt was wrapped around him and they were settled before the fire, he raised a brow at her.

"You were saying?" she said.

"I was saying that my wife was in this cottage in a thunderstorm and I had to get to her," he said, turning toward her.

"Why?"

With a smile that did not fully stretch across his mouth, he sighed. "Because I realized that I've been a bit of a dunce as of late. And when you come to understand that someone loves you as entirely yourself, you realize you have to tell them as quickly as possible, no matter the weather."

"Someone who loves you?" she asked. "Harrison, what do you mean? Of course I love you."

He nodded. "We'll get to that part in a second, but first, I need to apologize." Harrison rose onto his knees, the worn quilt wrapped around his shoulders like a knight. "I know that I've been guarded since we've come here and I'm sorry. I've let my fears guide my decisions and, in the process, I might have marred what is without a doubt the greatest love of my life. Because it is, and you are, the greatest love of my life. And I was afraid I'd ruin it.

"When I was younger, I learned quickly that you had to be valuable for someone to love you. My mother cared very little for me until I became the heir, and even then, her love came with conditions. I changed my posture, my smile, the way I talked and walked, all with the hopes that in doing so, I would finally please her. That she would finally love me. For the longest time, I thought that if I were anything less than perfect to everyone else that their love would be taken away from me, and in doing so, I lost myself in their expectations of me. As long as they were pleased with me that was all that mattered. And when you've played by a specific set of rules for such a long period of time it becomes really hard to change them. And then you came into my life.

"You are so unabashedly yourself, aware of things others may see as flaws but to you they're just facets of your personality. You know who you are, Phoebe. You like who you are." He smiled. "I like who you are. But your freeness is something I've never been able to do. You said you loved me with ease, as if it were a fact found in a history book, and it scared me because love has always had a price, and I didn't want to let you down. I didn't want to lose you. But I realized, after having it pointed out rather succinctly to me, that I would never expect you to be perfect to be allowed my love because that isn't love. And if I would never ask you to do something like that, I shouldn't expect it of myself.

"I'm new at this, but I'm trying. I know what I need to do to be a good partner for you and I promise that in those times where old habits creep up, I will work to implement what I know to be true. I know that I deserve to be loved for who I am, warts and all." He cupped her face, his hands now warm, "And I also know that I love you. That your love is a gift that I don't have to be perfect to receive, and thank you for loving me anyway."

"I don't plan on going anywhere anytime soon so you'll have a lot of time to practice," Phee said, wrapping her arms around his waist over the quilt. "I love you, Harrison."

"I love you, Phoebe," he said, kissing her forehead, her cheek. "I should have shouted it from the top of the Tower of London that I love Phoebe Metcalf and that she loves me."

Phee groaned. "Thank heavens you didn't. I would have hated the attention."

Harrison smiled, kissing her lips. "Then I shall tell you. Every day. Every hour until the end of time. I love you, Phoebe. I love our life and our home and our kitten—"

"Silly man," she said kissing his mouth.

"I love you, Phoebe," he said, the words soft against her lips.

Pushing the quilt from his shoulders revealing all of his brilliance, Phee ran her fingers through his hair, the strands still damp from the rain. The storm showed little sign of slowing but she had a couple activities in mind that would keep them busy. "I love you."

CHAPTER THIRTY-ONE

October, 1822
One month later
London

A LETTER FROM Meg addressed to the both of them arrived with the post, and Harrison wasted little time searching out his wife so they could read it together. She no doubt was checking on her bees, ensuring that the hives were thriving during the cold that had swiftly fallen over London.

She had discussed nothing but a process called "dead out" for the past week after the temperatures had dropped rather suddenly, worried that the hives would not have enough honey to survive and so she had taken it upon herself to not only check on them daily but to feed them crushed sugar cubes to ensure there was enough food for the lot of them. And he had taken it upon himself to ensure that while she worried about her bees that she was taken care of, bringing her inside to eat and warm by the fire with some tea and accompanying her in the evenings to check on the hives so she could go to bed without worry.

In the garden, his wife stood with a heavy coat around her as she placed small dishes of sugar water around a hive, her gloves missing from her fingers, the warm air of her breath escaping in puffs as it met the slight chill of the London air.

"You promised you would wear the gloves," he said, coming up beside her and taking her hands in his, rubbing some warmth into the skin.

"It's harder to do things with them on," she said, moving closer to him and pressing her cold nose to the side of his neck. She was just like her bees, busy and hard at work but drawn to any heat source provided.

"We have a letter from Meg." Tucking her hands into the inside of his coat, Harrison wrapped his arms around her, pulling her closer to warm her up further. "Let's head inside to the library. I'll have some tea brought in and we'll read it together."

"The hives—"

He kissed the top of her head. "You have fed them all?"

"Yes," she said.

"And you've checked on all of them?"

"Yes, but—"

"Then you require a reprieve. We'll return this afternoon and check on them again, if you'd like."

With a sigh, Phoebe nodded and Harrison led her inside, his arms still wrapped around her, determined to work some warmth back into her.

"I'm worried they'll die," she said as they entered the library and he directed her toward the fire.

"I know," Harrison said. "You have taken phenomenal care of them, love, but there is only so much you can control. As horrible as it is, sometimes nature is unfair even when we try our best."

Phoebe's lips twisted, but she nodded, the battle going on in her head so obvious that it made him smile.

After requesting tea and something to nibble on from a footman, Harrison grabbed a blanket from the back of the sofa and brought it to Phoebe, wrapping it around her shoulders. "Want to read the letter?" he asked, kissing her neck. "I'm sure Meg has some wonderful gossip about Averndale."

Phoebe nodded and followed him to the sofa. "I can't believe he decided to stay in Woodingdean. He was in such a rush to leave. I wonder what changed."

"Your guess is as good as mine. I imagine he's trying Oliver's patience as there is surely no way he has taken it upon himself to work the manor."

"Perhaps her note says he headed back to London?"

Harrison smiled. "Let's find out."

Breaking the seal, Harrison unfolded the letter.

Dearest Harry and Phee,

I'm so happy to hear that you made it back safely and that your trip was simple. I detest riding in a carriage very much, so I'm glad you were able to occupy yourselves during the long journey.

Harrison looked at Phoebe and chuckled at the smile that had captured her lips. "It would seem that Meg might not partake in the same activities that we do during our long journeys."

Phoebe laughed, pushing at his shoulders. "Hush. Everyone is different." Kissing his cheek, she rested her head on his shoulder. "Keep reading."

The new beekeeper is working out wonderfully,

I'm so glad your beekeeper at the Dorset estate recommended him. He has said he isn't too concerned with dead out but he agrees that your notion of feeding them sugar granules is a good idea. As hard as these things are, sometimes we have to let nature take its course.

Harrison raised a brow at Phoebe who merely stuck her tongue out at him.

Averndale has been such a surprising help around the manor and at the inn. He's taken up helping Marty at the inn every night which has given me more time to help at the manor. Marty seems rather neutral of him which is the strangest thing as I've never seen her unaffected by anyone, but only time will tell on how they decide to reach some sort of companionship. Oliver was certain he was going to be more of a nuisance than help but he's been happily surprised at the change he is seeing in Averndale. There has been several mornings the past week that Averndale did not join us for breakfast and we learned he had already left the manor to help Marty at the inn. Is it possible our friend is becoming a saint?

"Averndale is helping at the inn?" Phoebe asked, pulling her head from his shoulder to look at him.

"That's what she says. Surely, she has to be joking?" Harrison reread the paragraph, his brow furrowing. "He's waking before them and going to the inn to help with the guests? Has he been possessed? Did he injure his head and no one noticed?"

Phoebe shrugged. "Maybe he's found something worth enjoying? Who's to say why people change."

"I'm not sure a trip to the doctor is unnecessary."

"We'll see," Phoebe said.

I'm so glad we were able to spend a month together but hope that your next visit will be for a bit longer. It was like having family to visit and I don't think I realized how nice that was. We'll need to plan our next gathering soon. Stay warm and healthy during this winter and we look forward to hearing from you both soon.

All our love,
Meg and Oliver

Ps. Harry – Perhaps you should write Averndale just to be sure all is well. Oliver thinks he may have suffered an injury that we are unaware of.

"I knew there was a reason I liked the man," Harrison said with a chuckle.

Phoebe shook her head. "Something is seriously wrong with the both of you, assuming that Averndale is injured as the only probable cause to why he's acting the way he is."

"When you've known Averndale as long as we have you begin to learn that only an act of God would cause him to make such drastic changes." Folding up the letter, Harrison set it on the low table. "I'll write to him this evening just to be sure all is well. Ask him a couple of questions to ensure he hasn't been swapped out with some changeling during one of his trips through the woods."

"Leave the man alone," Phoebe said, leaning back

against the sofa. "Perhaps he's fallen in love with someone at the inn?"

Harrison shook his head. "No, that can't be it. Lust would make more sense." Shrugging, he sat back as well and pulled her into his arms, warmth finally apparent in her cheeks. "It's only a matter of time until whatever caused this change leaves him bored and he returns to London."

"We'll see."

That night, Harrison slipped from the bed where Phoebe and Mildred slept peacefully, his mind playing its typical game of overcompensation. Something about Meg's letter had wiggled free a small shred of worry that perhaps he could be doing more to help his friends and to help Phoebe. Instead of allowing the impulse to take hold, as he used to do, he headed to the conservatory, hoping that the spinning of the wheel and the soft clay in his hands would work out whatever criticism he seemed to have found.

That was how Phoebe found him, the soft *woosh* of the wheel masking her steps as she padded into the room, her hair in a braid down her back, a plum wrapper pulled over her nightgown, its presence unnecessary in the warm room. "Harrison?" she said softly.

Looking up at her, he smiled. Her eyes were soft from sleep, her hair in slight disarray, and there was an imprint on her cheek from her pillow, but it mattered not at all, for she was still utterly stunning.

Dipping his hands in the bucket of water at his side, Harrison scrubbed off the remnants of clay before drying them on the towel at his lap. "Come here," he said, holding his now clean hand out to her. She came happily, sliding into his lap, her arms wrapping around his neck as she laid her head on his shoulder.

"Trouble sleeping?" she asked, looking at the attempted water bowl before them.

"Working out some thoughts."

"Anything I can do to help?" she asked, raising her hand to cover a yawn.

Harrison smiled, kissing her nose. "This is perfect," he said, pulling her closer to him. "Just what I needed."

She gave a soft chuff on a laugh before releasing a sigh. "What are you making?"

"A water dish for Mildred."

"Is molding the clay hard?" she asked.

"Not once you get the hang of it. It's a rather unruly medium." Nuzzling her cheek, he asked, "Would you like to try it?"

"All right," she said, turning toward the wheel.

Harrison scooted back on the stool creating a space for Phoebe between his legs. Kicking his foot against the bottom wheel, he began to move the top wheel at a sure speed before them. "Get your hands wet," he said, pointing to the water bucket.

Phoebe dipped her hands into the bucket, then placed them on the piece before her, the clay gliding through her damp fingers as she pushed against it.

"Good," Harrison said, resting his hands on her thighs. "Make sure you keep the clay wet or it'll be unmanageable."

Phoebe nodded, her focus on the wheel before her, her head cocked to the side as she formed the edges of the bowl before dipping her hands into the water again. Her brow was furrowed, her mouth in a slight pucker of concentration as she rounded her hands around the clay, molding and shaping it to her will.

With a smile, Harrison let his lips fall to her shoulder where her wrapper and nightgown had fallen baring her silky skin to him. His lips traced the line of her shoulder, stopping to tease the jointure where it met her neck, and Phoebe hummed a husky note as she wiggled her bottom back against him. "Don't forget to keep your hands wet," he said, as the thumb of his hand that sat at her thigh drew small circles while his mouth teased her exposed flesh.

"Wet," Phoebe said, the word breathy. "Right." She dipped her hands back into the water and returned to the bowl, pressing her back against his chest while the thumb that had drawn the circles moved onto figure eights. Each time the digit neared her core, Phoebe's breath would catch, her thigh tensing beneath his hand before relaxing again as the thumb moved by.

"All right, Phoebe?" he asked, running his teeth softly across her skin.

"Yes," Phoebe said as she tensed once more against his hand, his wily thumb sliding past her cunny and back to the top of her thigh.

"Stay focused on the bowl."

She nodded, dipping her hands again, the wet slap of their return hardening Harrison's length to painful proportions. His breaths were sharp against her neck as he watched her cup and shape the clay, the damp bowl shifting under the slightest pressure from her fingers, and his eyes nearly rolled into the back of his head as he imagined her doing the same to his cock, the same sure fingers molding his heat until he burst.

"I want to touch you," he said, the words a growl against her neck. "Do you want me to?"

Phoebe nodded, her focus on the bowl loosening as she moved against him.

"The bowl," he said as he softly bit at the juncture of shoulder and neck.

Phoebe whimpered as she returned her attention to the clay, her thighs shaking beneath his hands. "Touch me."

Harrison's hand slid to the center of her thighs, his fingers brushing against her heat, and Phoebe let out a moan that nearly sent him spurting in his pants. Damp heat covered her nightgown, her want so apparent he bit the inside of his cheek as he took his two fingers and rubbed over the top of the swollen nub, the nightgown giving friction to the motion.

"Christ," he said, the words choked from him as he massaged, capturing the bud between his two fingers and circling the spot while she panted before him. His foot slid off the wheel, falling to the floor to brace himself as she leaned against him, pushing her quim into his hand.

"The bowl," she said with a gasp.

"Fuck the bowl." Taking his free hand, Harrison gripped her thigh, lifting it over his, opening her wider while his other hand rubbed at her cunny, circling the swollen bud as she squirmed against him. Her hands, covered in clay, lifted to his hair and he bit down gently on her shoulder as he fucked her with his hand.

Phoebe screamed as her climax took her, her body

shaking against him, and Harrison grit his teeth, the feel of her in his arms as she came nearly making him spill his seed in his pants. Dropping kisses down the length of her neck, Harrison stroked her as she came down to earth, her body jolting with each pass of his hand and he closed his eyes forcing his breaths to even out.

"So much for the bowl," Phoebe said, her head resting in the curve of his chest.

"I'll make Mildred another one," he said, his hands falling to her waist.

"Oh, good."

Phoebe turned her head toward him, her lips puckered for a kiss. Harrison brushed his lips against her mouth.

"Are you planning to do that now?" she asked as she traced her tongue against the seam of his lips.

Harrison laughed, the sound loud and joyful, filling the conservatory with the echoes of his happiness. "God no," he said, picking her up in his arms and marching for the door. "I'd much rather pay homage to my queen."

EPILOGUE

P HOEBE'S CRY OF distress sent Harrison to his feet as he waited in the hallway outside her bedroom. She had been in there for nearly an hour with only a maid running back and forth to bring hot water and warm towels, and no one had given him an update in at least twenty minutes. It was utterly nerve racking to be forced to wait through such a huge life moment while his wife undoubtedly needed him on the other side of the door.

When the door did open, his housekeeper, Mrs. Beatley, peaked her head out, her normally perfect coiffeur in disarray and a pink flush to her cheeks.

"Well?" he asked.

She shook her head. "Nothing yet, my lord. She's in a lot of misery which makes sense given how small she is. She's screaming with each pain as if it's tearing her insides."

Harrison groaned. "What can I do to help?"

Mrs. Beatley gave him a sad smile. "There's nothing to do, my lord. We just have to allow nature to take its course with these things, I'm afraid. Perhaps you should go to the library and get yourself a drink? It might be a while."

"No," he said with a shake of his head. "No, I'll wait here."

"Mrs. Beatley," Phoebe cried out and the housekeeper pulled her head back inside the room and slammed the door shut.

The anguish in Phoebe's voice was terrifying, and he wished he could be there beside her as she navigated this new point in their lives, but she had expressly told him he would only get in the way. She had been adamant that his worrying would cause her more distress than it would help and had summarily banned him from the room when the time came. She was right, of course. He hated seeing those he cared for in any amount of pain, so perhaps his hallway banishment was necessary.

The door opened once more and Mrs. Beatley stuck her head out. "We have one!" she said, before closing the door behind her.

Surely, given how tiny she was, there could not be any more than that?

But to his utter astonishment, the screaming began once again and sweat broke out on his brow. What on earth was he to do with more than one? Understandably this was the way these things went, but for some unknown reason he had only imagined one inside that tiny belly. There was hardly room for anyone else.

"Two," Mrs. Beatley shouted through the bedroom door.

"Dear god," Harrison said, sliding to the floor. Two? That meant double of everything. That meant two terrors running around the home, breaking things and ruining furniture. He would have to increase the staff's salary tenfold just to ensure they stayed on.

"Three!"

"Fuck," Harrison said, pushing up off the floor. Perhaps he would get that drink.

In the library, Harrison poured two fingers of scotch before taking a well-paced stroll around the room. A basket sat by one of the armchairs, filled with strings and little woolen mice toys. A deck of cards sat on the low table, awaiting their nightly game, although he had a sneaking suspicion that tonight's game would be postponed. With all the bustle going on inside the home it only made sense that silly things such as card games would fall to the wayside. No, there were more pressing matters.

Three new little urchins who would need to be looked after with care and comfort, taught what it was to be raised in the Everly home. Obviously, their mother would help with feeding them and keeping them clean, but it was anyone's guess how long that would last.

"Harrison?" Phoebe said from the door.

Harrison looked up. His beautiful wife stood before him with cheeks flushed, hair a mess, and the most beautiful smile on her face.

"Would you like to meet them?" she asked.

Harrison smiled, setting the glass down on the table before taking his wife's hand and following her upstairs. Inside their bedroom, tucked into a corner by the fireplace sat a deep wicker basket covered with a fluffy blanket and some towels. Small cries sounded from the basket and Harrison hurried over, kneeling down to peek inside.

Mildred lay on her side, three small kittens nuzzled against her stomach eating hungrily while she groomed them. It was unfathomable to think that they had all come from such a small cat, but here they were, of varying sizes and colors. Poor Mildred looked tired, her eyes soft, and she nuzzled her head into his hand as he scratched her cheek. "What a brave girl you are," he said.

"She was phenomenal," Phoebe said beside him. "I think I was more worried than she was."

"Was your mother a nuisance?" Harrison asked the cat.

Phoebe laughed. "You would have been worse."

Nodding, Harrison sat on the floor, crossing his legs before him as he looked at the newest additions to his family. "I hope she knows that we're never letting her outside the house again," he said, looking at each kitten to see if they looked anything like their sire. "I don't plan on letting a single tom near her ever again."

Phoebe sat down next to him and took his hand, resting her head on his shoulder. "She's going to have a tantrum for a month."

"I don't care. Nobody takes advantage of my little girl."

"You're still certain you don't want children?" she asked.

Harrison kissed her forehead and squeezed her hand. "Still certain. You don't want them, it's your body and I support whatever you want to do. This is my family. This is all I want."

Phoebe smiled before reaching forward and itching Mildred on the white tuft on her head. "I love you, Harrison."

Harrison looked down at his wife, the soft smile on her lips as she watched Mildred with her kittens making his heart skip. He was not perfect, nor would he ever be, but here, in this moment, life was perfect. Phoebe by his side, a new collection of kittens to worry over.

Perfect.

"I love you, Phoebe."

August 1819

THE EARL OF Everly was dead, thank God.

The bastard had met the grim reaper in his sleep at the ripe age of sixty-six, an easy way to go for someone so terrible as him, but nevertheless, he was dead. Margaret Reedy, Countess of Everly, watched the carriage pull away, the black plumes on top of the horses' heads dancing in the wind as they merged into the traffic of Mayfair. Everly would be buried at the family estate in Salisbury, and Margaret, being a lowly woman, was not allowed to attend the proceedings. Not that she would have. Her husband was a miserable man who had made it his purpose in life to ensure her days were a living hell. No, she would bid goodbye to the arse from the front steps of their Grosvenor Square home, then head inside for a nice cup of tea and some biscuits.

"How are you, dear?" her mother, Lady Veerson, asked from the couch of the sitting room. Her blue day dress showed nary a wrinkle as she sipped from her teacup, her perfectly coiffed grey hair immaculate, not a single strand out of place. The woman had not moved from the spot since she arrived that morning, and Margaret envied her carefree existence, but that was it. Her mother, after all, was married to her father and that was a sentence she would not wish upon anyone. It had been her sire who had determined the trajectory of her fate, forcing her to marry the aged earl, a man nearly forty years her senior, and sentencing her to an existence of wretchedness that only death could save her from. Unfortunately for them all, her father was very much alive.

"I'm well. Ready for this all to be completed." She brushed at her black crepe dress before sitting and taking the proffered cup of tea from her mother.

"The hard part is over, dear. The earl will be buried and once his will is read and Lord Harrison officially takes over the title, you'll be the dowager countess. Do you have any notion of what your settlement will be?" Lady Veerson sipped her tea so delicately at the question it set Margaret's teeth on edge.

She shook her head. "Walter wasn't too forthcoming about what his plans for me were once he perished. I'm sure he intended to outlive me."

Her mother frowned at her words. The acknowledgment of oppression she had been dealt at the hands of her husband was a topic her parents wanted little to do with. Just the mere mention of Walter's domineering personality sent them both into lamentations of her being overly dramatic. It had not mattered when Everly demeaned her in public, calling her all sorts of horrible names, and it certainly did not matter now. No, her parents cared very little for the well-being of their eldest child, only that she married well, and gained a title in the process. After all, what were a few harsh words when you could be a countess?

Margaret pasted a smile on her lips. "I can only hope Daphne's marriage is nothing like mine. It's a shame she could not come today."

"What nonsense, Margaret. She's at finishing school, readying herself to become a nobleman's wife. That is much more important than sitting idly by as her sister tends to her husband's funeral." Lady Veerson glanced at the clock but shook her head as she realized the timepiece remained unmoving because of mourning constraints. "I should be off. I have my monthly orphan society meeting. You should be grateful I was available to support you in your time of need."

"Of course, Mother. You are very thoughtful." The words left her lips with force, their necessity grating, given the circumstances.

Lady Veerson nodded. "I am." She set down her teacup and stood. "Let me know once the will is read and you learn your fate. Your father and I will be happy to have you return home for the duration of your mourning. I know he is eager to begin the search for your next husband."

Margaret bit the inside of her cheek to hold in her retort. Her mother did not need to know that she would never remarry, nor that she would rather live in a shack than return to her parent's household. No matter the outcome of the will, Margaret knew this was her chance for a new beginning, and she was not intending to let it pass without a fight.

After her mother took her leave, Margaret walked the home, her fingers dancing over the furniture that Everly had picked. Walter designed each room to his taste after he stated without affliction that she had little knowledge of what was up to fashion for the home. He had picked each piece meticulously. And he had lorded each room over her, another dagger in his reasonings for why she would never be a good wife and countess. The temptation to break each piece had her removing her hand and holding them tightly behind her back. Lord Harrison would not appreciate learning the items had become damaged in a manic rage, no matter how terrible her husband had been.

Yet the idea held merit. She imagined lining each precious possession on top of the dining room table, then maliciously hitting each of them with a Pall Mall mallet. Margaret smiled at the joy the image brought, allowing her mind to run through each cherished item Everly had boisterously taunted her with. She catalogued them from most hated to least, then imagined each swing and the resounding crash of the beloved item as it met its end. In terms of comfort, it was minimal, but she would take what she could get. After all, anything was better than Everly being alive.

The clearing of a throat behind her brought her out of her musings and she smiled at their butler, Sterns. "Sorry to interrupt, my lady, but the solicitor is here. I've already informed Lord Har-er, I mean the earl, that I have set him up in the study."

Margaret chuckled at his stumble of the title of the new Earl of Everly. It seemed it was not just her that was adjusting to the new life that did not include a temperamental old man with a penchant for malevolence. "Thank you, Sterns. If you could have some refreshments sent in, it would be greatly appreciated."

The butler nodded. "Of course, my lady."

Heading to the study, Margaret could not contain the nerves that danced around in her stomach threatening to bring up her breakfast. Her impending fate would decide the entire trajectory of her escape, and if Everly had ensured she be in hell even after he was gone, she was uncertain what her next steps would be. But she would escape, of that she was certain.

Inside the study, Lord Harrison Metcalf sat across from the solicitor, who presided over the previous earl's massive desk, the ankle of one leg resting on his knee as his brown eyes met hers, his usually meticulous blond hair falling over his face. A single sheet of paper sat before the solicitor, a stoic-looking man, and Margaret swallowed the bile that attempted to rise from her throat.

"My lady," the solicitor said, bowing to her. Lord Harrison nodded his head at Margaret as if to reassure her that all would be well. He had been her biggest champion and closest confidant during her marriage to the earl, and his friendship now was invaluable. And if the will read as she suspected it would, Lord Harrison would no doubt do everything in his power to ensure that she was taken care of. While she was grateful for his thoughtfulness, it did not escape her notice that she would be indebted to another man for the rest of her life.

Lord Harrison had been Walter's nephew and only heir, his presence truly underscoring the age difference in their marriage, but Harrison's always ready smile and quick wit had soothed the sting of her husband's vicious treatment. Within very little time, his weekly dinners with the earl had become the highlight of her week, the only bright spot in an otherwise dreary landscape of her marriage.

Taking the seat beside Lord Harrison, Margaret folded her hands primly in her lap and took a deep breath.

"First, I want to extend my condolences to you, Lady Everly, on the passing of the earl. I wish you comfort and support in this terrible time," the solicitor said, his voice a croak.

Margaret nodded even as his words made her hands tighten. "Your words are more comfort than you know," she said, forcing a smile to her lips. "I've rung for some refreshments before you read the will."

The solicitor nodded his head. "Thank you, my lady, but that will not be necessary. It seems the previous earl kept his legal matters rather simple, so I do not believe it will take much time at all to go over it."

Margaret's stomach dropped at the words. "What do you mean?"

The solicitor rubbed at the back of his neck before adjusting a pair of spectacles and picking up the solitary piece of paper that sat before him. "Perhaps I should just get to it." He cleared his throat, not that doing so would make the croaking of his voice any less pronounced, and said, "I, Walter Reedy, twelfth Earl of Everly, being of sound mind and body declare this to be my last will in testament. To my wife Margaret Reedy, Lady Everly, I leave the jewelry I gifted to her, which includes a pearl necklace, a sapphire ring, and a pair of emerald earrings. I also leave to her the unentailed property known as Baron Manor with the hopes she puts the same amount of love and care into it as she has shown to our other homes." The solicitor adjusted his spectacles once more. "He mentions your marriage settlement, where it seems a provision of ten pounds a year is allotted if you should become a widow."

Lord Harrison growled beside her. "You cannot be serious. How is she expected to live off ten pounds a year?"

"I believe the intent was for the countess to return to her family with the hope that she remarries," the solicitor said, swallowing audibly at Lord Harrison's rough tone.

"She is the Countess of Everly. The only one to decide she should remarry should be herself. This is unacceptable." Lord Harrison stood as if to lunge at the man, but Margaret placed a hand on his arm. His knight in shining armor act, though thoughtful, was entirely unnecessary. Walter's will, evil as it was, was set in stone and there was nothing either of them could do to change it.

"It's all right, Harry," she said, even as her mind replayed the solicitor's words on repeat, a soft chant that slowly grew louder as the moment went on.

"It's not all right, Meg. The bastard gave you a rundown property to call your home as a dowager and almost no money to get by. I won't stand for it."

Margaret squeezed his arm before turning back to the solicitor, who seemed paler than he had before. Poor dear. "Please continue."

The man nodded and glared at the paper before him. "I'm afraid the rest is regarding the new earl and the entailed properties that come with the title. I'm sorry, my lady, but that was the only mention the previous earl made regarding your settlement."

"That's quite all right. If you'll both excuse me, I'll leave and allow you to get on with the rest of the will." Margaret stood and smiled at the solicitor before nodding her head to Lord Harrison and taking her leave. Her hands shook as she headed to her apartments and quickly shut the door behind her, turning the lock. Leaning against the portal, Margaret took a deep breath.

She was free.

Most widows would respond to her settlement with shouts of outrage followed swiftly by someone fetching the smelling salts, and yet Margaret could not contain the smile that overtook her face. The jewelry meant nothing and could easily be sold for a respectable profit, but the house, oh heavens, the house.

Everly had referred to Baron Manor as Bitch Manor, the estate he had relegated his late mother to. Their relationship had been tenuous at best, and he had found much delight in telling all and sundry the story of his mother's involuntary isolation in Woodingdean. After she passed, the home sat in disarray and disrepair and was no doubt in a rather shabby state, but it was hers. Never mind that Everly had gifted her with the manor he most hated, never mind that he had written a final barb to strike her heart in his assumption that she would never care for it. The blighter could kiss her arse, thank you very much, because what he failed to realize in his idiotic attempt at revenge was that she could purchase an unentailed property. And now, not only did Margaret have the funds, but she had very little fears when it came to getting her hands dirty.

The smile that took over her lips was painful it was so large, and even as tears filled her eyes, she could not help the laughter that bubbled from her lips. It began quietly, then turned into a raucous noise. Combined with the tears, the pair of emotions were so contradictory yet meshed with one another in a display so awful, so joyful, that, for a moment, fear nearly overcame her. It was like a dream and Margaret was scared she would awake at any moment to find Everly still alive and the gilded bars to her prison firmly in place.

A knock at the door had her jumping, and she shook her head, wiping away the tears. Unlocking it, she found Lord Harrison on the other side. "May I come in?" he asked.

"Of course. It is, after all, your house now."

"Meg…" he said, his tone exasperated.

"Harry."

"Meg, let me help. You can stay here, or if you insist on going to Baron Manor, I'll pay for the renovations. I'll hire a full staff and make sure the place is at least habitable before you journey there."

She shook her head at him. "No. I'm going to do this on my own."

"Why must you be so stubborn? That bastard left you a dilapidated building that he called Bitch Manor and barely enough funds to pay for food and clothing, let alone renovate an entire home. Half the rooms aren't even safe enough to venture into."

Margaret laughed at his outrage. "Well, then I shall just avoid those until they are repaired."

"Repaired by whom? And with what money?" Lord

Harrison stalked the floor of her sitting room, his brow in a deep furrow. "You're talking nonsense. Why won't you let me help?"

"I know you won't understand, but I need to do this on my own."

"That's utter bullshit and you know it." Lord Harrison rubbed at his face. "I'm sorry, Meg. I just hate knowing that he's done this to you." He sat in the chair near the fireplace, his hands clenched together as he stared at the floor. "I wish you'd let me fix this."

"There's nothing to fix. Whether or not you see it, Walter gave me the key to my cage and I'm going to take it." She smiled at him. "If I promise to ask you for help should I need it, will that pacify you?"

"I think the only thing that will pacify me at this point is bringing the blighter back from the dead so I can kill him." With a sigh, Lord Harrison stood and walked over to her, placing a comforting hand on her shoulder. "Shall I send up some maids to help you pack?"

Margaret smiled at him. "Not for packing, but I would appreciate the help."

He raised a brow at her. "Do I want to know what you have planned?"

She went to her closet and examined the mass of gowns inside. "I plan to take my life back."

ABOUT THE AUTHOR

Emmaline Warden lives in Colorado with her four kids and an ungodly number of animals and plants. Her love of romance began with an accidental copy of Susan Elizabeth Phillips and a trip to D.C. She's been reading and writing romance ever since.

emmalinewarden@gmail.com
Instagram: authoremmalinewarden
Twitter: @emmalinewarden
Facebook: emmalinewarden
Goodreads:
goodreads.com/author/show/18507128.Emmaline_Warden

Sign up for her newsletter and receive, **HEART OF STONE,** a historical paranormal short, as a special gift! www.emmalinewarden.com